Also by A.P. McCoy

A.P. McCoy: My Autobiography

McCoy: The Autobiography

The Real McCoy: My Life So Far

Winner: My Racing Life

Novels

Taking the Fall

NARROWING THE FIELD

NARROWING THE FIELD

A.P. McCoy

First published in Great Britain in 2016
by Orion Books,
an imprint of The Orion Publishing Group Ltd
Carmelite House, 50 Victoria Embankment,
London EC4Y 0DZ

An Hachette UK company

1 3 5 7 9 10 8 6 4 2

A CIP catalogue record for this book
is available from the British Library.

ISBN (Hardback) 978 1 4091 5202 6
ISBN (Export trade paperback) 978 1 4091 5203 3
ISBN (Ebook) 978 1 4091 5205 7

Typeset by Input Data Services Ltd, Bridgwater, Somerset

Printed and bound by CPI Group (UK) Ltd, Croydon CR0 4YY

The Orion Publishing Group's policy is to use papers that
are natural, renewable and recyclable products and made
from wood grown in sustainable forests. The logging and
manufacturing processes are expected to conform to the
environmental regulations of the country of origin.

www.orionbooks.co.uk

NARROWING THE FIELD

1

September 1980

Duncan is in his element. On a horse, in a race, riders packed tight around him as they approach the last fence. His mount is unfamiliar, so is the course – he doesn't know what he's riding or where he is but it doesn't matter. All that matters is staying in control of the galloping animal beneath him, harnessing its power, waiting for the moment to make his move. There are three horses ahead of him, running abreast, with no daylight in between. His mount clears the obstacle sweetly and hits the ground at full run, threatening to pull his arms off. He can see that the three in front are flagging on the run-in. Get past them and the race is his.

He's about to switch to the outside when an opening appears. Two of his rivals drift left, the other goes right. He gives his fellow a squeeze and they're off through the gap, afterburners on. It's a feeling like nothing else, man and beast working together to blow away a top-class field. Suckers. They've handed him victory on a plate.

Only they haven't. The leaders have shifted left and right to avoid an obstacle in the middle of the racetrack. Duncan barely has time to react. One moment he's flying arrow-straight and swift, the next moment instinct takes over, yanking the horse's head off course, taking emergency avoidance action. But the thing in his path is too close, he saw it too late, they are going too fast. There's a smack and a crunch and the object is gone, blown away by half a ton of charging horse, *and Duncan himself is launched into the air. He thumps into the firm turf, curling into a ball as he has been taught in order to minimise the chance of being trampled by following runners. But oddly there are none, just two stewards, running towards him.*

Duncan scrambles to his feet. Mustn't show he's hurting. There'll be other races. He's set to protest that he's OK but the men run past him, out on to the course to the scene of the collision. He runs after them. What bloody idiot put something in the middle of a racecourse? And what the bejesus was it?

One steward is on his knees, the other stands looking down. Stretched out on the grass between them is a man in a three-piece suit, charcoal-grey pinstripe with a pale grey waistcoat rapidly turning bloody black. His dark brogues, flecked with grass, gleam in the pale afternoon sun.

The steward on his knees is becoming agitated. He shouts at the immobile form, 'Sir! Can you hear me, sir?' and places his cheek next to the man's lips. 'He's not breathing.'

Duncan looks around. The course is empty. No sign of his horse – of any of the horses. The stewards are trying mouth-to-mouth resuscitation now but it's no use. They turn to look at Duncan and one says, 'You've only bloody well killed him.'

Duncan stares at the corpse. At the Savile Row tailoring and expensive footwear. At the elegantly manicured hands and the diamond winking in his pinkie ring. He knows this man.

Duke Cadogan's bulbous eyes blink into life and fix him with a hypnotic stare. The thin lips part in a familiar sneer. 'Happy now, Duncan?'

Duncan sat at the kitchen table in the half-light, shaking. It had been half an hour since he'd woken in a muck sweat and his heart still raced. Jesus, what a thing to dream. Today of all days.

A shuffle of feet came from behind him and the ceiling light flickered on.

'I might have guessed it.' Kerry, his friend and fellow jockey, stood in the doorway, a ragged T-shirt and boxers covering his skinny frame. 'Can't sleep before the big day?'

'Turn the sodding light off, will you? And go back to bed.' Kerry might be his mate but Duncan didn't want company right now.

'After I've made you a nice cup of tea.' Kerry walked to the sink and splashed water into a kettle. 'I didn't think TLC in the middle of the night was expected of a best man but I'll not let you down.' Plainly it wasn't going to be easy to get rid of him.

In the bright light, Duncan took in the burned-out pans on the cooker, the overflowing rubbish bin and the sink full of un-washed dishes in which Kerry was rummaging for mugs.

'This place is toxic. Why don't you ever clean up?'

'I used to have a flatmate who was very good around the house.' Kerry poured boiling water on to tea bags and sniffed at a half-empty milk bottle. 'Only he sodded off to live in a mansion and have his arse wiped by maids and butlers. I doubt if he knows what Fairy Liquid even looks like these days. Do you, Duncan?' He dumped two mugs on the table and slumped into a chair opposite.

Duncan ignored the jibe. He'd moved into the flat with Kerry last autumn but his circumstances had changed since then. Despite the squalor he felt a pang of nostalgia for life here in Banbury.

'I don't understand why Roisin doesn't crack the whip. Make you put the Marigolds on.'

Kerry grinned. 'She might but we meet up at her place. She's never round here.'

'Why's that?' Kerry and Roisin Quinn, the knock-out lady jockey at the yard which supplied most of their rides, were an item. Had been for the best part of a year.

'Well, you know. It's just the way it is. Not every man wants a woman in his hair every waking minute.'

Alarm bells were ringing in Duncan's head. Kerry could charm the knickers off a nun if he set his mind to it. Maybe there was a reason he kept his girlfriend out of his bachelor pad.

'I hope that doesn't mean what I think it does.'

Kerry said nothing, just grinned some more.

Duncan put down his mug. 'Seriously, mate, if you screw it up with Roisin you belong in a loony bin.'

The grin disappeared and Kerry got to his feet. 'If you say so.'

'Not only will she kill you but her dad won't give you any more rides and you'll have to throw being out of work into the bargain.'

'You think I don't know that?' Kerry leaned back against the kitchen worktop and folded his arms. 'Look, I'm not the one who's about to chain myself to one person for life. You might at least look cheerful about it. That was the most miserable stag night I've ever been to. You'd better stay married 'cause I'm not bloody well doing it for you ever again.'

Duncan reflected that his mate had a point. It had been down to Kerry as best man to organise the stag outing and Duncan had made him promise not to go over the top. All things considered, he'd kept his word – a room upstairs round the corner at the Banbury Cross, just the lads from the local yards and only one stripper. All the same, Duncan had wished it over long before it was and nursed a vodka and slimline tonic the best part of the evening. He'd seen too many grooms at their wedding suffering from the night before and tomorrow – today! – he needed

4

a clear head. He'd made the usual excuses for staying off the booze – 'Got to make the weight at Towcester on Monday, haven't I?' – but he knew he'd not fooled Kerry.

'Sorry about that. I guess I was a bit of a wet blanket. I appreciate all you've done, honest.'

Kerry nodded, accepting the apology. Duncan hoped that was the end of the matter and his pal would head back to bed and leave him to sort out the turmoil in his head. But Kerry was standing his ground, chewing on his lip. He had something on his mind and plainly felt duty-bound to spit it out.

'You're not getting cold feet, are you?' His trusting hazel eyes bored into Duncan's. 'I mean, it's perfectly natural. Every bridegroom gets last minute nerves.'

Duncan smiled. Last-minute nerves, if only that's what it was. 'No, don't worry, mate. I'm really happy about getting married. I'm committed.'

'Then for Jesus' sake act like you're happy! Look, I know I said that about chaining yourself to one bird but I didn't mean anything. I swear Lorna is the most fantastic girl on earth – excepting, well you know, 'cause I hear what you say about Roisin – but she's the most fantastic girl for you and every guy there last night was shamrock green with envy to think who you'll be cuddling up to every night for the rest of your natural, you lucky bastard. Not to mention the rest of it.'

Ah, the rest of it. The rest of it was what they never actually discussed, because it was too hard to deal with. It was the wealth that came with the lady: the palatial house and servants, the fleet of vintage cars, the stables of horseflesh, the stocks and bonds and gambling largesse. Now Duke Cadogan was dead, his daughter, Lorna, Duncan's red-headed teenage bride, was a gold-carat copper-bottomed heiress.

5

'Happy now, Duncan?' the dead man had asked in his dream. He knew he should be, but he wasn't.

Duncan went back to bed but he couldn't sleep. He didn't expect to but at least in here Kerry wouldn't hover over him and ask more awkward questions.

The room – his old room, now a dumping ground for Kerry's racing mags and spare riding gear – was a decent size, with a double bed, sturdy wardrobe and space for two easy chairs in front of the electric heater in the old fireplace. He'd been over-joyed with it when he and Kerry had moved in. Just what the doctor ordered – a quick journey to Petie Quinn's Warwickshire yard in the morning, handy for motorway travel and the race-tracks and two doors down from a decent Chinese takeaway where the owner rarely let them pay.

But now, lying here felt weird. He'd been at Lorna's place for months, keeping up the rent till Kerry found someone else, which he hadn't because, frankly, there was no pressure to do so. Now the bed felt lumpy and the hissing of the dodgy cistern in the toilet next door got on his nerves. Was he turning soft?

He'd not told Kerry a lie. He was committed to marrying Lorna, but the wedding day ahead filled him with dread. So many things could go wrong and almost all of them because of his father. Since Charlie Claymore's fall from grace – thrown out of racing because he opposed the corrupt powers-that-be – his dad had been a broken man. In less than three years Charlie had gone from being a successful National Hunt trainer with a middle-sized yard packed with classy contenders and good-looking prospects, a man sought after by owners and respected by the industry at large, to a listless shell of a man. His success had made him enemies and those men had sold him down the river on trumped-up doping charges. Charlie had been warned off racing for nine years. At the age of sixty that had been the end of his life as a trainer. In some respects, it marked the end of his life.

Charlie was no longer capable of living independently. The upright fearless figure who had single-handedly raised a son and built a business was now diminished in every sense. He'd sit in his room at the Grey Gables care home unaware half the time whether it was Christmas or Thursday. Duncan sincerely hoped his father would remember that today was his son's wedding day. But he was taking no chances – he was going to fetch the old man in person.

The problem was that, deep down, Charlie was still the fiery and fearless man who had forged his way in life. The bloody-minded crusader who had taken on the dark forces of racing was still alive inside the vacant husk that he had become and he would come out fighting when he was provoked. What provoked him was being in the company of racing people, being reminded of the world to which he once belonged, a world which had unjustly spat him out. And half the guests invited to the wedding would be those very people – jockeys and trainers, stable lads and lasses, and a smattering of the industry establishment. It couldn't be avoided – the wedding was going to be well attended. Much as Duncan might have wanted a modest ceremony, there'd never been a chance his young bride would fall for that.

'There's been so many sad things,' Lorna had announced. 'Daddy's funeral and the inquest and everything. I want a big proper do where everyone's happy and getting on and no one cares about the past. I want a dress with a train and the tallest cake and buckets of champagne and bands and dancing. I want a real occasion! It's our wedding and we've got the money, so let's flash it around. That's what Daddy would have done.'

Duncan hadn't had an answer to that. In all honesty, he wanted that too.

The easy thing would have been to keep his father out of it, leave him staring at the walls in the Grey Gables and get on with having a good time. But he couldn't do that. Like his father, he didn't do easy. Duncan gave up on trying to go back to sleep and got dressed quickly, pulling on jeans and an old flannel shirt. His new suit hung in its Harrods bag on the wardrobe door. He'd be back to change for the wedding later. Now he had to clear his head in a place he felt more comfortable.

The Quinn yard was twenty minutes away, less than that at six in the morning with few cars on the main road and nothing stirring on the country lanes. There was activity in the yard though, where business carried on 365 days a year. The horses didn't know or care whose wedding day it was and they came first. Stable staff were busy mucking out their charges, doubtless many of them thick-headed from the do the night before. Not everyone had been as abstemious as Duncan.

Petie Quinn, shouting instructions at a group of lads, raised his eyebrows at the sight of Duncan but he nodded agreement to the jockey's request to join first lot. Duncan tagged along at the rear of the first group of riders taking the back lane up on to the gallop which Petie shared with two other nearby yards. He was on an old favourite, Water Colour, a twelve-year-old chaser at the end of a decent career who'd put on a bit of weight over an indulgent summer. Petie's instructions were to give him a regular blow to get him back into shape and, to be fair to the horse, he enjoyed his morning exercise. Duncan's anxieties melted away as he pushed Water Colour into some serious work and the sun began to thin the milky autumn mist that hung over the broad green gallop. What the hell was he worrying about? he thought as they made their way back down the track. Today was going to be a great day.

As he headed back to his car, conscious that he now had to get a move on, he passed an old row of stalls that Petie was planning to replace. A regular commotion was coming from the one on the end, as if someone was taking a sledge hammer to the walls. In the gloomy interior Duncan made out the large pale shape of a horse he did not recognise, kicking the back wall with the full force of his hind legs.

'Hold on, big feller,' he called out as he approached. 'You're going to bring the whole place down.'

The horse was indeed big, muscly and deep-chested with a dappled grey coat. When he saw Duncan he charged straight ahead, slamming into the wooden door and baring his teeth. His great white head thrust forward, finishing just inches from Duncan's face.

'Jesus!' Duncan took an involuntary step back.

'No, Sammy!' A small blonde figure darted from nowhere and placed herself between Duncan and the agitated horse. He found himself gazing down on a petite female figure wearing a green sweater a few sizes too big for her. He bit back the warning that was on his tongue as she raised a small hand and laid it on the great column of the horse's neck. He guessed she knew what she was doing.

At her touch the horse seemed to come to his senses; his entire body calmed instantly. Keeping her hand on the horse's neck, the girl turned to look at Duncan. 'He's still upset about the ferry and everything. He's a lovely boy really.' She spoke with a soft Irish accent and her big chocolate-brown eyes seemed to widen as she looked at him. 'Ooh, you're Duncan Claymore, aren't you? You've been all over the papers.'

He was puzzled by that but replied, 'Who are you?'

'Michelle O'Brien. But I'm kind of one of the Joyces, a cousin. We're like a big family, you know?'

He didn't really but he recognised the name Joyce as one of Petie's Irish connections. Now he remembered that some Joyce or other was sending over a horse. He hadn't realised that a girl was coming over as well.

Michelle soon rectified his ignorance as a stream of chatter bubbled from her lips. It seemed she was really a jockey, desperate to work in an English yard and she had jumped at the chance to bring Sammy – Prince Samson – over to England. He could be a bit of a bad boy but she knew how to handle him and could get him settled in a new home, no bother. Mr Quinn seemed a bit of a gruff old stick but her cousins said he was a trainer who liked to give youngsters a chance and if she played her cards right maybe she'd get a few rides – what did Duncan think?

Duncan thought there wasn't a cat in hell's chance that Petie would rush to put this little elf up on one of his animals. For all her soothing effect on the fearsome Prince Samson, she didn't look strong enough to pilot an athletic racehorse. And there were other obvious obstacles.

'You know he's already got two other girls begging for rides, don't you? There's his daughter, Roisin, and Fee, who's been grafting away here all summer – she's pushing for her chance, too.'

'Then perhaps I could get rides instead of some of the boys. Like you, maybe?'

Duncan laughed. Not because the idea of women riding races was alien to him – he was all in favour, provided they could do the job – but because this girl's cheek was infectious. Her eyes flashed and her smile almost split her face in two.

'You read about me in the paper? What race was that?'

'It's 'cause you're going to marry the heiress. The poor girl whose father up and died so tragically and him owning all those fine horses. That's you, isn't it?'

'That's me. We're getting married this afternoon in fact.'

'No! So what are you doing here gassing to me?'

Good question. He grinned sheepishly and strode off to his car.

The inquest for Duke Cadogan had been held at the end of April, a month after his death. It had turned into a bit of a circus, due to the press hassling Lorna outside the court. The racing journos had been civilised about it but the tabloid news reporters had laid siege to her on arrival and departure. Duncan had been tipped off by his friend, TV journalist Maddy Gleeson, that there might be a bit of a scrum and he'd prevailed on Kerry to come along with him and give Lorna some protection. Duncan had been serving a two-day ban which, for once, came at the right time, but Kerry had given up a ride at Exeter to attend. 'I'd do the same for you,' Duncan had said. 'No, you wouldn't,' had been the reply and, though he had protested, Duncan suspected his friend was right. For him, giving up rides was like shedding blood.

He'd been glad Kerry had been by his side on the hard benches of the coroner's court. On his other side Lorna had sat rigid, like a pale and beautiful ghost. Next to her was her Uncle Rodney, Duke's elder brother, the only Cadogan family member, it seemed, who had ever kept in touch with the flamboyant owner. 'Black sheep,' Rodney had said to Duncan at the funeral. 'He wasn't christened Duke, of course. Didn't seem to think David was special enough.'

Rodney was a thin elderly gent with a limp handshake and a

11

remote manner. He had endured Lorna's heartfelt hug of greeting and sat next to her with a long-suffering air, regarding the inquest proceedings with evident distaste. However, he glared intently at the witnesses and fiddled nervously with a retractable pen in his hand, click-click, click-click. Even if Lorna had not marked his card it would have been plain to Duncan that the old boy was anxious.

'Uncle Rodney is worried they'll say it was suicide,' she'd said.

It wasn't a new notion. Cadogan had been found dead after a clay-pigeon shoot on his estate. He'd taken the full force of the blast from a twelve-gauge shotgun in the face. Nobody else had been present and police statements at the time described his death as a 'tragic accident'. Later some of his guests told reporters that Duke had been drinking heavily all afternoon. Then the papers began dropping hints that Duke Cadogan's manic high-living masked an unbalanced nature and that the black dog of depression had finally claimed him. Or possibly that he was up to his neck in gambling debts. Or even that his complicated love life had left him lonely and bereft in his middle years. Or any old rot they chose to dream up to make a story. The dead can't sue, after all.

The verdict of the coroner was anticipated with interest all round, not least by Duncan. As witnesses came and went – guests at the shoot, staff assisting at the occasion, the police officers who attended the scene – he tried to conquer the irrational fear that the coroner would turn to him.

'I see Mr Duncan Claymore is present at this proceeding. Would you mind answering a few questions, Mr Claymore?'

He wouldn't have any choice. He'd have to swear on the Bible and tell the truth. That would be awkward.

'You say you rode one of Mr Cadogan's racehorses at the

Cheltenham Festival six days before he died. What instructions did he give you before the race?'

'He just told me it wasn't the horse's day.'

'What did you understand him to mean by that?'

'That he didn't want Ra-Ho-Tep to win.'

'But he did win, didn't he? Why did you disobey the deceased's instructions?'

'Because I always ride to win! I've never thrown a race and I never will.'

'So, let me get this straight. There were a number of people – dangerous people – under the impression that Ra-Ho-Tep would not win that race, and by winning, you knowingly put the deceased in danger. Is that right?'

'Yes. But I never thought they would kill him!'

'And when you later told a third party that it was Mr Cadogan's desire that you should win because he had placed a substantial bet on the outcome, that was a lie, wasn't it?'

'Yes.'

'And why was that?'

'Because I placed the bet myself. In his name, on his account. He didn't know a thing about it.'

'What reason did you have for placing a bet without his knowledge?'

'I wanted his associates to think that he had betrayed them.'

'Would it be accurate to suggest that you set Mr Cadogan up?'

'Yes.'

'And what bearing do you think your actions had upon his death?'

'I didn't know they would kill him!'

'But you did want revenge on Mr Cadogan. Isn't it true that he was responsible for destroying your father's career?'

'He was a bastard who'd ruined my dad but I never wanted him dead!'

'However, that was the consequence of your actions, wasn't it, Mr Claymore?'

Yes. He'd almost spoken the word out loud in the court. That was the consequence of what he'd done. He'd not foreseen it and would never have wished for it but the father of the woman he was going to marry had been murdered on his account. That was the truth.

'Duncan, are you OK?' Lorna was squeezing his hand, looking urgently into his face. He was conscious of murmurs in the courtroom, people turning to look at them.

'Yes, I'm fine.'

He saw Rodney smiling at Lorna. 'Thank God for that,' the old man muttered. 'Never would have lived it down otherwise.'

He turned to Kerry. 'What's happened?'

'Trust you to drop off, you dozy bugger. The verdict's in – accidental death.'

In the car going home, having fought their way through the press scrum, Lorna buried her face in his shoulder and cried. Her sobs came from deep within and he held her close, as if he could absorb her pain and take it for himself. He deserved it, not her. Since her father's death she'd been in shock, her emotions locked inside her. She'd always said her father didn't love her and she'd professed not to care for him but Duncan guessed that such things were easily said.

In the aftermath of Cadogan's death she'd asked Duncan to marry her and he'd said yes. What else could he say? She was alone in the world at the age of nineteen and it was his fault. In the weeks since then he'd wondered at the wisdom of his promise. In the cold light of day, she was a spoilt rich teenager who'd never had to lift a finger for herself and he was a semi-educated roughneck scarcely older than she was, with a passion to make it in racing. Would she turn out to be just a moody millstone round his neck? Sure, she was sexy and passionate and they had a laugh together but how long would that last? In recent weeks there'd been precious little passion and even fewer laughs.

But he knew as he held her weeping in his arms that he couldn't abandon her. They had a bond. They'd make it work. He owed it to her.

Eventually she calmed down and raised her tear-stained face. 'I'm so glad that's over. Now we can put all that behind us and be happy, can't we?'

'Yes,' he said. And he meant it.

Just as long as she never found out the truth.

2

The Grey Gables wasn't the most luxurious of care homes. The rooms were on the small side and it didn't have a conservatory or a cinema or a lake in the grounds like some Duncan had found when searching for a refuge for Charlie. But it did have a pretty garden, decent food and the friendliest staff they had encountered. It was also free from the depressing odour of cabbage and pee that clung to even the fanciest places. So, though he'd installed his father at the Grey Gables with a heavy heart, all things considered it could have been a darned sight worse.

It would have been better, however, if he could ever persuade his father to leave the premises. Charlie might no longer be the man he once was but he was in better physical shape than any of the other residents. He was hale enough to go on trips around the country. Even if racecourses were off limits, he could have enjoyed restaurants and movies and the theatre – not that Charlie had ever set foot in a theatre, as far as Duncan was aware. But he could start now. His father's life didn't have to end just because his racing life was over. But even though Duncan said this until he was blue in the face, he got nowhere. Charlie just didn't appear to understand his words. And if he pressed for a response all he got was, 'No.' Just like he was getting now.

'But it's my wedding, Dad. You're all the family I've got. I need you there.'

'I'm sorry, son, but I can't do it. I'll not go.'

Duncan took a deep breath and stared at the rose-patterned wallpaper and ill-matching brown-swirled carpet and the small boxy television with a bent aerial positioned in front of his father's armchair. This was his dad's entire world. A haven he wouldn't leave even for his son's wedding. Duncan could scream.

'I'll not go,' Charlie repeated. 'I'll not go with those bastards there. No.'

'What bastards? What are you talking about?'

But Duncan knew well enough. There'd been three men in the conspiracy to ruin his father's career. One of them was no longer in the land of the living and the other two were not on the guest list – he'd made sure of it.

'You don't have to worry,' Duncan continued. 'Duke's dead and the others aren't invited.'

Charlie, who'd been staring out of the window, turned to fix Duncan with a glare he knew well. The vacant look had gone, dispersed by steely blue venom. *'She'll* be there,' he spat. 'Cadogan's daughter.'

For a moment, Duncan was at a loss. He thought he'd smoothed over the difficulty of marrying Duke's daughter. Charlie knew that Lorna was an innocent party in his downfall, that she'd had her own problems with her father – Duncan had explained it endlessly.

'But you like Lorna,' he protested. It was true. She'd made a genuine effort with his dad and often visited when Duncan was off racing and couldn't make it.

'Yes,' Charlie agreed. 'Lorna's a grand girl, it's Cadogan's daughter I can't stand.'

Duncan was at a loss. Sometimes his father's mental confusion rendered him speechless.

He was rescued by a knock. Mrs Solanki, Charlie's carer, stood in the doorway holding a crimson carnation, its stem wrapped in silver.

'He says he's not going,' Duncan said.

Mrs Solanki's smiling face fell as she stared at Charlie in dismay. 'But I went to get you this buttonhole special.' She held it up. 'Isn't it pretty? You're going to look so handsome.'

Charlie said nothing, just turned to stare mulishly out of the window.

Mrs Solanki looked at Duncan. 'You want to leave him with me for one minute?'

Half an hour later Duncan drove out of the gates of the Grey Gables, his father in the passenger seat in his suit, carnation in place. A deal had been struck, for behind them sat Mrs Solanki, without whom Charlie had refused to attend. Mrs S. had been most apologetic when she'd explained to Duncan his father's demand but he was too relieved to care.

'That's great,' he'd exclaimed. 'But what about you? We'd be delighted to have you – if you're prepared to come.'

It turned out that she was and, after a brief negotiation with her supervisor, she was given permission to attend the wedding as Charlie's personal carer. First, though, she had to be driven home to change into something more suitable than a housecoat and trousers. The delay was frustrating but the important thing was that Charlie would be by his side. While Charlie was getting spruced up, Duncan rang the venue and asked for another place to be set on the top table. It was something of a relief to think that Mrs S. would be on hand to keep his father sweet.

Duncan drove to Mrs Solanki's tiny, brick terraced house where he waited with a degree of impatience for her to transform herself. Charlie sat beside him with his vacant face on, which, for once, was a relief. Conversation with his dad could be a minefield and he could do without Charlie exploding at this point. Finally, Mrs Solanki appeared at the door. She had changed into a beautiful crimson sari with silver embroidery and had painted a red bindi on her forehead. At the sight of her Charlie sprang into life, leaping out of the car and opening the rear passenger door. 'You look stunning,' he said. He helped her into the car and climbed in beside her, leaving Duncan alone in the front.

Right, thought Duncan. Let's get going.

As he put his foot down on the accelerator he was glad he hadn't chosen the two-seater Lamborghini. Among the Cadogan collection of vintage cars was a Roller, a Merc and a vintage Simca 5. For this occasion he'd picked out a 1960s Dodge Dart, partly because it looked good as a wedding car with its rocket fins and a white ribbon stretched across its huge hood but also because he'd wanted to have a go at driving the magnificent fuel-guzzler. He was aware he made a bit of a spectacle, driving an American classic car to a traditional English wedding with an Indian lady in a sari in the back seat. But why not? This was how life was these days. This was the eighties.

Unlike Duke Cadogan, Duncan wasn't impressed by fancy motors and he knew Lorna didn't give a hoot about them. With her agreement, he'd decided to sell the collection after the wedding. Maybe they'd keep one or two for sentimental reasons, such as the yellow Lamborghini. He and Lorna had taken it without her father's permission on the first day they'd spent together and ended up making energetic love on the front seat on the way back from Doncaster races. He had very different ideas to Cadogan about the best uses for a classic car.

Eventually, after impatiently barging through the west London traffic, Duncan drew up outside the church where he was accosted by a figure in a morning suit. Kerry wore an anxious frown and had the car door open before Duncan had even come to a halt.

'Thank God, you're here. The church is almost full. You'd better get inside quick – I'll take care of the motor.' As Charlie held the car door open for Mrs Solanki, Kerry slid into the driver's seat. 'I'll see you inside. Did nobody ever tell you, it's just the bride who's allowed to be late?'

There were grins and smiles all round as they walked up the aisle to take their places at the front, some confusion too at the sight of the little Indian woman by Charlie's side. Someone on the groom's side – populated entirely by Duncan's racing mates – was heard to murmur in a bad effort at an Indian accent, 'Well, goodness gracious me!' Charlie stiffened and would have stopped had Duncan not prompted him to keep going.

'It's harmless, Dad. Someone's a bit pissed already.'

As they took their places, Duncan looked around. The church seemed full to bursting. Behind him sat row upon row of men and women in wedding suits and fancy dresses. He didn't recognise many on his side of the aisle as they were Lorna's guests but across the way familiar faces in unfamiliar clothes were smiling at him. He picked out Petie Quinn and Roisin, sitting next to a strange bulky shape in an orange check tweed suit and a spotted bowtie. The vision grinned gap-toothed at him and held up a gnarled thumb. Good God, it was Gypsy George, once Charlie's horse guru, now whispering his unorthodox brand of equine wisdom into Petie Quinn's ear on a daily basis. Duncan had never seen George in anything smarter than a holey vest and stained tracksuit bottoms.

A flushed-faced Kerry was striding briskly down the aisle towards them. He slipped into the pew beside Duncan and whispered in his ear, 'She's on her way. You ready?'

Duncan took a deep breath. Everything was finally in place. His father was here. His friends were here. His enemies and the mistakes of the past no longer existed. This was his future and it was looking good.

'I'm ready,' he said as the organ struck up the Wedding March.

The ceremony went without a hitch. Lorna looked magnificent as she swept down the aisle, her red hair tumbling over the breast of her white silk taffeta dress, followed by a gaggle of bridesmaids. She was given away by her Uncle Rodney, standing in for her father, who even managed a smile for the occasion. Duncan anticipated that Kerry would pull the oops-forgotten-the-ring stunt but he played his part straight, sincere pleasure shining in his eyes.

The reception was held at the Grand Conservatory in Roystan Park, beginning with champagne and canapés served on the lawn in the late afternoon sunshine, and followed by an extensive sit-down banquet that satisfied all parties – except those, like Duncan, who were expecting to make a weight the following Monday. But Duncan wasn't bothered by that, he was too nervous about delivering a speech, not something he'd ever had to do before. In the event he was guided by Lorna's uncle and kept it short – 'Bare bones, old man' was Rodney's advice – thanking all for attending and declaring that Lorna was the woman of his dreams, which was met with a collective sigh of approval. He was followed by Rodney himself who failed to take his own advice and rambled at length, inevitably making extensive reference to his younger brother David. Duncan had been amused to see how long it took some people to work out who the uncle was waffling on about. Happily the reference to Duke appeared to go over Charlie's head. Not so Lorna, of course. Duncan gripped her hand under the table as the light dimmed for a moment in her sparkling green eyes.

Then Kerry lifted the mood with a traditional best man's speech in which he revealed three things guaranteed to embarrass Duncan and then was foolhardy enough to rave about the sexiness of the bridesmaids – friends of Lorna's – and earned himself a poisonous glower from Roisin. He concluded on a safer note by proposing a toast to bride and groom and everyone stood at his request and clinked glasses. The music started and, to cheers and applause, Duncan led his beautiful bride on to the dance floor.

If anyone was surprised to see a lady in a sari take to the floor with the bridegroom's father, they kept their mouths shut. Charlie looked very happy by Mrs Solanki's side as he squired her around and, for her part, Mrs S. appeared to be having the time of her life. Considering that it was Charlie's first social occasion since his fall from grace, he was doing well. Duncan, who had relinquished Lorna into the arms of others eager to dance with the bride, watched his father's progress with pleasure and an unavoidable knot of irritation in his gut. See? The old bugger wasn't incapable, after all. He could still get off his arse and have fun. Surely he had many good years ahead of him yet.

After a couple of dances Charlie and Mrs Solanki left the dance floor. She patted his hand and turned towards the door which led to the cloakroom. Charlie made his way over to Duncan and sat down heavily, somewhat out of breath.

'All right, Dad?'

'Oh aye. Right as rain. It's a first-class do, this.'

The words filled Duncan with pleasure. Getting his father to the wedding had only been half the battle, ensuring he enjoyed himself was the other.

'One thing, son.' Charlie leaned towards him confidentially. 'Whose wedding is this?'

Duncan's heart stopped for a moment. Dismay threatened to overwhelm him, but he smiled right through it.

'Mine,' he blurted.

Charlie stared at him open-mouthed. Then he recovered. 'Of course, of course. I'm only joking.'

But Duncan knew it had been no joke. For a moment his father had lost it. Maybe he was kidding himself about the old man's condition. He was relieved to see Mrs Solanki returning and watched as Charlie's face lit up at the sight of her.

He left the pair of them to it and stepped outside, avoiding the group of happy revellers by the door and heading out on to the lawn for a moment of peace – though he was not destined to find it.

The one man he wanted to avoid seemed to materialise out of the dark. If he could have crossed any name off the guest list Lorna had prepared it would have been that of George Pleasance. But despite Pleasance's involvement in Duke Cadogan's death, the two had been close and Pleasance had known Lorna since she was a girl – 'I know they say horrible things about him but George always stuck by Daddy. That's what Daddy said. And they owned horses together – like Princess Lorna.'

Princess Lorna, named for Duncan's new bride as a tenth-birthday present, was a racing legend. In her short but brilliant career she had won the Champion Hurdle at Cheltenham, only the second mare to do so. Duncan knew he couldn't fight that, even though the 'horrible things' that Lorna had referred to included words such as 'drug-smuggler' and 'gangster'.

For a big man, Pleasance was precise and elegant in his movement. His mane of black hair flecked with silver was meticulously groomed and he was always immaculately dressed. His voice was soft and a smile was ever-present on his lips – as it was now. He held his arms out wide and Duncan couldn't avoid the bear hug that enveloped him.

'Congratulations,' Pleasance purred as he released his grip. 'You've just done the finest day's business of your life. That girl is gold dust.'

'I'm a lucky guy.'

'Well, luck's on Lorna's side too. Not every man would jump into the breach the way you've done. I don't presume to talk for the dead but I'm sure Duke would be very happy to know you've taken on responsibility for his little girl.'

Duncan said nothing. The mention of Duke had thrown him.

Pleasance moved on smoothly. 'Remember, I'm always on hand should you newly-weds need me. Always at the end of a phone. A chat. Advice. Some money. I'd be happy to help out.'

'That's kind of you, George, but I don't think I'm in need of anything.'

'Maybe not now but circumstances can change very fast. Not only in the racing game.'

'Right, yeah. I'm sure that's true. But, look, I've got to get back.'

'Of course. You mustn't neglect your guests. Just don't forget, if you need a helping hand don't be too shy to ask.'

Duncan almost ran across the lawn to get away from Pleasance, back to the bright lights and cheerful music of the reception. What was the man on about? What could he possibly think Duncan would need from him? George bloody Pleasance – the last man on earth he would turn to in a crisis.

He couldn't deny that marrying into money made a difference to his outlook on life. There'd not been much of it around when he was growing up. Charlie had put everything he had into establishing his business. He used to say that horses had had

Duncan's pocket money. They often had his wages too; money Charlie had owed him for helping out at the yard before school.

He'd not realised it when he was a lad but there'd been a history of money troubles in his dad's life. Charlie had confessed to his gambling habit when he'd caught Duncan in the bookies at the age of fifteen. 'You've heard of the AA? Alcoholics Anonymous. They give up the booze but they know they still have the addiction. It's the same with us Claymores only we're in the GA – Gamblers Anonymous. My father lost everything gambling and so did I. I even lost your mother. So don't you ever start with the bets. Gambling's in your blood and it'll ruin you too.' Duncan might not have taken much notice of this speech if Charlie hadn't backed it up with a threat to ban him from riding out at the yard if he ever caught him again.

Coming in to Cadogan money was a windfall that he had not sought but it was a fact of life. What's more, it was obvious to everyone that he had come into riches. So why would Pleasance offer him money? It made no sense.

The wedding festivities were continuing. The Bee Gees were blaring out over the sound system and all the guys were doing their best John Travolta. Lorna and her pals were deep in the mix and even Charlie was busy discoing with Mrs Solanki. But other activities caught Duncan's eye.

Petie, Roisin and Gypsy George were huddled close together at a table in the corner. Coffee cups and brandy balloons had been pushed to one side and Roisin was making notes on the back of a menu. Duncan took a seat. 'What's this – a kitchen cabinet? I hope you're not talking shop.'

Gypsy George leaned back in his seat. 'Watch it, the owner's turned up.'

'The owner' was what George called him whenever the topic of Cadogan's horses came up. At the time of his death, Duke had owned forty jump horses so now, given that Lorna had abdicated responsibility for them, Duncan was effectively their owner. By some judicious selling they'd managed to reduce that number by half but it was still a substantial accumulation of horseflesh and the one part of Duke's legacy that was of genuine interest to Duncan. The horses had been at the yard of William Osborne. Osborne was one of National Hunt's most successful trainers and he'd played an integral part in ruining Charlie's career in racing. Osborne had been on the original guest list to the wedding that Lorna had compiled and Duncan had quickly removed him. Though he was determined to take no further action against the men who had wronged Charlie, he didn't have to invite them to his family engagements.

'What's up?' Duncan said. 'You're not working now are you?'

Over the summer, once new stalls and other facilities had been installed at Petie's yard, Cadogan's horses had been transferred from Osborne's. The influx of twenty animals had at a stroke significantly expanded Petie's complement of horses in training and at present they were still trying to assess the capabilities of the new intake. Further sales were likely and the best of them would be kept, but at present no one could be sure exactly which. A lot of lists had been compiled and then redrafted. Duncan assumed that Roisin was working on another right now.

Petie took the menu card from Roisin and folded it into the inside pocket of his suit. 'You're right, Duncan. We're out of order talking business at your fancy knees-up.' He got to his feet. 'I think I might be trying a little of that Saturday Night Fever meself. Roisin?' He held out his hand to his daughter.

'My God, Dad, I thought you'd never ask.' And, stifling laughter, she allowed her father to steer her towards the dancers.

Duncan looked at the old gypsy. 'What about you, George? Are you tempted to take to the floor?'

The old fellow appeared to consider his options. 'You know, I used to be quite quick on my toes when I was your age. Do you think there's any chance of getting Charlie to let go of that nice Indian lady?'

Later, Duncan and Lorna were driven back to the Cadogan estate by the family chauffeur in the Rolls-Royce. They went straight to bed, exhausted. There was to be no honeymoon, at least not for the time being. Duncan was racing again in two days' time.

'And how was the day, Mrs Claymore?' Duncan said, cradling his new wife in his arms.

'Wonderful,' Lorna said sleepily. 'Almost perfect.'

'Almost?'

'Well, you know – I wish it had been Daddy giving me away and not Uncle Rodney.'

There was no answer to that.

3

Two days after the wedding Duncan was in the saddle at the start of a two-mile handicap hurdle at Towcester in the rolling Northamptonshire countryside. He had unhappy memories of this place. On a bitter day in February with snow in the wind, the going had often been so heavy that he'd felt his mount slipping backwards on the final slog to the winning post. But today, in the balmy autumn sunshine with the trees in full leaf, the track was a picture. He rather envied the spectators in the old wooden stand who would enjoy a glorious view of the big square course. Armed with a decent pair of binoculars, this was one racetrack where you wouldn't miss any of the action out in the country.

But Duncan was here to work, not to spectate. He wasn't given to overconfidence but as he lined up at the start with the ten other runners, he expected to open his account as a married man with a victory. His mount was Ansible, a six-year-old chestnut gelding and the most fancied of the Cadogan horses that had come over from the Osborne yard. Thanks to a win at Huntingdon and a close-fought second at Fontwell at the end of the previous season, Ansible was giving away five pounds to his nearest rival and starting as the 2-1 favourite. The horse had schooled intelligently at Petie's and showed a fair turn of speed on the gallops, so Duncan reckoned the bookies had it about right.

The only blot on the landscape from Duncan's point of view was that he was dressed in the white silks of Cadogan emblazoned with a deep crimson star on his chest. He'd worn these colours before but he'd justified it to himself then as a necessary part of his plot to bring Duke down. Now they were a disturbing reminder of a past he wanted to forget.

He'd tried to wriggle out of this predicament by suggesting a change of colours to the owner. That owner, of course, now being Lorna. He'd seen the problem looming before the start of the season and had broached it then. He'd found that she was resistant.

'Change Daddy's colours? Why?'

He couldn't give her an honest answer so he'd said, 'Because it's a fresh start. You're the new owner, racing out of a different stable. It makes sense.'

'It doesn't make sense to me. Jockeys on our horses have always worn white with a big red star. It makes them jolly easy to see.'

He'd tried another tack, one a bit closer to home. 'It's just that I don't know how my dad's going to react when he sees me in those colours. There's bound to be races of mine on TV.'

That hadn't gone down well either. 'Well, I can't help it if your father goes bananas about anything to do with mine. And I don't think you should pander to him on everything. You've said yourself he's not in his right mind half the time. I've grown up with those colours. I've said you can decide everything else about Daddy's horses but those were his colours and now they're mine.'

For once Duncan had recognised an argument he couldn't win and he'd dropped the matter. But he'd brought it up again that morning as he was dressing in the early morning light. Lorna was still in bed, where the pair of them had been for most of the time since they'd returned from the wedding reception. Racing had decreed that a honeymoon was not on the cards but he'd tried to make it up to her in other ways.

Now seemed a good moment to revive a delicate subject. 'Sure you don't want to come racing today? Watch me win on your horses?'

'Do you mind awfully if I don't?' She yawned. 'I've got to catch up on my sleep and it's all your fault.'

'Then I suppose I'd better bring you back a racecard as a souvenir. You realise it's going to say "Owner: Mrs L. Claymore"? Not "Cadogan" any more.'

'Gosh, I'd not thought of that. It makes me sound very grown up.'

'You are grown up. A proper married woman and the owner of a string of racehorses. Everything's changed. I really think you should be sending them out in different colours.'

'But I like the old ones. We talked about it.'

'Yes, but—'

'Hey, I've just thought of something. If I'm the owner, I'm supposed to give you riding instructions, aren't I?'

'The trainer does that, really.'

'But I could, couldn't I? Well, I've got some riding instructions for you – take your clothes off and come back to bed.'

It was tempting but he hesitated. 'What about the colours, Lorna?'

She didn't reply, just looked at him with her full lips set in a thin line. Then she'd pulled the sheet up over a bare golden shoulder and turned her back. So he'd blown her an unseen kiss and left. It wasn't how he'd wanted to leave her on their second morning as husband and wife.

Now he tried to clear his head and forget about it. Whatever silks he was wearing there was only one thought he could allow himself during the next four minutes – how to win the race.

The two-mile course at Towcester started on a small spur leading directly on to the straight that ran uphill past the stand and the winning post, where the race would end on the next circuit. The top of the straight was the highest part of the course and there the track took a sharp right-handed turn and led downhill out into the country. The entire field, grouped together, negotiated this without problem, but this section of the contest was the easy bit. There was only one hurdle along the top straight and then man and beast could revel in the thrill of thundering down into the next bend. Two more obstacles came and went as they galloped towards the bottom of the course. The business end of the contest was getting closer.

Duncan had positioned Ansible on the outside of the pack as the runners swung round the long bottom curve. It meant they travelled further but there was no chance of getting boxed in and he had a clear view of the runners ahead of him. The field was beginning to stretch out now as they jumped the third to last hurdle and the ground beneath began to rise. From here it was a long uphill grind to the winning post, still a good half-mile off. This was what made Towcester such a challenging course. Some said it was the stiffest track in the country. Whether that was true or not, it was a proper test of stamina for a horse. But he was feeling confident about Ansible. His race at Fontwell back in the spring had been over two miles and six furlongs in heavy going – he ought to be able to handle two miles on good ground today.

Duncan gave the horse a tap on the shoulder with his stick – time to get going. Ansible obediently quickened and moved past three horses on the inside. As they approached the final bend there were two horses ahead, Client Trust the second favourite, who still looked full of energy, and the leader, a big black horse who had made all the running so far. Duncan discounted the leader. Towcester was a tough track to make and he reckoned the animal must be tiring rapidly.

Into the home straight there were two hurdles left to clear and the incline was even stiffer. Over the first obstacle, Client Trust landed ahead of the leading animal and Duncan tracked him, a length behind. The black horse was out of the picture now: there was just the two of them. All thoughts of Lorna and Charlie and past quarrels were gone from his mind. There was just him and Ansible, joined together like one creature, timing their moment to fly past their rival and take the race in a symbolic victory – his first on a former Cadogan horse, his first as a married man, his first of a new winning partnership.

They took the last hurdle abreast of Client Trust. Now was the time for Ansible to give him the turn of speed he'd shown at home and Duncan gave him a quick reminder – the race was theirs, he had no doubt.

Only, it wasn't. Ansible seemed to stumble and Client Trust forged ahead. Duncan wielded the whip, urging the animal on. But no matter how hard he pushed and kicked, it was plain that his horse had nothing left to give and the race was lost.

The black horse who had led for so long overtook them on the run-in, his rider flogging him to the line. Duncan made no effort to contest the runner-up spot. Punters might complain, but he didn't believe in bullying a horse into the secondary places. To his mind, you won the race or you were nowhere. And, as he crossed the line on the exhausted Ansible, nowhere was a bitterly disappointing place to be.

'Not bad,' said Petie, as he walked with them back to the enclosure.

'But not good enough,' Duncan growled. 'He's not fit.'

'Well, we can fix that. Come on, knock that devil off your shoulder.'

Knock that devil off your shoulder. It was what Petie said when he meant cheer up. The trouble was that the devil on Duncan's shoulder would never be satisfied. Even if he'd won, his elation would soon have been replaced by another anxiety, another demon on his shoulder. Like, where's the next winner coming from? But he hadn't won and that burned him inside. Duncan was a victory junkie. He needed it in his veins.

The next race was a blank as Duncan didn't have a ride which, after a loss such as the one he had just sustained, was a pity. After he'd weighed in, he sat silently on the bench by his peg in the changing room. His valet rolled his eyes but said nothing and the other jockeys ignored him, familiar with his moods. Finally, he roused himself. The best thing to clear the disappointment from his head was to immediately face another challenge. He couldn't afford to indulge himself for too long. These days he had to look outside his own little bubble. After all, he was more than just a jockey now.

He met Petie in the parade ring ahead of the fourth race on the card. He didn't have a ride in this either but he did have an interest. Hotandcold, another Cadogan horse, was in the field with Petie's second female jockey, Fee Markham. In other circumstances, Duncan might have coveted the ride himself but he couldn't deny that Fee, who'd been up to her knees in horse muck at Petie's yard all summer, deserved her chance. In any case, as the owner's husband, Duncan had another function.

'Go out there and enjoy yourself,' he said to the trim figure in boots and britches, ignoring the irritation of her red and white Cadogan silks. 'As long as you and the horse come back safe and sound then me and Lorna are happy.' It was all he ever wanted owners to say to him before a race.

Fee's anxious face broke into a grin. She thought he was taking the mickey. 'It's hardly the Grand National, Duncan.'

'Maybe not.' Petie fixed her with scowl. 'But three miles over hurdles round this course is no picnic. You tuck your lad in and take it easy. No heroics. Concentrate on getting him round. And if you end up with a chance of a finish, that's a bonus.'

She nodded seriously. Duncan had no doubt she was noting every word. Slim, pretty and always up for a laugh, Fee had ambitions and the nerve to make the most of them.

As Petie legged her up, he was hailed from across the ring.

'Hello there, Quinn!' Two hulking men dressed identically in dark suits, pink shirts and blue ties had disengaged from a group on the far side and were barrelling in their direction.

'Who the hell are they?' Duncan muttered but the men were on them before Petie had a chance to reply. Handshakes and backslaps took place all round. The men seemed extremely pleased at this surprise meeting, although their Irish accents were so thick that Duncan missed half of what they were saying. However, he soon discovered that these men were the Joyce brothers or, rather, two of them. It seemed there were more, the youngest being Michael who was riding in this race.

'We'll watch it from the bar,' announced the senior brother, Martin, and Duncan found himself swept up in the group heading for the second floor of the members' stand. The raucous Irish intervention shattered the funereal atmosphere in which serious race-goers were indulging their twin passions – the study of racing form and the downing of alcohol. Despite the interruption, the cloth caps of the members barely lifted from their copies of *Sporting Life*.

'You're the lad who just got married, aren't ya?' said Patrick, the other Joyce, as Martin and Petie negotiated at the bar.

'Our Michelle says you were up at the yard the day of your wedding. She couldn't get over it.'

Ah, the Michelle connection. These must be the cousins. It explained the ebullient friendliness. Petie was doing them a favour, taking in that slip of a girl and her mad horse.

'I hope she's finding her feet. Likes her digs and everything.'

'Can't say. I only heard this second hand from her ma, Auntie Kath. Knowing Mich she'll be sleeping with Sammy anyway, till he gets settled in.'

Sammy the mad horse. In Duncan's opinion that wouldn't be any time soon.

Martin and Petie returned clutching pint glasses of bitter, even one for him. Petie shrugged, as in 'I tried to stop him but couldn't' as Duncan politely refused.

'Well, it won't go to waste,' said Martin. 'Let's watch the race outside.' He shouldered his way through the door, a glass in each hand.

As Duncan suspected, they had a fine view of proceedings from up here. The three-mile course started halfway along the top straight running downhill out into the country. From there the runners followed the circuit down into the dip, then up the gradient into the home straight and past the spectators along the rails and in the stand – before taking on another complete circuit. It was a fair old slog, even in the mild conditions of a pleasant autumn day. Duncan was pleased to see that Fee had followed instructions and positioned Hotandcold in the pack to the rear of the eight-strong field. He noted that the horse was clearing each hurdle nicely. Fee's white and red colours, he had to admit, made her progress easy to follow.

Irish eyes, however, were on the pink silks of the jockey tucked in behind the leader as the horses swept past the stand for the first time.

'Go on, Michael, my boy!' roared Martin into Duncan's ear. 'You're doin' grand.'

On the other side of him Patrick was adding to the racket, which echoed round the stand and over the spectators below, some of whom looked up to see who was getting worked up so early in proceedings.

'Michael's got this one sewn up,' said Martin. He'd finished his first pint and was working on the second.

'There's still a long way to go,' Duncan said, irritated by too much Irish triumphalism.

'Right enough but Michael's on a lot of horse. With respect to your little lady there who's doing a grand job, I don't think he's got a lot to beat.'

And so it proved. As the race proceeded the field unravelled until a string of horses covered the best part of half a furlong. Michael Joyce held his position, never falling more than three or four lengths behind the leader. As they jumped the second to last in the home straight he moved up to sit on the front runner's shoulder. They jumped the last together and then Michael kicked on to leave his rival floundering on the run-in and won by a clear five lengths.

Martin and Patrick went bananas with excitement and Duncan was swept up in a beery embrace. He hadn't taken his eyes off the course, however, and had seen Fee's steady progress through the tiring field, picking off flagging runners one by one.

'Did you see that?' he said to Petie.

'Aye, she finished in the frame.'

In some circumstances, Duncan reflected, third place wasn't such a disappointment after all.

*

Duncan had few expectations of the penultimate race on the card, a three-mile-one-furlong chase over eighteen fences. He was riding another Cadogan horse, The Black 'Un, a small seven-year-old named, Duncan assumed, for his glossy raven-dark coat. He'd not had much time to get to know the horse. He'd only sat on him once and had concluded that he was a lazy lump, certainly he'd not put himself out on Petie's gallops. His past form didn't show much. After an undistinguished career on the Flat he'd done nothing over hurdles in his first jumps season and sat out the whole of the next with a stress fracture that wouldn't heal. The only bright spot on his CV was a victory in a novice chase at Bangor. But that had been before his injury and, on the evidence so far, Duncan feared it was destined to be the horse's one moment of glory.

Before the race he'd looked for Michael Joyce in the changing room. Petie had marked his card about the Joyces as they'd left them heading back to the bar. 'Irish raiders,' he'd muttered. 'Their speciality is turning up and nicking the good prizes. Bloody irritating but you can't help admiring the crazy bastards.'

'So what's with the grey horse – Prince Samson?'

'The boys are looking for an arrangement this side of the water. I've still got a few pals in Ireland and they put in a word for me. If we can get Prince Samson in shape, there'll be better prospects to come.'

'And the girl?'

'I'm taking her on to keep the Joyces sweet. She's wanting rides already so that might be tricky. I've got enough on my plate with Roisin and young Fee nagging me.'

'Michelle knows how to handle Prince Samson. That's something.'

Petie had ignored the remark. 'I'll put up with her as long as it takes to make this thing work with the Joyces. I can rely on you to help out, can't I?'

Duncan had not been entirely sure what the trainer meant but it was with those words in mind that he'd sought out Michael. 'Nice ride in the last. Well done.'

'And who the feck are you?' Michael was a sandy-haired fellow with freckles. His pink silks didn't do him any favours.

Duncan introduced himself. 'I met your cousin the other day up at Petie Quinn's yard.'

'Michelle? She's a darling. Fantastic wee horsewoman too. You'd better treat her right or you'll have me and my brothers comin' after yer.' That was a daunting thought. 'So no hanky-panky, all right? Keep your hands to yourself.'

Duncan laughed. 'You don't need to worry about me, mate – I got married on Saturday.'

'Get away!' The Irish lad slapped him on the back. 'So what are you doing here, you silly bastard? Why aren't you on honeymoon? Cuddling up on some sizzling beach with your missus.'

'That might come later. I've got a job to do. You don't ride winners on beaches.'

'And you don't ride them here either,' Michael said. 'Not if I'm on a decent prospect in the next – which I am.'

So here they were, lining up for the start of the chase. Duncan was amused and irritated by the Irish rider's words. He'd love to put the cheeky sod in his place but for that he was reliant on the diminutive black animal underneath him. At least The Black 'Un was keeping calm, ignoring a frisky horse who'd suddenly backed out of the line and upset the start. Some of the other runners showed signs of agitation at the delay but the black horse was unfazed – or half asleep. The latter was more likely, Duncan thought. They were left standing when the starter finally sent them off.

'Come on, you dozy bugger,' Duncan swore as they ran to the first fence in last position.

They were still last as they approached that same fence on the second circuit, though the field had thinned somewhat; there had been two fallers and another horse had refused at the open ditch at the top of the course. Duncan had to concede that The Black 'Un could jump. He'd been mulish and uninterested when schooling over fences at the yard but here he was accurate in take-off and landing, taking all the obstacles in his stride. If only Duncan could get a turn of speed out of him, there might be some hope after all. But The Black 'Un seemed to have only one gear, a low one. They'd get round all right but unless the rest of the field took a tumble they wouldn't be making any punters happy.

All the same, they sailed over the water jump and took the fence that followed sweetly. Then it was over the open ditch and into the long uphill to the home straight. They were among the other runners now and some of them were plainly flagging. Duncan anticipated that The Black 'Un would also be feeling the pain but if he was he didn't show it. Instead he ploughed on without faltering and turning for home they were only halfway down the field. Well, at least this wasn't turning out to be a disaster.

The little black horse stood off the second to last fence and cleared it with a mighty leap, landing upsides of the second favourite. Ahead, on the inside, two horses were having a private battle and in front of them, a good half a dozen lengths clear of the field, were the silks of Michael Joyce on the most fancied animal in the race. Duncan gave his horse a couple of sharp taps with his stick. The animal took no apparent notice, just continued to gallop on.

As they passed the two on the inside Duncan glanced across and saw that the pair were treading water, being kept going by the furious exertions of the men on board. He himself was doing nothing but staying balanced, making it as easy as possible for the horse beneath him who, he now realised, had reserves of stamina no one had suspected. He may not possess a quick change of pace but he could move up the gears all the same. It was barely credible but, after three miles of up hill and down dale over fences and ditches and water hazards, they were flying along.

Duncan knew this was too good to be true and as The Black 'Un took off over the last fence he half expected the horse to crumple on landing. Or for fatigue to come down like a hammer on the run-in. Or for the horse to just simply stop. But he didn't. He kept charging remorselessly on, catching a surprised Michael Joyce in front of the stand and winning by a clear three lengths.

Joyce caught up to him on the other side of the winning post and held out a hand. 'You fecker. I'll get you next time,' he said with a grin.

To Petie, Duncan said, 'The little bugger fooled us all along. We're keeping him.'

'You've cheered up then.'

Duncan couldn't argue with that. There was nothing like winning.

Duncan took his time in the shower, savouring his victory. Thinking back over the afternoon, it hadn't been that bad after all. Three of the Cadogan horses had run and all three had finished in the places. Ansible had disappointed but then maybe expectations had been unrealistic. And anyway, The Black 'Un had more than made up for it. He had the feeling the small black horse could turn out to be something special. Grudgingly he admitted that Duke's trainer, William Osborne, had done a pretty decent job. But then he was the champion trainer and had been at the top of the tree since the sixties – he ought to know what he was doing.

Duncan had given Petie a lift to the course so the Irishman could experience the Lamborghini that was Duncan's favourite among Duke's cars. The trainer had not been impressed. 'Jesus, it's doing my back in,' he'd complained. 'It may be all right for bendy lads like you but I'm going to need a stepladder to get out of this thing.' So Duncan had expected a similar earful on the way back but Petie had other things on his mind.

'I ran into Martin Joyce just now. He was cheesed off. He thought they had the last one in the bag till that Spring Moon hacked up.'

Spring Moon, trained by William Osborne, had romped home in the two-and-a-half-mile handicap hurdle that had wrapped up the afternoon. At 40-1 it was the longest-priced winner of the day and consequently the most surprising. Michael Joyce's runner had finished second.

Duncan shrugged. 'Osborne's smart. Our horses did OK today – I suppose we've got to give him a bit of credit.'

'I won't tell your dad you said that.' Petie gave him a long look from the passenger seat. 'You must be mellowing in your old age.'

Duncan let that pass. Not mellowing, just prepared to see the bigger picture maybe. Keen to bury the hurts of the past.

4

Duncan wasn't feeling quite so charitable the next morning when he turned the yellow Lamborghini into the driveway of Petie's yard and found a sleek black Porsche parked in his usual spot. He knew that car.

There was activity going on at the back of the stables, near the five-bar gate that led out to the lane up to the gallops. He could see four figures grouped around a horse and a mounted rider. The horse was being a bit skittish and he could identify the stocky figure of Petie Quinn holding the reins. Roisin was there too: her slender silhouette was easy to spot. The other two were fairly new stable staff.

He also recognised the horse. Destiny's Dream, a nine-year-old bay gelding with a white blaze on his face, one of the horses to have come across from Osborne's stable. A mud-loving steeple-chaser, the horse had been a regular winner for Cadogan the previous winter, landing some decent prize money in a sequence of victories at Sandown and Newbury. He'd gone on to win the Armagnac Bowl at the Grand National meeting at Aintree and was a horse Duncan had earmarked as central to his campaign for the season.

But there, sitting astride Destiny's Dream, reins in one hand, the other resting arrogantly on his hip, was another rider. The owner of the Porsche. Osborne's stable jockey and champion for the last three seasons. For all his intentions of burying the past, there was only one way Duncan thought of Sandy Sanderson. He was the enemy. Sanderson, along with Osborne and Cadogan, had been responsible for Charlie's downfall. It was not something that Duncan could forgive.

Roisin looked up and quickly looked away.

'Mornin',' Petie said cheerfully.

When Petie said good morning in cheerful style you knew there was nothing to be cheerful about.

'What's going on?' Duncan asked.

Sanderson flashed his teeth at Duncan, all smiles and no words.

'Sandy here is helping us out,' Petie said. 'Just for a while, like.'

'Helping us out? How is he helping us out?'

'Well you said yourself yer man here was a bit frisky.' *Yer man* was Destiny's Dream, who seemed to have calmed down to listen to all this with interest. 'I think Sandy could get the best out of him.'

Duncan clamped his jaw shut. Roisin walked away, heading back up to the house.

It was true that Destiny's Dream was a difficult animal. It wasn't just the question of him jamming on at his hurdles, he was unpredictable, volatile even. He could float like a cloud one minute, no trouble at all. Then for no apparent reason he might want to take a bite out of another horse or cow-kick one of the stable lads. Duncan had been on his back several times but he hadn't yet got the measure of him. It was proving tricky.

'Let's get going,' Sanderson said, ignoring Duncan. 'I don't have all day.'

'Just don't think you'll be riding him next time out, that's all,' Duncan said.

'You might have to rethink that, son,' Sanderson said.

'Petie?'

'Listen,' Petie said, 'you've not got the mastery of him just yet. I've called Sandy in to help us out and he's said he would. No need for you to feel your nose is out of joint.'

'He's young,' Sanderson put in, 'and he doesn't realise sometimes you need to match the jockey with the horse.' There was something lizard-like about him, Duncan decided. The years exposed to the elements on the back of a horse had left him with a scaly, weather-beaten complexion, and he had a habit of darting his tongue out before speaking. 'Best man for the best job and all that. He'll learn.'

'Aren't you both forgetting something? I'm the owner of this horse. I'll decide who rides him.'

'No,' Petie said sharply, 'I'm the trainer and I'll decide what's best. And if you want to make this an arse-kickin' competition and speak to me like a stuck-up owner all ye need to do is pay me the stabling fees you owe me for all these horses you've got here. Meanwhile go and see Roisin and she'll let you know your schedule for this morning.'

Sanderson smirked openly. The stable hands, silent throughout this exchange, looked away, embarrassed.

Sanderson trotted Destiny's Dream towards the gallops.

Lorna arrived late at La Tante Claire in Chelsea. But then, she rarely arrived on time for anything, especially lunch with a man. In her experience chaps were usually very pleased to see her and made allowances for any delay. As they jolly well should, given that she'd probably taken extra time to make herself look nice for them. On this occasion she hadn't gone to too much trouble, just a little black jacket worn with a raspberry polka-dot dress that wrapped over at the front. Though he'd never made a pass at her, Uncle Willy would appreciate it, she was sure. All middle-aged men, unless they had an eye for boys, liked a hint of cleavage.

As she had expected, William Osborne showed no displeasure at her tardiness but rose swiftly from his seat to greet her with a kiss on the cheek. He was a tall, lean man with a foxy face and a ready smile. As one of her father's companions while she was growing up, he'd never been less than charming to her. But this was the first time they had been on their own together as equals, with no prospect of her father walking through the door. Lorna didn't know quite what to expect.

'You're looking radiant,' he said. 'Just like a beautiful bride. I understand the wedding was a famous success.'

'It was lovely. Everyone had a wonderful time.' She hesitated. 'I'm sorry you couldn't be there but – you know.'

'It's all right, my dear, I'm not mortally offended. I know the reasons and they are nothing to do with you.'

It was a relief to have got that out of the way. A glass of champagne had appeared in front of her and, though she had resolved to stick to orange juice, she sipped nervously and reached for the menu. It was written in dauntingly complex French. A waiter was already hovering expectantly.

'What do you fancy, Lorna? I can recommend the chef's signature dish – that's what I'm having.'

She quickly agreed, happy to solve the problem. French had not been her best subject at school – not that there had been many of those.

'Where is Duncan today?'

'Ludlow. He's got three races. I'm surprised you don't know that. One of your horses is up against him this afternoon.'

'Of course. The thing is, Lorna, I have horses running at

45

different meetings and I sometimes lose track. I'll be dashing off to catch the last couple at Plumpton after this.'

'I'm surprised you could find time to fit me in.'

'Have you told Duncan that you were meeting me?'

'I haven't had the chance.' She wondered if he'd spot the outright lie.

'I'll be honest, Lorna. Your new husband dislikes me so much that I couldn't see him allowing me to talk to you. But I was one of your father's oldest friends and I'm concerned for you.'

'Why's that?'

At that moment, waiters arrived and served their food with a flourish. She found herself confronted by a suspiciously shaped log of meat covered in a rich chocolate-black sauce next to a small mound of creamed potato topped with a wafer-thin crisp. It was elegant and daunting. The waiter declared its identity in precisely enunciated French. This time she caught a phrase: *pieds de cochon*.

'Pigs feet?' she murmured in horror.

'Stuffed with morels and sweetbreads,' Osborne replied. 'This restaurant is famous for it.'

'Gosh.' She prodded the potato with her fork and wished she had the nerve to ask for something else.

'As I was saying,' Osborne swallowed a mouthful and fixed her with his pale brown eyes, 'I'm concerned about your situation. Duke was a bit chaotic with his spending, and I say that as one of his closest friends. I imagine his estate will take some ironing out. So if you need any help you'd better come to me or I'll be very cross.'

'Help how?'

'If you need any money.'

Lorna looked startled. 'But we're fine. For money, I mean.'

'I'm pleased to hear it but probate can take some time to come through, you know.'

Lorna had no experience of these things but she was finding out. She'd visited her father's solicitor shortly after his death and taken Duncan along, which had seemed sensible but hadn't made the meeting any easier.

As soon as they had walked into the offices of Pargetter & Jolt and met the elderly Mungo Pargetter, Duncan had decided the lawyer was a wrong 'un. 'What sort of a name is Mungo anyway?' he'd muttered loudly.

Lorna shushed him. She'd met Mr Pargetter before, when he'd been a guest at the house. Her father had often crossed business with leisure. In fact it seemed to her that all of Daddy's 'friends' were also business associates. Everyone who had turned up at her father's funeral had had some sort of business connection with him.

Pargetter was a bald man with unfashionable mutton-chop sideburns that did little to disguise his heavy jowls. He sat in the gloom of a walnut-panelled office surrounded by shelves of leather-bound books which looked like they hadn't been opened this century.

'My commiserations to both of you,' the solicitor said, looking over the top of his tortoiseshell-rimmed spectacles.

'Thank you,' Lorna said.

'I was of service to your father for a long time and I'm happy to take charge of probate. You'll want me to apply for a letter of administration.'

'What?'

'Your uncle was named as executor. He has told me he doesn't want anything to do with it. You are the only person named in the will, Lorna, so that makes you the administrator. But I have to apply.'

'How long will that take?' Duncan asked.

Pargetter peered at Duncan for a moment and spoke slowly to both of them, as if to children. It occurred to Lorna that, in these matters, that's exactly what they were.

'Here is what has to be done: value the estate and speak to Mr Cadogan's banks to get a grant of representation; complete the relevant application and inheritance tax form – you will of course be subject to inheritance tax; send the forms to the Probate Registry and Her Majesty's Revenue & Customs; attend in person at a probate venue or at the office of any commissioner for oaths to swear an oath; wait for the grant of representation to arrive in the post – banks and other organisations will ask to see this before they allow access to the deceased's assets; pay any debts owed by the estate and then distribute the estate.'

'Christ! It's a full-time job!' Duncan burst out.

'Quite. That is why you require my services.'

'Have Daddy's bank accounts been frozen?' Lorna asked.

'That is correct. It's standard procedure pending probate.'

'The thing is,' Lorna said, 'we've got staff to pay, and other expenses.'

Pargetter cleared his throat. 'That's understandable. We'll make an application to the banks to cover funeral and legal costs etc. But you will have to make a separate application to the banks to cover wages and other outgoings. A loan secured by the house or other assets on the estate would do it.'

'How long?' Duncan asked again.

'Six to nine months, if we're lucky. But I really can't say at this stage.'

'Jesus!'

'It's not a horse race, Mr Claymore,' Pargetter had pronounced with satisfaction and smiled affably at the pair of them as they left the room.

It struck Lorna now, sitting across the table from Osborne, that it been almost six months since that meeting and they'd heard nothing recently from the solicitor. She'd tried to forget all about money and Daddy's estate and all that probate gobble-degook while burying herself in planning her wedding. But she was aware that cash was getting tight. It had turned out that her father had a company called DC Equine under whose banner he managed his racing affairs. They had been permitted to use the company account to pay for the upkeep and training of the Cadogan horses – which was considerable – but she'd seen a recent bank statement that Duncan had left lying around just before the wedding and, if she understood it correctly, the company money was now all gone.

Osborne was regarding her shrewdly. 'When Duncan moved your father's horses out of my yard—'

Lorna interrupted. 'It's not like he didn't ask me, you know.'

'Quite. I'm sure it's entirely understandable that you chose to support your fiancé. However, when those horses left, I was upset to lose some first-class prospects, animals I'd invested a lot of time in. And there's the issue of a breach of contract. I want you to know that I'd be prepared to buy one or two of them back, at top prices, any time you want.'

'Oh.' Things became clearer. 'So this is why you invited me to lunch.'

'I've invited you to celebrate your wedding – in view of the fact that I wasn't able to do it at the time. It also gives me the opportunity to propose a truce with Duncan and I hope you'll be the intermediary. Let me buy some of Duke's horses. I've a feeling you're going to need some cash before his estate is wound up.'

'That's kind of you, Uncle Willy, but I'm sure we're OK. And I don't know about the horses – that's all down to Duncan now.'

'Really? You can't just wash your hands of your father's

business and leave it to hubby. I didn't think you girls were such pushovers these days.'

She felt a spark of anger light within her. She wasn't a pushover, was she? She'd not let Duncan get away with changing Daddy's colours.

'You know, if we could come to some arrangement about one or two horses,' Osborne continued, 'I'd be more inclined to drop my case for breach of contract.'

'I didn't realise you were filing a law suit against us!' Lorna said hotly.

'It's not that I want to, but it's business and I've got to look after my own investments. You can understand that, I'm sure.'

'If you're as concerned about me as you say, you should drop it anyway,' she said, more loudly than she'd intended. Suddenly she felt close to tears.

He reached across the table. 'Don't get upset. Like I said, it's just business, my dear. A negotiating tactic.'

She didn't know what to think. Maybe she shouldn't have come.

'Look,' he continued, still holding her hand, 'I've got another idea that might make things better all round. Why doesn't Duncan ride a few horses for me?'

She pulled her hand away. 'He'd never agree to that.'

'Why not? He's ridden for me before. And, let's be honest, he's still a youngster making his way in the game. It's only a couple of years since he was a conditional. I could put him on a couple of sure things and give his career a boost.'

Lorna frowned. Something didn't quite add up. 'If Duncan's so inexperienced, why would you offer him your best horses. Sanderson's your stable jockey.'

Osborne smiled expansively. 'Sandy and I make a good team. But he's his own man at the end of the day and sometimes his plans don't coincide with mine. I need more than one top rider if Sandy's off doing his own thing.'

'You mean Sandy's getting rides from someone else?'

Osborne laughed. 'Of course. They all do it. Don't expect fidelity from a jockey. Oh dear, I shouldn't have said that, should I? I'm sure your husband is an entirely different animal.'

Lorna decided not to take offence but she'd had enough. Some of the things he'd said needed thinking about. She began to make her excuses. 'I'm sorry about the food,' she said. She'd hardly touched it. 'What are sweetbreads anyway?'

'Calves pancreases.'

She blanched. There were some tastes she didn't want to acquire.

Osborne paid the bill and accompanied her to the door. 'Just bear in mind what I've said, Lorna.'

'Honestly, Uncle Willy, we don't need any money and Duncan won't want to ride for you, I'm sure of it.'

'Really? He might if you ask him nicely. I'm sure you can be very persuasive.'

She left him at the door and almost ran down the street.

The meeting at Ludlow was a complete washout for Duncan. His first ride gave all he had but finished sixth out of eight runners, his second went to sleep at the start and was never in the race, and his third dumped him at the open ditch on the far side and ran off, leaving Duncan to walk back in the rain that was blowing in from the Brecon Beacons. So Duncan was bruised and pissed off when he arrived in the owners' bar, where he'd arranged to meet his agent, Mike Ruddy.

Mike was a former jockey whose moderate success in the saddle had been eclipsed by his meteoric rise as a jockeys' representative. Since he had sweet-talked Duncan into being his first client he had built a proper business for himself, starting something of a fashion for jockeys who had previously had to do their own haggling. They'd jumped at the chance of a big mouth like Mike doing the dirty work on their behalf – for a percentage, of course. The owners and trainers hated the idea of negotiating with an agent instead of with a jockey, whom they could stiff pretty easily; but as a former rider Mike knew the game only too well and it wasn't possible to pull the wool over his eyes. Nowadays he was working hard at expanding his influence through clever PR and his remarkable gift of the gab.

A bottle of champagne stood on the table. 'I thought you might need a bit of reviving,' Mike said as he popped the cork. 'You still in one piece?'

'I'll live, I suppose.'

'Well, cheer up then, you grouchy sod. Have you met Rita and Vanessa?'

Nowadays Mike never appeared at any racetrack without two beautiful leggy 'assistants'. They both carried clipboards but they never did anything except fetch drinks from the bar, light Mike's cigarettes and help him into a taxi at the end of a hard-working, heavy-boozing evening. They were models, hired by the day. But the jockeys were suckers for the air of glamour it created around Mike and they came running to be on his books. These days he could pick and choose who he wanted to represent.

For all his flash ways, Mike was a man you could trust. Duncan had confided in Ruddy about the cash-flow problems he and Lorna were experiencing while waiting for Duke's money to come through. In particular, Duncan was concerned about the bill that was mounting with Petie Quinn now the DC Equine account had run out.

Mike poured the champagne. 'I've got some news. There's a group of City brokers all ready to go clay-pigeon shooting at your gaff.'

Duncan groaned. They'd talked about this idea already, with Mike explaining how it worked. 'The big thing is corporate weekends for business colleagues. They shoot some old parrot out of a tree and it's called team building.'

'Parrot?'

'Pheasants. Partridges. You know. Get them shooting pheasants, or each other. Who cares? Accommodate them at the house. These Hooray Henry boys are awash with cash. And cash is what you need. Don't put it through your books, because it's all still subject to probate.'

Duncan had dismissed the idea then and now Mike was bringing it up again.

'Look, there's only a couple of dozen of them. You clear out, the bosses stay at the house and the rest of them shack up at a nearby hotel. We lay on the bubbly and—'

'Who's we?'

'Me and the girls. If you want to organise it, go ahead. Otherwise we'll do it for you, won't we, girls?'

'Oh yes!' said Vanessa, narrowing her eyes at him. 'We'll be brilliant.'

'She doesn't even know what it is,' said Mike, 'but they'll be good at it.'

'And you'll handle it all. For ten per cent I guess.'

'Of course it's ten per cent. I'm your mate not bloody Santa Claus. It's a lot of work. But it's big moolah for you. These City boys have got money coming out of their ears.'

Duncan shook his head. It sounded like a complete pain. 'Thanks for the thought, Mike, but it's no go. We're not that desperate.'

The agent shrugged. 'Let me know if you change your mind. Anyhow, I've got another scheme for you.'

'Let's hear it then.' Duncan was beginning to feel more civilised.

Mike turned to the two models. 'Pull us in another bottle of fizz, would you, girls?' They knew better than to be asked twice and swished off to the bar.

Duncan watched them go. How did they manage on those heels? When they were out of earshot he said, 'Which one are you bumping?'

'Guess. You can't go wrong.'

'Not both?'

Mike's grin was melon-sized.

'You jammy sod.' Another thought struck Duncan. 'Together?'

'You've got a filthy mind for a married man. Actually, I haven't figured out a way to ask. Not yet anyway.'

Duncan sighed. His days of bachelor lechery were behind him. 'So what's this plan?'

'Consortium buying. These horses you have. Petie won't want to buy them all off you. So we sell them to a small group of these lads from the City. They're into doing the same thing with artworks, so why not horses? They operate as a group so they spread the risk.'

'What's in it for them?'

'Racing is a glamour sport and they can brag about owning a racehorse. Plus it gets them on the inside. Meet the jockeys. Visit the stables. Access to the owners' bar.'

Duncan looked round the bar. It wasn't exactly jumping. A lot of men in Barbour coats sat around with jockeys still red-faced from their exertions.

Mike read his thoughts. 'What you don't understand, Duncan, is that glamour isn't the reality, it's the perception of reality.

Look at Vanessa over there. You take all that make-up off and put her in an M&S frock and she's Miss Nobody.'

'And you think they'd want to own a horse?'

'I don't think, I know. They just want to swan around parade rings, talking bullshit, pretending they know what they're doing. They don't want to interfere. They just get to visit the stables. Everything is as it is already. Except we get you a nice price for a second-rate horse.'

'What, we swindle them? I'm not playing that game.'

Mike rolled his eyes. 'Look, there's a difference between swindling someone and getting the best possible price. If I got the worst price for my client what sort of an agent would I be? A horse is worth what someone will pay for it.'

'I dunno, Mike. I'm not sure about it. And I don't know what Petie would think.'

'Here he is now,' Mike said as the bar door opened. 'Let's ask him. Girls! Where's that fizz got to?'

5

It was ridiculous, Duncan thought, he was living in paradise but it felt like hell.

He was lying in the king-sized bed in the master bedroom of the Cadogan mansion which Lorna had commandeered. Duke had not used it in a dozen years, not since his wife's death, and Lorna had refurnished and modernised it for their use. The room now contained a cutting-edge sound system and the biggest TV on the market; there were his-and-hers walk-in closets and the adjoining bathroom boasted a sunken whirlpool bath and a double shower. Duncan had been indifferent to the rearrangement but had not thought it his place at the time to interfere. Besides, it had given Lorna a project at a time when she needed it. Now he looked round at the fancy gadgets and luxurious fittings and thought, how much did that cost?

It had been a drag of a journey in the wet back from Ludlow, even in the Lamborghini. Just because you were in a luxury motor most people would kill for didn't mean you could drive through the rush-hour Midlands traffic any quicker. He'd travelled back on his own – not surprisingly Petie had refused to accept another ride in the 'yellow sickbag', as he'd referred to it. But Duncan had been happy to do without Petie Quinn's company. The Irish trainer might be the anchor in Duncan's career now his old man was out of the game but Petie could be a devious bastard. Right now Duncan had a bone to pick with him – a weather-beaten, lizard-faced bone known as Sandy Sanderson.

Duncan had history with Sanderson. Leaving aside the fact that he was Osborne's man and that the pair of them and Duke Cadogan had driven Charlie out of racing – he'd put that behind him now – Sanderson had always been an irritant. Although he was a brilliant horseman who currently dominated the riding fraternity, that didn't mean the long-standing champion jockey was a likeable guy. Though quick to smile for the public, always with a ready joke for the camera or a PR agent, forever bigging up his charity work in the press, in the changing room or out on the course, Duncan had found Sandy to be a mean-spirited little shit. And he wasn't any nicer to his nearest and dearest, Duncan knew that for a fact – though the source of his information, the glamorous Christie Sanderson, was strictly off-limits these days.

As he'd driven back, Duncan's mood – briefly lifted by the diverting company of Mike and his little harem – had nosedived. And when he'd finally reached home he'd dumped it all on Lorna: the foul drive, the hopeless rides, the bruised elbow from his fall and, above all, the early morning sight of Sanderson at the yard on Destiny's Dream. It came spilling out in one long whinge of complaint as his wife eased him out of his clothes and ministered to his hurts, ran him a bath and fetched him supper on a tray so he could eat it in bed where, soon afterwards, she arranged herself for his pleasure and whispered in his ear that she loved him and made rude suggestions that he had followed almost without thinking. Finally she had managed to shut him up.

Now Lorna was in the bathroom next door, getting ready to return to bed and resume her role of the devoted and sympathetic new wife. By rights, of course, he should be squiring her around the Caribbean or somewhere suitably exotic – cuddling up with her on a sizzling beach, like Michael Joyce had said. Jesus, what must she be thinking about him and his moans? Why couldn't he ever just lie back and be happy?

The truth was that he had fallen in the shit and come up smelling of roses. Duke's death wouldn't go away. He had to live with the fact that, though he hadn't intended it, he was responsible. But because of it he was now married to a woman who doted on him and he was about to come into a fortune – including a string of horses which could be the stepping stone to his ambition of being the number one jockey in National Hunt racing. Looked at that way, he was truly a lucky bastard. He had to keep the big picture in mind. So what if Sandy Sanderson blagged a few rides off Petie? The guy couldn't go on for ever. He might be top of the tree today but, if Duncan worked hard and kept focused, tomorrow was surely his.

He turned as Lorna came into the room. She wore an over-sized blue-and-white pyjama top – one of his – and nothing else. She looked fantastic. He held out his arms.

'Come here.'

Lorna had been in turmoil as she brushed her hair in the bath-room. Every moment of her lunch with Uncle Willy replayed in her mind. Why was he so keen to offer her money? Did he know something she didn't about the estate and the lawyers? He'd made offers to buy back horses and drop the breach of contract lawsuit that he was threatening. She knew these were important proposals and ought to be debated properly. But what did she know about dealing with these kinds of things? There was only one person she could discuss them with and that was Duncan – who was bound to go potty when he found out she'd had lunch with the trainer. In fact, she'd sworn to herself when she'd accepted the invitation that she would never tell him. Now she didn't see how she could avoid it.

If only Duncan wasn't such a baby where his father was concerned. Charlie had such a terrible persecution complex about the way he'd lost his yard. Daddy had discussed the matter with her when he'd found out she was serious about Duncan as a boyfriend. He'd explained that, though Charlie was a brilliant man with horses, the trainer had mental problems and he felt sorry for him. He'd even gone out of his way to defend Charlie in the press when Duncan's dad had been accused of doping a horse. 'If he did do it, Lorna,' Daddy had said, 'it's only because he wasn't thinking straight. Someone needs to stand up for him.' But for all Daddy's efforts things had gone against Charlie and he'd been banned. And he and Duncan somehow blamed it all on Daddy and Uncle Willy and Sandy Sanderson – which was mad. But then, Charlie *was* mad some of the time, and Duncan just couldn't see it.

So now what should she do? She'd thought about it all afternoon and decided it was just too sensitive a matter to bring up with her husband. And, in any case, the resulting explosion might prove entirely unnecessary. Daddy's money would come through eventually. And though it might be awkward to suffer the lawsuit maybe it would never come to court anyway. And hadn't Uncle Willy said it was just a negotiating tactic? So maybe he wasn't serious about seeing it through. And anyway, even if they lost, they could pay whatever it cost out of the estate. In which case, she didn't need to mention any of it to Duncan. And that had been her conclusion until he'd walked through the door this evening, tired and bruised, and spitting blood about Sandy Sanderson riding one of her horses up at Petie's that morning.

She'd tried everything she could to shake him out of his bad temper. So this is what marriage is really like, she'd told herself as she'd pandered to him. She'd played nurse and mummy and sexpot and, she had to admit to herself, had still failed to bring him round. There was one card she had left to play and she reckoned it was a winner. But how damaging was it going to be for her to play it? She put down her hairbrush and considered herself in the mirror. Her auburn curls glistened, falling artfully to the shoulders of her pyjama top which skimmed the top of her pale slender thighs. She knew how good she looked. She also knew it wasn't going to save her from her husband's anger.

'Duncan, I've got a suggestion. I know how you can get your own back on Sandy Sanderson.'

That stopped Duncan's hands from roving beneath Lorna's pyjama jacket. He'd pulled her into bed, determined to apologise to her in the best way he could. He wasn't much for the lovey-dovey speeches, he was better at the actual lovey-dovey. But her words stilled him and they faced each other across the pillow, nose to nose, breathing each other's air.

'What do you mean?'

She repeated what she'd said. 'That's what's eating you up, isn't it? Sandy on a horse you reckon is yours.'

'Yes, of course.'

'Well, suppose you ride some of his.'

He laughed. 'That's impossible. Osborne would never let me near any of his horses.'

'Why don't you ask him?'

'Don't be silly, Lorna, I can't do that. It's not how it works.' He began to fondle her again, still chuckling at her naivety. Then he registered her cool, green-eyed stare. She wasn't laughing with him. She was serious.

He pulled his hand away. 'You know something, don't you?'

Then she told him. It came out slowly and calmly. That William Osborne was proposing a truce. That he wouldn't take them to court over a breach of contract concerning the removal of their horses from his yard as long as Lorna sold him some horses back. That Osborne wasn't exclusively committed to Sanderson. Suggesting that top rides would be available to Duncan at Osborne's yard. That Osborne could help Duncan's career.

But Duncan couldn't take it in. Couldn't get beyond one basic thing – that his wife had gone behind his back to meet his father's enemy. It was betrayal.

He slept in a spare bedroom – there was plenty of choice. Husband and wife in separate rooms on only the fourth night of their marriage. As he lay in the dark he wondered whether this was some kind of record.

Duncan was late leaving in the morning. He'd been too wound up over Lorna and Osborne that he'd not fallen asleep until the small hours, and then he'd overslept. As he'd left the spare bedroom along the landing he'd run into Mary, the housekeeper, who'd looked startled to see him emerging from that quarter. Lorna had insisted they kept Duke's staff on to run the big house but it still made him feel bloody uncomfortable to have servants bustling around – he'd never thought he'd ever find himself living in a real-life episode of *Upstairs Downstairs*. But that was how his wife had grown up. The more he thought about it, the wider the gulf between them yawned.

The black Porsche was parked in the same spot in the yard. He'd had a faint hope that Sanderson's visit yesterday was a one-off but it seemed there was no chance of that. The champion jockey was the kind of man who'd cut his grandmother's throat to keep a ride, he obviously wasn't going to relinquish his hold on Destiny's Dream – and who knew how many of the other horses which had come over from Osborne.

Roisin came out of the office as he crossed the forecourt in front of the old stalls. 'First lot's long gone,' she said.

'Yes, well . . . sorry I'm late.'

'I scratched you. Dad said you were a bit sore after yesterday's fall.'

'No, no, I'm fine.' His elbow hurt like stink but it wasn't his policy to let on. Even though Roisin was a fellow rider and a mate, as Petie's daughter, she also counted as management.

'Look, I'm glad I caught you. Dad won't say anything but we're behind on the training fees.'

'He did say something, actually. Yesterday when we were having that argy-bargy about Sanderson on Destiny. You must have gone by then.'

'Oh.' She looked surprised. 'So he has noticed. He always gets me to do the dirty work and chase people up.'

'So you're chasing me up, are you?'

'Well, it's just a friendly word. Maybe the bill got lost in the post.'

No, it hadn't got lost, but he wasn't going to tell her that. 'Could be,' he said. He didn't feel proud of himself. 'I'll try and sort it out.'

'That's great. Thanks.'

He looked at the row of stalls behind her. All of them were empty, even the one on the end that Prince Samson had been doing his best to destroy. 'How's your house guest?' He knew Michelle was staying with Roisin for the moment. Petie hadn't wanted her exposed to the suspect facilities of the lads' hostel.

Roisin shrugged. 'OK, I think. We haven't talked much. She's either up here with that horse of hers or running up my phone bill. She's been ringing round every trainer in England trying to get rides.'

Duncan could imagine how that might irritate Roisin. But then Roisin didn't have to blag her way on to horses, she only had to smile sweetly at her father.

A throaty roar interrupted their conversation and they turned to see a clapped-out Hillman Avenger lurch to a stop next to the Porsche and the Lamborghini. Kerry leapt out of the car.

'Nice motor pool,' he cried. 'What a beautiful morning!'

Roisin's jaw set. The beauty of the morning evidently cut no ice with her. 'Where the hell have you been?' she demanded of her smiling boyfriend. 'I suppose it's a coincidence that both of you have turned up late.'

'Well.' Kerry's smile grew even broader. 'It's true that the hospitality at Claymore Towers was generous last night. I'll be sending Lorna a small token of esteem from Interflora once we're done here this morning.'

Duncan kept his face straight as Roisin turned to him. 'You never said he was with you last night.'

Kerry was still smiling but his eyes pleaded.

'Sorry, Roisin. I thought you knew.'

'It was very last minute, my darling.' Kerry slipped an arm round her waist. 'Or else I'd have taken you along too. I heard Duncan had taken a bit of a tumble up at Ludlow so I dropped in to check up on him and ended up chewing the fat all night. Now, any chance of a cup of tea before second lot?'

Duncan left them to it. The last thing he needed was to get tangled up in Kerry's dodgy doings. He found Gypsy George supervising a horse and rider tackling the practice jumps in the back pasture. Michelle was schooling Prince Samson.

George turned to see who had taken a place beside him then

resumed his position, leaning on the fence, eyes fixed on the small figure on top of the grey horse.

'How's she doing?' Duncan asked.

'Not bad.' Not bad in George's book was pretty bloody good in anyone else's.

Small though she was, Michelle appeared to have the horse firmly in hand. There was no twitching or rearing or other sign of nerves from the big grey, on the contrary, he seemed calm and content, even as she put him to the big practice ditch. He sailed over it with ease.

Duncan was impressed. 'I see what you mean.'

'Fine animal, that one. No bloody use to us though.'

'What do you mean, George? He looks the business.'

'Yes, but he only looks the business when she's on him. He loves her but he don't like anyone else. They've all had a try on his back and he goes berserk.'

Duncan remembered the crazed animal he'd seen the other morning. Berserk was about it.

'It's still early days, George. It might just take him a long time to settle.'

'He is settled when his sweetheart's around.'

'Maybe she should ride him then. Find a modest race and put her up. That should keep the Joyces happy.'

'Huh. She might be all right back here but how's she going to hold him in a race? Look at her – she's knee-high to a flea and about as strong.'

Duncan knew that George was old school when it came to female jockeys.

'Come on, George. Some of these girls are good. Don't go talking like that around Roisin and Fee.'

'Those two have got more meat on them. Roisin's a strong lass and that Fee's a sight tougher than she looks. They're

64

proper grown-up women; this one looks like a schoolgirl.'

The schoolgirl had jumped Prince Samson neatly along the row of five practice fences and now trotted the horse over to the watching pair.

'So, Mr George,' she called out, her face pink from exertion, 'what do you think?'

'He's OK,' said George grudgingly.

'He is, isn't he?' Michelle was rubbing the horse's neck and he stood obediently, enjoying her touch. 'Will you put in a word for him with Mr Quinn? And for me?'

But George had already turned his back, heading off across the yard to the lane to hail a couple of riders. First lot was returning.

'What do you think?' she said to Duncan. 'Is there any chance Mr Quinn will find him a race?'

'He hasn't been here a week,' Duncan said. 'And he's not the easiest, is he? George says you're the only one he gets on with.'

'So? That means I'm the one who should be riding him. I can't wait to have a crack at an English racetrack.'

The excitement shone from her gleaming brown eyes and he didn't want to dampen her enthusiasm. It was infectious.

'I know,' she continued, 'you think I'm just some silly wee eejit from the bogs who fancies herself bolting up at Cheltenham without doing any work but that's not so. I'm a grafter, you ask my cousins. I'll go anywhere, do anything – I'm just looking for a chance to prove myself.'

He laughed. 'It's OK, I believe you. The way you handle your fellow there is amazing. And Michael Joyce told me up at Towcester that you're a fantastic horsewoman.'

'Did he?' She looked like she'd burst with pleasure. 'Michael's my favourite cousin. We grew up like big brother and little sister, you know.'

'Well, he's no fool in a race. Bit of a cocky sod though.'

Throughout this exchange Duncan had been keeping an eye on Prince Samson. The horse was docile but Michelle had kept him at a short distance from the fence where Duncan stood. He could tell the animal was aware of his presence and only tolerated him being this close because of the rider on his back.

'Look, Michelle, Petie's not going to take Sammy seriously if he freaks out with everyone except you. Other people have got to be able to work with him.'

She considered this for a moment. 'Suppose I show you how to make friends with him? And you persuade Mr Quinn to give me a ride?'

'It doesn't work like that. I can't persuade Petie to do anything he doesn't want to do.'

'But you can try, can't you? You've been the nicest to me here so far – and you know Michael! Come on, say we've got a deal?'

A commotion from across the fields interrupted them. Hearty male laughter. Duncan turned to see a group of riders and horses turning out of the lane into the courtyard where Petie's Land Rover was now parked. Sandy Sanderson was among the group on a bay with a distinctive white blaze on his face, exchanging loud banter with Petie. It burned Duncan up to see the pair of them so matey.

'Duncan, did you hear me? What do you say?'

He turned back to Michelle, her small, pretty face eager to hear his reply. She was a sweet kid who needed friends in this treacherous business.

'OK,' he said. 'I can't guarantee anything but I'll help you if I can. And I'd love to ride Sammy – he's a real prospect.'

He knew that if she could have jumped over the fence to kiss him, she would have.

*

Duncan accepted a lift to the pub at lunchtime with Kerry. He wanted a word with his friend.

'You do realise you're playing with fire.'

'Don't know what you mean.' Kerry shot him a look of wide-eyed innocence as he piloted the noisy Avenger along the country road.

'If you're playing away from home, I don't want you sucking me in to your scheming. I could have shopped you earlier.'

'Ah, but you didn't. That's because you're watching my back like I'm watching yours. Like I was when I did you the honour of being your best man only as recently as last weekend.'

'But I'm also watching your back when I tell you you're an idiot if you piss off the boss's daughter. She's no mug.'

'D'ye think she knows?'

'No. But if she finds out you'll be gelded with a hot iron in your sleep.'

Kerry did not reply, just concentrated on the road ahead. Duncan didn't feel up to pursuing the matter. He had his own worries.

As they turned into the pub car park he said, 'What's going on with Sanderson? Have you heard anything?'

'Don't you know? Petie says he can ride Destiny's Dream at Uttoxeter in a couple of weeks.'

Duncan felt his blood boil as he jumped out of the car and made a beeline for the pub entrance. He hated that Sanderson was at the yard, and now he was taking Duncan's rides. It was a kick in the teeth. He hadn't come to the pub for food or drink but because he couldn't use the phone in the yard for the call he now urgently needed to make. He picked up the pub's pay phone and punched in a number.

'Can I speak to William Osborne, please?'

The female voice on the other end was apologetic. 'I'm sorry, sir, Mr Osborne is occupied at present.'

'Tell him it's Duncan Claymore. I'm calling from a phone box and I've not got much change.'

It did the trick. Duncan hadn't spoken to Osborne for many months and he felt all the old familiar resentment as the trainer's voice came on the line.

'Duncan – what a pleasure to hear from you. How's married life?'

'Didn't Lorna tell you? When you had lunch with her yesterday?'

'It was delightful to see her. She looks well.'

'She says you might have some rides for me.'

'And if I have, would you be interested?'

That was the question. Despite Duncan's resolve to bury the pain of the past, it still went against the grain to team up with a man who had plotted his father's downfall. But this was a new day, with new pressures – like Sanderson stealing his rides and a lawsuit threatening their already tight funds.

'Yes, I would be. I'll ride for you, Mr Osborne.'

In the following pause Duncan heard what might have been a satisfied sigh. 'That is excellent news,' said Osborne. 'I can't tell you how pleased that makes me. I'll need a little time to consider the best options but I promise I'll be in touch shortly with some firm proposals.'

'And the lawsuit?'

'Yes, yes, I'll keep my word on that score, Duncan. Consider it dropped.'

'OK. I'll wait to hear from you.' The deed was done. It didn't make Duncan feel any better.

'One other thing while I have you on the line, Duncan. Who exactly is Michelle O'Brien? She keeps calling me from

Quinn's yard and leaving messages. I've never heard of her.'

'She's a young jockey just over from Ireland.' Duncan remembered his promise to speak up for her – why not now? 'She's related to the Joyce family in Limerick and looks to have bags of talent.'

'I see. Thank you. Maybe I'll have a word next time she rings.'

With that out of the way Duncan had one more call to make. He wasn't much good at saying sorry – he'd not made a habit of it. But in this case maybe his actions would speak for him.

He was thrown when Duke's answering machine picked up – he still wasn't used to it.

'Hi, Lorna, it's me. I've been thinking about what you said last night and, well, maybe it makes sense. Anyhow, you might like to know I've just called Osborne and agreed to ride for him. I'll see you later. Oh, and if anyone asks, Kerry was round at our place last night. OK?'

He hung up feeling better. Though not much.

6

Duncan was pleased to see Michelle making herself useful at the yard, bedding up stalls with fresh shavings and helping put horses on walkers, as well as mucking out. His advice to her had been to lend a hand wherever she could and not just devote herself to Prince Samson.

'You need to get yourself in Petie's good books if you want him to take you seriously,' he'd said. 'There are plenty of animals here who need attention, not just Sammy.'

This morning, as a further mark of her progress, he'd noted that she'd been on the gallops riding Glendora, a little mare who was coming back from a sprained tendon. Glendora was a favourite of Petie's, a neat jumper with a rock-solid temperament. Duncan had no doubt that was a good sign – maybe Petie was thinking of pairing them up? He had no intention of saying that to Michelle, however, and getting the little Irish girl over-excited.

Michelle wasn't the only one prone to excitement. When Fee and Roisin returned from third lot, Petie was waiting in the yard. Fee had been riding Because I Said So, who had had won the Hexham Silver Bell Novices' Chase over two miles last season when every other horse in the race had fallen. Both girls were covered in mud from the gallops and exhilarated from the morning's work.

Though Petie's habitual scowl didn't waver, Duncan guessed that he had some good news in store as he strode across to Fee. 'I expect you'll be wanting to ride him at Chepstow on Wednesday?'

Fee stared at him, as if she hadn't understood. Then she dismounted and flung herself on the trainer, raining mud and kisses on his jowly face.

'Gerroff!' cried Petie. 'Or I'll change my mind, so I will!'

'Oh no you won't!' shouted Fee, still clinging to him.

'Will somebody disconnect this bloody woman from me?'

'What the heck is going on?' asked a voice. Sandy Sanderson had arrived during the commotion and now stood watching them, hands on his hips.

'Fee is riding Said So at Chepstow,' Roisin said.

Sanderson scowled. 'If God wanted women to be jockeys,' he said, 'he would have put a dick halfway up a horse's back.'

'But he did,' said Fee, turning to grin at him. 'That's why you're here.'

Everyone laughed at that, including the champion jockey. However, Duncan noted the venomous look that he darted in Fee's direction before he joined in. She might have just made herself a powerful enemy.

Duncan travelled to Chepstow with high hopes. The yard had four runners, all decent prospects in his opinion, two of which were now owned by Lorna. The only blight on the day was her refusal to attend. Though he could understand that she wasn't much of a race-goer, he'd thought she might be interested to see how her own horses performed. 'I will come sometimes,' she'd promised when they had discussed the season ahead. But that had been months ago and she still hadn't shown up. With the

71

way things were between them at the moment – still frosty after their argument about her lunch with Osborne – he'd not wanted to insist.

However, here was Michelle leading up Flapdoodle, one of Cadogan's horses that they were still dithering about whether or not to sell. Roisin was riding him in the first race on the card, a two-and-a-half-mile novice hurdle.

Duncan was once more playing the part of the owner. He had a proprietorial eye on the smiling groom as she led the horse over for Roisin to be legged up.

'You're getting everywhere now, I see,' he said to Michelle as Petie instructed Roisin.

'Right enough. And I bet you I'm wearing silks next time you see me in the ring,' she replied.

Duncan doubted it, though he kept his thoughts to himself. This was one determined young woman.

Chepstow was a left-handed oval made up of two long straights and two tight bends with plenty of up and down – which defeated Flapdoodle, who tipped Roisin out of the saddle after stumbling at the fourth hurdle. The horse recovered his footing and carried on running, doing his best to interfere with the remainder of the field. Roisin was helped to her feet by a solicitous St John's Ambulance man and she walked back to the changing room holding her arm, in obvious pain.

It was not a good start and the Quinn yard's fortunes did not get much better, though Fee did put up a decent show as she drove Because I Said So to the runners-up spot in a two-mile-and-half-a-furlong chase, the horse's preferred distance. Claiming 7 lb as a conditional, she jumped off to a good start, was always in contention and eased into the lead just before the last fence. She might have won the race but was beaten into second on the run-in when the horse ran out of gas.

'You did good,' Petie said as she unsaddled.

'I could have done better. He faded.' Fee was out of breath. 'That's not like him.'

'Maybe the going was a wee bit soft.'

'No.'

'Cheer up, girl. I'll take second.'

But Fee wouldn't be cheered – she took defeat hard which Duncan, on hand to console her, thought was a good sign for her future prospects. He felt exactly the same way about losing, which he did throughout the afternoon. His mount in the fourth race failed to get out of second gear and in the last race – the brewery-sponsored Old Muckster's Maiden hurdle whose prize included a dozen barrels of Old Muckster's Jubilee Ale – he led until the penultimate obstacle and then was swallowed by the pack.

So for all the hard work in training, at the end of the day the Quinn yard only had a second place for a conditional jockey and an injury. No barrels were rolled out and any beer had to be paid for.

Back at the yard the next day, Roisin's dislocated shoulder complicated Petie's plans. Petie had wanted her to ride Drap D'Or in a chase at Warwick the following Saturday and she was keen to get back on the French gelding who had given her a Cheltenham victory last season, but the doctor had ruled it out. Everyone could see that she was in a great deal of pain. Drap D'Or was a big-hearted, lovable mare with an awkward jumping style who responded well to a lighter jockey. Roisin, also still a conditional, could claim weight, though not quite so much as Fee since Roisin had more winners under her belt. Roisin suggested that Fee replace her, but Petie decided she wasn't ready, so he asked Duncan. Then something happened to make Petie change his mind.

The *Punter,* a new weekly racing magazine, had just hit the news-stands. It was full of glossy photographs, features and opinion pieces but, in contrast to the regular racing publications, light on facts and statistics. The reporting style was sensationalist rather than balanced. The writers sought controversy where there wasn't any and engineered dispute where no one actually gave a toss. This week's edition – only number three in its history – led with the headline *'Women in Racing – Just What is the Point?'*

Inside was an article headed by photographs of six women jockeys, including Roisin and Fee. A sub-heading read: *'We agree they look good, but are the punters being served?'* The piece, not short of a few sniggers and leering remarks, went on to suggest that there was a serious point behind the jokes. The question was whether horses were being ridden to their full potential by women jockeys, and if they weren't then the bookmakers were taking easy money from their clients. In support of these arguments, the article pointed to the record of each of the six jockeys pictured. Roisin Quinn, it said, after the false promise of a win at Cheltenham last season had already fallen twice this year. Fee Markham, the piece declared, had lost her backers the last race through inexperience by taking the lead too early. It was all very well, the journalist wrote, for husbands and fathers to indulge their girls, but it was the punters who supported the game on a regular basis who were being fleeced. One of the featured women jockeys was married to a young trainer and two of the others were daughters of trainers, one of those being Roisin.

Petie stormed across the yard waving the magazine in the air. 'I'll cut this rag into squares and hang it behind the bog door!

No! I won't hang it behind the bog door! It's not even worth the shit and the flies!'

'Forget it, Daddy,' Roisin said. 'It's just entertainment. You can't take it seriously.'

But one person who didn't treat it as a joke was Fee. She was in pieces. Everyone told her not to take it to heart – the journalist was ignorant; she'd ridden a great race. But her confidence was shattered. She left work early that day and she failed to turn up the next morning.

They discussed who should go and get her. Duncan and Kerry offered but Petie said, 'No. I'll bring her back.'

He returned some hours later with Fee in tow. He'd found her curled up in bed in the little house she shared with two other girls. He'd persuaded her to get up and get back to work because he needed her to ride Drap D'Or in the 2.10 at Warwick that Saturday. 'You'll want a bit of practice,' he told her.

Duncan was upset to see Fee so distressed and made a call to Mandy Gleeson, a presenter of a weekend TV racing programme and an old love interest – not that he'd ever managed to sweet-talk her into bed. Which was probably a good thing, he reflected, as she was a clever journalist and well clued-up on the dark side of racing. Sometimes it was better to have a reliable old friend than an embittered old flame.

'Have you seen the article in the *Punter* about female jockeys?' he asked her.

'Yes. What about it?'

'We've got a kid in our yard. She's really good, Mandy. She could go on to make it. But right now she's in bits 'cause of what they said about her. I'm looking for a way to build her back up again and I wondered if you could feature her in a small way.'

'I can do better than that. Does she look good?'

'As it happens, yes, but whose side are you on?'

'Hers, of course, but I work in the real world. Look, as long as she doesn't have a face like Brigadier Gerard I'll get her on. Could we film her on Friday?'

True to her word, Mandy turned up at the yard with a cameraman and a sound guy. She got Fee to brush her wild black curls and slap a bit of lippy on, and then she completed a short interview about Fee's ambitions as a conditional jockey. They also triggered a few frames of her riding out on the gallops. That was it. Mandy said she was going to make it part of a longer feature that would go out between races on Saturday.

At Warwick racecourse that Saturday morning it rained, making the going a trifle soft. Fee was like an exposed wire, keyed up to run in the third race on Drap D'Or. Seeing Fee buzzing like that actually made Duncan feel more relaxed: normally he was the one fizzing with nervous energy while Kerry talked him down. It was fortunate he didn't need Kerry on this occasion as he was riding for another trainer up at Catterick.

Drap D'Or had been moved up a class to compete in the Backman TV Handicap Chase over three miles and two furlongs. All the same, the horse had been working well at home and if Fee kept her wits about her she was in with a chance. However, there were two things that unnerved her on the day. One was that the race was going to be televised. 'That's why it's called the Backman TV Handicap,' Duncan said, ''cause it's on TV.'

The second thing was that she was riding against Sandy Sanderson on The Salamander, one of Osborne's geldings. 'He's only the champion fudging jockey,' she said. 'And he hates me.'

'He may be a good jockey,' Roisin said, 'but he's on an inferior horse. Plus he's carrying more weight than you.'

Fee wasn't allowed into the changing room. It was a place where they made no concession to women jockeys. Strictly speaking, she was allowed access to the weighing machine and the tearoom adjacent to the changing room. But the changing room was the 'real' weighing room, where all the banter took place and jockeys gossiped and learned from each other. There, dozens of jockeys ambled around completely naked. The only feminine thing about the jockeys' changing room was the sight of so many men slipping on a pair of ladies' tights to prevent chafing under their jodhpurs.

'Del' Delores Cunningham, one of the first women to place in the Grand National at Aintree, famously threatened that if changing facilities weren't offered then she would walk in on the willy festival of the changing room and strip off regardless. It was only then, as a grudging concession – driven by the outraged morality of the Jockey Club and not by any sympathy for women jockeys – that facilities were made available. Such 'facilities' as there were at Warwick amounted to a battered old caravan somewhere out of the way near the horseboxes complete with mildew and mushrooms growing in the corners. So women jockeys were treated like the horses, only not so well and with fewer catering services.

But in the tearoom, where Fee was allowed to show her face, the two of them spied someone that Duncan was pleased to see. Bare-chested and in white jodhpurs as he sipped tea, Aaron Palmer, aka 'the Monk', sat quietly apart from the other jockeys. The Monk was in the last years of his jump-racing career. No one knew whether his nickname had come about because of his tonsure-like haircut or because of his intense, blue-eyed stare and aloof manner. He was riding against Duncan in the first race.

77

Duncan and Fee sat on the bench next to him. 'Aaron, I want you to meet a young jockey. This is Fee.'

'Pleased to meet you,' Fee said, flashing her eyes at the older man. She offered him a hand to shake.

The Monk looked at her. With infinite slowness he took her hand and shook it briefly. He didn't crack a smile and neither did he speak a single word. Not even a grunt. A close observer might have said that those penetrating blue eyes blinked once. Duncan saw that Fee was unnerved. He knew that look, as if the Monk was somehow reading you. All the same, she returned his stare.

'I'm having the first race,' Duncan said.

'You'll do well if you do that,' Palmer said, still gazing at Fee.

'You can't get any edge with this guy,' Duncan said to Fee with a smile.

Fee was about to answer when the mood in the room was suddenly altered by the arrival of Sandy Sanderson who got a lot of greetings and nods from the other jockeys. He was well liked by people who didn't know him well.

He stopped when he saw the three of them. 'So, Duncan,' he said, 'I see the honeymoon's over.'

'What?'

'Obviously this little tart will be your first ride of the afternoon.'

Duncan felt his cheeks flame. He was about to leap to his feet when he felt the Monk's restraining hand on his knee.

With a smug grin, Sanderson moved on to the tea urn.

'You're too quick to bite,' said the Monk.

'I know,' Duncan said. 'Tell me – how come he's afraid of you? He looked me and Fee in the eye but he wouldn't make eye contact with you. He's scared.'

'Maybe that's because I'm of no consequence. I wouldn't say anyone is scared of me.'

'What?' Duncan said. 'You scare the sodding liver out of me. Still gonna beat you in the first race all the same.'

Duncan was riding Billy Blake in the first, a two-mile novice hurdle. Occasionally you win because you're the better jockey but more often you win because you're on a better horse. Unfortunately for Duncan, it turned out that Cherry Orchard, the Monk's horse, was superior on the day. Billy Blake didn't like the going, which had been softened by a sudden deluge, and he tired over the last furlong to yield the lead on the run-in. It was a disappointing start.

Fee and Drap D'Or were next to race and her nerves were getting the better of her. Duncan knew she'd twice gone behind the boxes to vomit. He did all he could to reassure her. They'd walked the course together earlier. Warwick was a tight left-handed track with pretty sharp bends. This meant that a horse with a strong galloping action would not get the opportunity to get into full stride, and that factor suited Drap D'Or, who could make ground on the jumps.

'Front-running favourites tend to win these chases,' Duncan told her. 'So don't be afraid of getting to the front.'

Fee nodded like she was taking it all in but Duncan could see her looking over his shoulder at the white TV van that would be tracking her round the circuit. She knew that today she was going to be scrutinised not just as a jockey but as a woman jockey. Her confidence had been eaten away by the article in that stupid rag. Having said all he could to boost her confidence, Duncan left it to Petie and Roisin to take over with Fee in the parade ring. He wanted a good spot from which to watch the race so he got himself on to the restaurant balcony and borrowed a pair of binoculars.

He saw Fee jump off to a nervous start. She was looking a bit stiff in the saddle. 'Come on,' he muttered to himself, 'settle down.'

Fee had been told that The Salamander, Sanderson's horse, was now 7-4 favourite and Drap D'Or, after drifting out for a while, had settled at 5-2 joint-second favourite. Not that the odds made any difference to the task ahead, neither did the TV cameras nor the reaction her appearance had caused in the parade ring. Some wag in the crowd had bellowed, 'Go home and cook the dinner!' The wrong sort of attention never seemed to stop.

She made a poor start and spent the run-up to the first fence just trying to get Drap D'Or balanced and in stride. The entire field was bunched ahead of her, with The Salamander and the other second favourite, Come Calling, showing near the head of the pack. She got Drap D'Or back on his hocks for the jump and he made a clean leap, then she settled near the back of the field. At the fourth fence a rider was unseated. Fee hadn't got a clue who it was – all she saw was orange-and-black silk rolling on the turf and a few of the runners lost ground in the confusion. Drap D'Or, though, avoided the trouble. He was now jumping cleanly and Fee's confidence began to return. She relaxed and, on the second circuit of the undulating four-sided circuit, she started to assess her rivals, looking for an advantage.

After they turned into the back straight Fee saw a gap. A firm shake of the reins was enough to push Drap D'Or forward. She heard someone in the Penderton colours shout, 'Come on, girlie!' but she hadn't the time to work out who it was; she just moved up, concentrating on jumping the succession of fences ahead.

Now she had the front runners in her sights. She could see the white camera van driving alongside them on the other side of the rails, but it didn't matter. She could hear the loudspeaker commentary, maybe even hear her name echo through the air, but it counted for nothing. She was in a bubble, and inside the bubble were only racehorses, jockeys and the loud drumming of hooves on soft turf.

A runner pulled up at the open ditch and another hit the deck at the fence after. The field was beginning to thin out. She decided to challenge the leaders. Duncan had told her not to leave it late. She tracked Come Calling who was stride for stride with The Salamander and two other runners as they jumped the final fence in the back straight. Into the final turn, the four horses in front of her were arrayed in one solid line, with Sanderson on The Salamander on the inside. Was there a big enough gap to squeeze through? She reckoned there was and urged Drap D'Or into the opening. But as she did so, Sanderson drifted left, shutting the door. A rider being overtaken is entitled to maintain his line but he must not ride off any horse trying to pass him on the inside. Sanderson was enough of a pro to ensure only the slightest drift, but it was enough.

Forced to take the penultimate fence just behind The Salamander, she decided to try again on the inside – she was certain there was a big enough gap. Drap D'Or charged into the opening and easily gained on The Salamander. She had the speed to take him and the champion jockey knew it.

Sanderson switched his whip from his right hand to his left. With his body interposed between the cameras and his challenger he raised his whip high, almost theatrically. He brought the stick down, lashing Drap D'Or square on the nose and making sure he brought the whip back on to the quarters of his own horse. Drap D'Or faltered but Fee pushed him on. The whip came down again, but this time it struck Fee's lip, jolting her head back, throwing her off balance.

Both horses jumped the last fence well but Come Calling had seized the advantage of the tussle between his rivals and streaked ahead to the finishing line, winning by a length. Fee was beaten into third, losing to The Salamander by a short head. As far as she was concerned it could have been by a dozen lengths. She felt sick to her stomach.

From the balcony of the restaurant Duncan had seen what had happened. Or rather, he'd seen what he thought had happened – that Sanderson had struck Fee and her horse. But Sanderson was way too smart to make any of his actions obvious. The only people who would know for sure were Sanderson and Fee, and maybe one of the other riders. But even if they had seen anything, the unwritten jockey's Law of Silence would prevent them from reporting it. Jockeys had their own methods of settling the score.

Duncan trained his binoculars on Fee. She was wiping something from the corner of her mouth. Whether it was mud or blood he couldn't tell. He watched Petie and Roisin go to her as she dismounted. Fee was talking and pointing as Drap D'Or was unsaddled. She looked upset. Roisin put her good arm around her.

Duncan had seen enough. As he made his way down the stairs he noticed that one of the small private boxes had been set up as a TV studio. Two chairs had been arranged around a table with a TV monitor and microphones. Mandy was there, making some last-minute notes. Duncan didn't stop to speak to her. He was too angry.

*

Fee weighed in. Her teeth were clamped shut. Sanderson gave her a wave and a smirk but she wouldn't acknowledge him. She returned to Roisin and Petie.

'I'm gonna say something.'

'Don't waste your time,' Petie said. 'You rode well. Let it be.'

'I can't. If I don't shout at him, I'll cry, and I don't want that bastard or anyone else to see me cry.'

'Listen,' said Roisin, 'you're on a hiding to nothing. If you kick off they'll say it's 'cause the girlie can't take losing a race, and if you can't take losing a race you shouldn't be in the game.'

'That's what you think, is it?'

'Of course not! You've told me what he's done and I believe you! But I'm telling you exactly what they will say about it.'

'Come on,' Petie said, 'let me buy you a drink in the owners' bar. Put it behind you.'

But Fee was still quivering with rage. She stormed back to the weighing room and shouldered her way between two valets into the changing room, looking for the champion jockey. She was confronted by male nudity at all points of the compass, but she took no notice of the thicket of waving willies. A cheer went up from the jockeys as they saw her charge in. One of the officials was protesting. A jockey was having his legs dusted with talcum powder to help his boots slip on and off. 'Hey there, Fee! How about slapping a bit of this talc on my arse!'

Laughter followed and rude remarks – she ignored it all, looking for Sanderson. She saw him stepping out of the shower, still dripping with water, casting around for his towel. He was bollock naked and she wished she had Petie's gelding tool with her at that moment. That would wipe the smirk off his slimy face.

She didn't know exactly what she was going to say to him but as she opened her mouth a valet laid a firm hand on her arm. 'I hate to break up you two lovebirds,' he said, 'but if you can get yourselves over to the lounge they're talking about you on TV.'

Mandy Gleeson had been anchoring the broadcast from Warwick that afternoon, linking the races with interviews of jockeys, trainers and owners. The programme also included a feature on some controversial or newsworthy racing item. Today's topic was titled 'Women in Racing: Can They Hold Their Own?' Joining Mandy in the studio to discuss the subject of women jockeys was none other than Aaron Palmer, 'the Monk'.

The Monk was seen as very much old school. As a rule he was for change in the racing game in the way a Catholic priest is for condoms. On the other hand, he was seen as scrupulously fair in his judgement and always good for a sound bite.

He opened by saying that he had no objection to women jockeys provided they were up to the job. 'That was just it,' Mandy said excitedly. 'Were they up the job?' As a means of answering this question they asked Palmer to review the most recent race on the monitor in front of him and to talk them through it, offering his assessment of the performance of Fee Markham.

They were already halfway into the replay on the studio monitor in front of them, when Fee, Sanderson and all the other jockeys in the weighing room tuned in.

'Right now,' the Monk was saying, ' she's doing everything right. She's hanging in there, jumping well and she's getting ready to go. This is a stiffish course, you know, and the going is a bit soft. Here she comes now, and here's where it goes wrong for her.'

On the TV, Fee started to move up on the champion jockey's inside.

'Looks like a bit of bumping and banging going on there,' Mandy said.

'There's always a bit of bumping and banging,' the Monk said. 'But look, Sandy edges her over here, and she's in danger of running out.'

'Isn't that interference?'

'If she's got the speed to go past he should let her go. That's the rule. But she should also be clear of the horse before reaching the obstacle. So I'd say it's about 50–50 there.'

'Are you saying she should have gone on the outside?'

'No. She wouldn't have made it. She did the right thing. But it's what happens next that's interesting. Watch her as she goes up again. Here, she makes the run, she's got enough to go past him and she looks like she will. But for some reason – let's freeze that right there – for some reason she loses her stride here.'

'So you are saying that she was impeded?'

The Monk smiled. 'Are you trying to get me into trouble? I've said no such thing. The camera can't show us what's happening in there. If you want to know you'll have to ask the jockeys. And because they're both professionals, they won't tell you. And quite right too.'

'So would you say that Fee Markham is a sound jockey?'

'Indeed she is, though she'll benefit from experience. Had that been me I'd have known what to expect. Sandy Sanderson is a man who'd die in the saddle before letting you have a bit of light.'

'Is the punter getting a fair return from these women jockeys?'

'I'd say he is. It's not Fee Markham the punter should complain about.'

'What do you mean by that?'

'If I were a gambler with a couple of quid on the champion

jockey in this race, I'd be asking, why was he was getting into a ruck with the third horse when he might have won the race. That's the question I'd ask.'

Then the Monk leaned back in his chair and gazed directly into the camera, giving the viewing public a look as old as time.

7

'I'm thinking of putting you up on Royal Enfield.' William Osborne's tone was friendly. 'He's a bit of a handful but he's got winner written all over him.'

Duncan had returned Osborne's phone call from the spacious book-lined office upstairs in the Cadogan mansion. He had retreated up there and closed the door because he didn't want Lorna overhearing the conversation, which was irrational as he would be bound to tell her all about it the moment he hung up.

However, he was torn about the ride. He'd just returned from seeing Charlie at the care home where the old man had whipped himself into a lather over the racing from Warwick, which he had watched on the television the day before. But it wasn't the skulduggery of Sandy Sanderson and the injustice of Drap D'Or's defeat that had got the old man so worked up. It was the sight of Duncan in the last televised race riding one of Duke's old horses and wearing the white and red of Cadogan.

Duncan had tried to explain. 'Lorna's sentimental about her father's colours. I've tried to get her to change them but she grew up with them. You've got to see it from her point of view.'

'Why should I? That man sold me down the river. I can't believe my own son would ride in his silks.'

'Dad, Lorna is the owner. Those are her colours now. It's different.'

87

But the colours were the same, no matter whose name was on the racecard, and they both knew it. It was a row Duncan had anticipated but there still had been nothing he could say to make it any better. He'd left Grey Gables in a fury and had been met at home with Lorna saying Osborne had rung in his absence. That hadn't improved his mood. No matter the circumstances, he still didn't like the idea of Lorna talking to the man. He wondered who had called whom.

However, he did want to get back at Sanderson, especially after Warwick. He wanted to get in with the champion jockey's main source of rides and steal what he could. Just as Sanderson was doing to him. So the idea of riding the five-year-old novice chaser at Nottingham was tempting, no matter who the owner was.

'He can be a bit of a bugger. But that's why I thought of you – I've seen you handle tricky horses before.'

'Has Sanderson sat on him?'

'Sandy was schooling him only last week, I believe. He was impressed.'

'Then why isn't he riding him?'

'Because I haven't asked him to. In any case, I believe he's engaged elsewhere – as he often is these days. You've seen quite a lot of him, I understand, up at Quinn's yard.'

And that was the point. This offer of a ride was payback from Osborne to Sanderson. And its acceptance was payback from Duncan.

'So, will you ride him for me?'

'Of course.' Despite his reservations, the outcome had never really been in doubt.

Lorna was thrilled. 'I think it would be great if you started riding regularly for Uncle Willy. Daddy thought he was the best trainer in the country.'

Duncan was pleased that at least he'd done something to get back into her good books. All the same, the idea of riding for Osborne went against the grain. God knows what he'd tell Charlie. He thanked his stars that the Nottingham meeting wasn't going to be televised.

Petie raised his bushy eyebrows when Duncan told him he was going to ride for Osborne.

'Excuse me, but I thought you hated the bugger.'

They were in the kitchen of Petie's hovel of a house. With a stables and training facilities worth millions, Petie could not be persuaded to knock it down and build himself somewhere decent to live. He stood over a grease-stained hob, frying bacon in a pan. Roisin and Kerry, who usually joined them for a late breakfast, were still in the yard. Duncan had seized his moment for a private word.

'Sure, I don't like Osborne but I'm a gun for hire and he's hiring. It's a professional decision. A bit,' Duncan couldn't resist adding, 'like you getting Sanderson up here to ride Destiny's Dream.'

The trainer chuckled. 'That really pisses you off, doesn't it?'

'Of course! You didn't have to invite him along. Not when you know what he and Osborne did to Dad.'

'I thought you'd put all that behind you. A new leaf, you told me.'

'Well, I have. But I haven't forgotten – Dad's never going to let me forget for one thing.'

Petie handed Duncan a chipped mug of tea the colour of rusting metal – all he ever consumed in here.

'Did you never think, Duncan, that even though he's a bit of a turd Sandy mightn't know a thing or two? Like how to ride that

89

fine horse belonging to your lovely wife, which no one else can figure out? The same animal, I have to remind you, you don't have a clue about either.'

'Yes, but—'

'There is no but, you young eejit. Until we can discover how to get the best out of Destiny's Dream we'll all have to put up with old Sandy, including you. Now I don't mind you having the odd ride for Osborne but don't do it just to play games. Even you have to grow up some time.'

'OK then, Duncan, come here and smell me.'

'You what?' Duncan stared at Michelle, not sure he'd heard correctly. They were standing in front of Prince Samson's stall and she was giving him her big Irish smile. He'd seen a lot of it lately and, with the enduring frostiness from Lorna at home, he was finding it less and less resistible.

'Come on, don't be shy – you're an old married man!'

The fact that he was a married man was precisely the reason he shouldn't be putting his face right next to hers and breathing in her scent. But he wasn't going to say that. Instead he stepped closer and lowered his head to hers.

'Do you smell it?'

Up close, a distinct and familiar perfume enveloped her, warm and flowery and – surprising.

He laughed. 'You smell like a little old lady.'

'Right. It's lavender. I wouldn't choose to wear it but Sammy loves it.' She produced a plastic bottle with a spray top and aimed it at Duncan and squirted his sweater generously.

'Jesus!' he protested as the musky scent enveloped him.

'Give me your hands.' She squirted them too. 'Now go and talk to Sammy.'

So far, talking to Sammy – doing anything with Sammy – had proved impossible. The horse had shied away from every approach Duncan had made.

Sammy had been watching them cautiously from within his stall. On past form he'd back as far into the corner as he could to get away. Now he remained where he was as the jockey walked towards him.

Duncan knew that horses, like most animals, had a sophisticated sense of smell, way beyond a human's rudimentary capability. But would this lavender business work? The horse looked at him. He thought he could read apprehension in those big amber eyes but for once the animal stood his ground.

'Hello, Sammy. There's no need to run away from me. Are we going to be mates, after all?'

'Sure, you are,' said Michelle from behind him. 'See, he's just working it out. Let him smell your hand.'

Duncan did as he was told, holding out his left hand, palm up, prepared to snatch it away fast should Sammy decide to go in with his teeth. But the horse just looked at him placidly, much as any other would. And he didn't veer away. This was progress.

'Rub his neck. He likes that.'

Duncan obeyed, placing his hand on that big white furry column as he had seen Michelle do. Sammy did appear to like it.

'Bloody hell,' said Duncan. 'Why lavender?'

'Sammy was bred by my grandma over in County Clare and she believed in herbs and oils, that kind of thing. She always said lavender was good for calming nervous horses. So you weren't wrong about little old ladies. Except Grandma Joyce was built like a rugby prop – you've seen my cousin Martin. Anyhow, Sammy was the last of the horses she bred and she was a bit soft on him. She left him to Martin in her will.'

'So that's the secret to Sammy? Lavender?'

'I use lavender oil – as pure as I can get. But yes, that's the key to Sammy and now you know. But can we keep it our secret for a bit longer?'

Sessions with Michelle and Prince Samson apart, Duncan wasn't enjoying life much. The business with Sanderson was an ongoing sore, his wife seemed to have a permanent headache (so much for passionate newly-weds) and he couldn't buy a winner on the racetrack. He'd instructed Mike Ruddy to get him rides wherever he could and, as a consequence, he'd spent hours behind the wheel travelling the motorways. After a fruitless trek to Carlisle, he'd run into the Monk as he headed for the car park.

'Duncan, I need a word.'

They stepped into the shadows. 'Go on,' Duncan said.

'I hear you're riding Royal Enfield.'

'Yes, in a couple of days. Why?'

'Don't.'

'But I've said I'll ride him.'

'Listen. There are difficult horses who can be managed and others that no one should go near. One day Royal Enfield will be sweet as pie then the next he'll buck, roll, run backwards – anything. Osborne won't have told you about how many of his stable hands that horse has put in plaster.'

'How do you know?'

The Monk's eyes glinted in the half-light. 'How do you think?'

'You've been on him?'

The other man nodded. 'The horse isn't safe. Sanderson knows what he's like and that's why he won't ride him.'

Duncan thought about the row with Lorna. 'It's a bit awkward.'

'Well, I've said my piece.' The Monk placed a leathery hand

on Duncan's shoulder and peered into his eyes. 'Be very careful.' Then he walked off.

That evening Duncan called Osborne to book a visit to the yard the next morning. If he could get Royal Enfield on to the gallops then he could make his own decision.

But Osborne said it was too difficult to organise at such short notice – in any case, he wouldn't be available himself. 'You only need a lad to open the stable door for me,' Duncan argued. 'I'll take it from there.' But that still wasn't good enough, it seemed. Osborne maintained a reasonable tone, but the excuses stacked up until it was blindingly obvious that Osborne was simply blocking him. He wanted Duncan to ride Royal Enfield cold at Nottingham

This wasn't uncommon. Because of their tight schedules, plenty of jockeys encountered a horse for the first time at the racecourse. Duncan preferred to have sat on his rides before a race, though it wasn't always possible. But this was different. Duncan had never been warned off a horse by the Monk before.

'In that case, Mr Osborne, I'm sorry but I don't want to ride him at Nottingham.'

'What? You're backing out?'

'I've heard he's a dangerous animal. If I don't have the chance to see for myself then I won't ride him.'

Osborne's tone changed. 'That's ridiculous. He can be a bit difficult but that's why I booked an expert horseman to ride him – at least, I thought I did. Obviously I was mistaken. You're scared of a challenge.'

That stung and Duncan was tempted to agree to ride just to prove the man wrong. But maybe that was point.

'I'm sorry, Mr Osborne. I appreciate the offer but I've made my mind up.'

'I hope your wife is happy about this. Lorna and I have gone to a lot of trouble to build bridges between us. I can see you don't care about her feelings.'

'It's because of her feelings I'm saying no. I don't think she'd want me riding an unsafe horse.'

But Osborne had already put the phone down on him. In truth, Duncan didn't think Lorna would be at all happy about him backing out but surely she'd be more concerned that he came home from work in one piece? All the same he expected some grief.

In the event, he didn't tell Lorna he wasn't riding for Osborne until the morning of the race. He'd got back late from Sedgefield the night before and she'd been asleep. Now he got up late and brought her a cup of tea in bed.

She sat up slowly. 'What are you doing here? I thought you'd be at work.'

'I've got a day off.' He explained the circumstances.

To his surprise she said, 'Oh good, then you can come with me to see the solicitor. He called me yesterday afternoon and insisted I saw him today. He said it was urgent.'

'Did he say what it was about?'

'Actually, it was his secretary. I couldn't get anything out of her.'

Duncan remembered the secretary, she was a bit of a dragon. 'Maybe probate's come through,' he said. 'Maybe you can finally get your hands on some money.'

'Do you think? Well, I don't mind going in that case. And you can come too – that's fab.'

She was smiling at him, which made a change these days, and he slipped an arm around her shoulders. She kissed him happily but as he made to slide into bed beside her she said, 'I'm sorry, Duncan, but I don't feel like it.'

He froze. 'You never do these days, do you?'

'That's not true, I do. It's just . . .' Her face crumpled, she seemed genuinely upset. 'I mean, I don't feel like I could.'

Whatever the reason, he got the message and stomped off downstairs to find the paper. He took it into the main drawing room with a view out over the lawn down to the lake – a room he scarcely ever had time to enjoy – and turned to the racing pages. His eyes scanned the card for Nottingham. Which mug, he wondered, had Osborne found to ride Royal Enfield? The answer had him sitting bolt upright in shock and fear. The jockey listed was Michelle O'Brien.

He hurriedly called the Quinn yard and got Roisin.

'Is Michelle there?'

'Haven't you heard? She's got a ride at Nottingham. She'll be on her way.'

Roisin would have been happy to chatter on about how all Michelle's ringing around trainers must have paid off but Duncan interrupted her. Could she find Petie and ask him for a number for the Joyces? When she heard why Duncan needed it, Roisin promised to call him right back. While he waited, he phoned the Nottingham course and got hold of one of the valets on duty that day – please would he ask Michelle O'Brien to call him as soon as she arrived? Then Roisin rang back with a variety of numbers in Ireland.

It turned out that the Joyce brothers – unbelievably, there were six of them in total – were not that easy to get to the phone. They were in paddocks and yards, on tractors and up on gallops, or in pow-wows with vets or feed merchants and couldn't be disturbed right now, though they all promised to ring back later. Duncan was getting anxious. It was now 11.30 and Michelle's race was due off at 2.30.

The phone chirped and he grabbed it. 'Michelle?'

'Do I sound like a girl, you eejit? It's Michael Joyce here. I'm told you've been ringing round half of Ireland trying to talk to one of us.'

Duncan blurted out the story. Michelle was down to ride a dangerous horse, way beyond her capabilities – at the very least, Duncan had to let her know what she was in for.

Michael, it turned out, was in England. What's more, he'd just finished schooling a horse at the Penderton yard just down the road from Petie's. It was a stroke of luck and Duncan seized it. 'If I pick you up in twenty minutes, we should be able to get to Nottingham before the race. If we both talk to her, maybe we can stop her riding. I've got a really bad feeling about this.'

'Hurry up then, man. I'll be waiting.'

Duncan had one more call to make before he broke the news to Lorna that he wouldn't be able to see the solicitor with her. His foot tapped impatiently on the hard floor as he waited for Osborne to pick up.

'Hello?'

'Osborne, it's Duncan.'

'Ah, Duncan. Changed your mind about riding, have you? Well it's too late, I've got a lovely little rider lined up for Royal Enfield. You recommended her to me, in fact. Do you remember?' Osborne's voice was friendly and reasonable, but Duncan detected a hint of malice beneath his words.

'I know who you've got to ride. Have you told Michelle that the horse isn't safe?'

'Like I told you, Duncan, there's nothing wrong with Royal Enfield that a strong rider won't be able to handle.'

'You know that you're putting her in danger. You should at least tell her that the horse has a difficult temperament. She should be warned.'

'Fine, Duncan. I'll tell her,' Osborne said, his voice disinterested and bored. 'I have to go. I imagine I will see you at the race.'

Without another word, Osborne hung up. Duncan swore. He was almost certain that Osborne had no intention of warning Michelle about Royal Enfield. Osborne wanted a rider in that race and he didn't care who he put in danger.

Duncan made his way quickly up the stairs and Lorna looked at him in dismay as he told her he couldn't accompany her to the solicitor.

'I'm sorry, sweetheart, but this is important.'

'More important than sorting out our future?'

'No, but no one's going to get hurt seeing that fat fart Pargetter, are they? You sort him out. It's your money, after all.'

He suppressed the urge to say there were worse problems in the world than going into London to pick up a lorry-load of loot. Just how tough could life be? Sometimes Lorna didn't know she was born.

Michael Joyce was waiting for him impatiently. 'You English jocks know how to travel incognito, I see,' he muttered as he climbed into the Lamborghini.

Duncan let that lie. Now was not the time to explain why he was driving a custard-coloured Italian sports car. He wished he'd travelled in something more modest.

Sports car or not, progress was too slow. It was now after midday and raining hard out of a mushroom-grey sky. Adrenaline was buzzing through Duncan's veins, making it hard to sit still. It seemed as though every light was against them, every roundabout blocked.

'Jesus,' Duncan said, banging his fist on the steering wheel as they hit a queue on the motorway. He craned his neck to look at the column of stationary cars ahead of them. He checked the time again. They were going to be cutting it pretty fine.

'You're sure this horse is a nutter?' Michael asked, chewing his lip.

'Palmer says he's put lads in hospital and I believe him.'

'Michelle won't want to hear it, you know. She says that girls have to take whatever chance they get. Jaysus, if anything happens to her, it'll kill my Auntie Kath.'

They fell into silence, haunted by their thoughts, willing the traffic to move so that they could get to the racecourse in time.

Lorna asked Len the chauffeur to drive her into London in the Rolls. She might as well travel in style to pick up her inheritance. Len beamed as he ushered her into the back, delighted to be taking her on a proper outing. Without Duke to pilot around the country these days, his life was reduced to working in the garage, maintaining a redundant fleet of cars. Lorna wondered why he stuck around. She suspected he was hanging on out of loyalty to her.

On reflection, maybe it wasn't such a bad thing that Duncan had ducked out of the trip to see Pargetter. The last time they'd visited the solicitor Duncan had made loud comments about lawyers being as bad as politicians and them all being on the take. Lorna knew he'd only done it because he'd felt like a fish out of water. She wasn't often conscious of the gulf in background between the two of them but, in the walnut-panelled offices of Pargetter & Jolt, Duncan had been a bit of an embarrassment.

All the same, she was nervous about facing the solicitor on her own. This meeting was a significant moment in her life and she

had to keep her wits about her and remember everything Pargetter told her. If only she didn't feel so dreadful. She'd not been
making excuses when she'd turned down Duncan's advances
that morning, or over the past week. She'd gone off sex and felt
permanently tired. Even the silky kiss of the Rolls-Royce's tyres
on the road was making her feel nauseous.

Len got her to the appointment ten minutes early and, to her
surprise, she was taken directly to Pargetter's office. That was
something, at least. With luck this would soon all be over and
she could go home to bed.

Duncan and Michael arrived at Colwick Park racecourse at 2.27 —
three minutes before the scheduled jump-off for Michelle's race.
Duncan threw the car in a space and they sprinted from the car
park. As they made their way towards the racecourse, Duncan
prayed that the start would somehow be delayed. Please, please
let there be some issue with the track, he thought. But as they
reached the nearest TV monitor, in the stand bar, he saw the
runners in the 2.30 already navigating the chase course.

Duncan felt as though the wind had been knocked out of
him as his eyes fixed unblinking on the screen. They were too
late. It was all his fault – if only he'd thought to check who was
replacing him sooner. If anything happened to Michelle now, he
would never forgive himself.

'Looks like she's doing OK.' The relief in Michael's voice was
tangible.

'I can't see her,' Duncan said, worried, a knot of panic forming
in his chest.

'In the leading bunch. The blue cap.'

Duncan identified the crouching figure balanced high on the
shoulders of a strapping mahogany-coloured animal with a wild

black mane. She was lying third or fourth. They were on the second circuit heading down the far straight with about a mile to go.

'She should just sit tight there,' said Michael. 'No need to do anything fancy.'

Duncan agreed but he didn't like the way the big horse was pulling. He could see Michelle trying hard to keep hold of him, but would she have the strength?

Royal Enfield burst clear of the pack approaching the last fence in the straight.

'Steady on, girl,' muttered Duncan, his heartbeat stepping up a notch.

Michelle was doing her best but it was clear the horse had decided to have his own way and there was nothing she could do about it. Heading into the fence, he suddenly took off. Too early. His front legs hit the stiff brush of the top of the obstacle and his body concertinaed, his rear quarters catapulting Michelle out of the saddle.

'Jaysus!' Michael's wasn't the only voice raised in alarm. Everyone in the bar was transfixed by the sight on the screen.

Michelle somersaulted in the air and landed on her back. The chasing pack of horses ran over her, obscuring her from view. Then they were gone, leaving her small body motionless on the turf.

Mungo Pargetter got up from behind his desk to steer Lorna to an armchair and sat down next to her.

'Thank you for coming in at such short notice,' he began. 'I'm sorry that your fiancé—'

'He's my husband now. We've just got married.'

'How delightful – congratulations – I'm sorry he couldn't accompany you but I didn't think this meeting should wait. Something has turned up that you ought to know about.'

'OK,' said Lorna, suddenly apprehensive.

'I won't beat about the bush. It's about the property. Did you know that shortly before he died your father had taken out a new mortgage?'

'No. What does that mean?'

'It means that effectively you don't own the house. Or indeed the grounds. And unless you have the means of servicing the debt, which is substantial, then you will have to reconsider your circumstances.'

'Oh. So you haven't dragged me in here to hand over Daddy's assets?'

'I'm afraid not.'

'I'm sorry'– she was having difficulty breathing – 'could you start again and make it very simple so I understand?'

And that's exactly what he did. Afterwards she walked down the hall to the ladies toilet and was thoroughly sick.

Duncan and Michael Joyce followed the ambulance into Nottingham to the Queen's Medical Centre. Though short, it was a horrific journey. They had just watched their worst fears come true and now they clung to a shred of hope that Michelle's injuries would not be as bad as feared.

'I'll kill Osborne,' Duncan said, his eyes fixed straight ahead. Anger coursed through him. 'I told him that horse wasn't safe. I warned him. I knew he wouldn't tell Michelle he was dangerous. I should have forced him.'

'I'm not sure it would have made a difference,' Michael said, his face chalk white and tight with worry. 'You've seen how she is with Prince Samson, she loves a challenge.' He fell silent for a moment. 'Ah Jaysus, let her be all right.' He turned his face to the window. 'She's got to be all right.'

Duncan kept silent. He'd seen the horses race over Michelle's body. He'd seen this happen before. He knew what the likely outcome was. But still, he drove quickly in the wake of the ambulance, terrified of what they would find when they reached the hospital.

The press had got wind of the accident and there was a flurry of activity at the entrance to A&E. Michael declared his connection to the patient and the pair of them were ushered into a waiting room by a sympathetic doctor.

They only waited half an hour but it seemed to stretch into eternity. Eventually the doctor returned. The grim news was written on his face.

'I'm sorry, Mr Joyce, but Miss O'Brien was dead on arrival at the hospital. There wasn't anything we could do.' He paused. 'I understand she was thrown from a horse.'

Michael stared at the doctor as though he couldn't process what he was saying. 'She's dead?' he asked dumbly. He shook his head. 'She can't be dead. She'll just have some broken bones, a couple of cracked ribs. Our Michelle's a fighter.' His voice broke as he said her name.

'As I said, Mr Joyce, I am very sorry for your loss. I was told she was trampled by a number of horses.'

'The runners behind couldn't avoid her,' Duncan said, his voice flat with shock. He reached out a hand and rested it on Michael's shoulder.

'In addition to substantial internal damage she sustained severe head and neck injuries. I imagine she would have died almost instantly.'

Michael didn't seem to be hearing the doctor's words. Duncan took charge. 'Thank you, doctor. It's no consolation, but it's good to know she didn't suffer.'

The doctor nodded at Duncan and left.

Duncan steered Michael towards a chair and sat down next to him.

'What am I going to tell the family?' Michael asked in a hoarse voice. 'How to I tell them that she's dead?'

'I don't know,' Duncan said honestly, his own mind reeling with the loss. 'But I think you should call them before they hear it on the news.'

'Aye,' Michael said, nodding mechanically. 'I'll do that.'

Duncan pointed to a pay phone in the corner and got to his feet. 'I'll stand outside and stop anyone coming in.'

Michael nodded again, his face blank with shock. 'Thanks.' He stayed still for a moment, as though he couldn't quite get his body to move. Then he looked at Duncan with wet eyes. 'I've got to say this. I wish to Christ you'd been on that bloody horse.'

With all his heart, Duncan wished it too.

It was late when Duncan drew up outside the Cadogan mansion. It seemed like he'd been driving for ever. After Michael had made his calls at the hospital – a lengthy process – Duncan had driven him to London and dropped him at Heathrow to wait for Martin, who was flying in from Shannon. Duncan had offered to wait with him but Michael had shaken his head and said, 'I'll be OK.' When Duncan had made to take his hand on leaving the Irish lad had pulled him into a wordless hug.

Now Duncan sat for a moment in the car trying to get his head together. The full horror of the day seemed to press down on him. Michelle was dead. Dead. It seemed impossible – she was so full of life with that smiling face and cheeky attitude. It felt incredible that he'd spoken to her only the day before. And now she was gone.

If only he'd told her about the horse. If only they'd got to the racecourse three minutes sooner. If only Osborne had bothered to tell her about the dangers of Royal Enfield – in ignoring Duncan's warning, Osborne had signed Michelle's death warrant.

Suddenly, Duncan's old anger returned. His hands were shaking on the steering wheel as he thought about all the people Osborne had hurt. His desire for revenge resurfaced, even stronger than before. He wouldn't let Osborne get away with it, not this time.

The only issue was how to prove that Osborne had known about the dangers of the horse before putting Michelle in the saddle. Everyone who knew Michelle knew that she was desperate to race. It was going to be difficult to make the case that Osborne had knowingly put her at risk. But if there was a way, he was going to find it.

Duncan took a deep breath and looked out of the car window, grappling to get his anger under control before he headed into the house.

Eventually, he made his way into the mansion, which seemed deserted. There were no lights on in the kitchen or the sitting room where Lorna usually watched TV. He found her upstairs in bed in the dark. He would have left her to sleep – why inflict his mood on her just yet? – but when he began to close the door she spoke his name.

'I'm sorry I didn't wait up for you,' she said. 'You were so long – what happened?'

'You mean you haven't heard?' He knew the accident had been all over the news. He'd even seen Michelle's face on the front page of the *Evening Standard* at the airport. But Lorna shook her head.

So he told her.

'How terrible! Who was she? You never mentioned her before.'

It was true. He'd never talked about Michelle to Lorna. Now he lay on the bed by her side and told her about the Irish girl and her big grey horse who had come to Petie's looking to make it on English racetracks.

When he'd finished, she squeezed his hand and said, 'That's so sad. But I'm glad it wasn't you on that horse.'

He said nothing and they lay there in the dark in silence for a minute. Then she spoke again.

'This isn't great timing, Duncan, but there's something you ought to know. About what happened with Pargetter.'

He'd forgotten all about the solicitor and how he was supposed to go with her to the meeting. All that seemed a lifetime ago.

'It turns out,' she said, 'that it wasn't to say that Daddy's money was coming through. Just the opposite really. He said that there isn't any money, just a massive debt on the house and the estate.'

'A debt?'

'Well, a mortgage that we can't possibly pay. And God knows what happened to the money Daddy raised – it's all gone. We can sell the cars – we were going to do that anyway – but we've got to sell the house.'

'And the horses?'

'They're mine but, frankly, Duncan, they're a liability. They cost a fortune to keep and they don't seem to win many races.'

That was true. There was his sole victory on The Black 'Un and Sanderson had won on Destiny's Desire at Stratford the week before but the combined prize money would barely keep Lorna's horses in feed for the month.

'Unless we can think of some other way out, I'll have to sell them too. I can always offer them to Uncle Willy.'

Never, thought Duncan, but he kept quiet. He didn't want to talk about Osborne.

'So' – she let go of his hand and sat up – 'the fact is, I don't have any money after all. I've married you under false pretences.'

'What are you talking about?'

'I've been thinking about this, Duncan. If Daddy hadn't died you wouldn't have married me. We'd have just carried on going out and who knows what would have happened. After all, you weren't exactly faithful to me before Daddy died.'

'Of course, I was.'

'Come off it. I know for a fact you were shagging Christie Sanderson and I bet there were others, but that doesn't matter any more. My point is that me having money and horses made me a more attractive proposition than I really am.'

'Jesus, Lorna—'

'Let me finish.' Her voice wobbled. He could tell she was close to tears. 'I want you to know that I don't hold you to anything. Circumstances have changed, that's how Pargetter put it. If you want to call off our marriage now I'm broke, then I'll under-stand. I won't fight it.'

He could make out her pale shape in the half-light from the bedroom door. She sat with her hands in her lap, her shoulders slumped. A curtain of hair obscured her face but he knew she was staring at him, trying to read his mind. What he said next would count for a lot.

'Lorna, sweetheart – we just swore to be husband and wife, for richer or poorer. So, as far as our marriage goes, nothing has changed at all – not as far as I'm concerned. We stick together whatever happens.'

'You're sure about that?'

'Yes. Completely. What about you?'

She fell forward and he caught her, holding her to his chest as, at last, tears began to fall.

'Don't cry, sweetheart – it's only money.'

She gulped in a breath and steadied herself. 'There's one more thing.'

'What's that?'

'I'm pregnant.'

8

December 1980

In the past, the elongated oval of Leicester racecourse had been a lucky venue for Duncan. He'd had a couple of winners there as a conditional early in his career on strong galloping types who had responded well to the long straights. He always looked forward to returning, especially on a pleasant late autumn day like this. A soft breeze ruffled the silks of the riders and the sun was surprisingly warm. But, six weeks after Michelle O'Brien's death, he could take no pleasure in the occasion. It seemed like everything he touched these days went bad. Even the horses were suffering. He hadn't had a winner in many weeks and Petie's yard was struggling.

Today he and Petie were involved in three races. Duncan had been unseated in the first and tailed off in the third, so he was keen to put his name on the penultimate race of the day. He reckoned he was in with a good chance to break his bad run as he was riding Delacroix, a big strong bay gelding of French origin who had won for him over fences last Boxing Day at Kempton. Petie had moved him up two classes.

'Listen,' Petie said, 'I'll just be happy today for you to get the trip.'

'Yeah, right,' Duncan said. It was nowhere in his soul to ride just to get the trip. Duncan had to win. If he was playing a game of Monopoly with Lorna he had to win. In racing it was a sacred matter. Duncan was also convinced that a jockey who cheated the punters was not a jockey. Shame on all of them.

Petie knew this perfectly well. He wasn't asking Duncan to go easy on Delacroix, but he believed in gradually bringing a horse to its peak. A horse pushed too hard in the wrong race only to get beaten could mysteriously lose its spirit along with losing the race. 'OK. I'm just saying don't thrash him to get there.'

Duncan smiled. When Duncan had first ridden Delacroix, Petie had warned him that the powerfully built horse would take some holding and to give him his head – holding a horse back too much could make him lose the desire to race. Now here was Petie saying the opposite. He must be feeling nervous about having jumped the horse up a couple of classes or else he was getting used to disappointment. Well, bugger that – Duncan was determined to get the win for all their sakes. They were due.

Delacroix made a decent start and Duncan kept him tucked just behind the leading two horses. They pinged the first fence nicely. The field of a dozen horses was bunched tight. Duncan could feel them over his shoulder, like bees around a hive looking for a way in. It was important not to give ground.

They cleared the second fence at a great pace for so early in the run. The rumble of hooves on the good going only excited the horses more. When they took the second together, Duncan felt Delacroix begin to pull. He'd had enough of this hanging back. He wanted to be in pole position and Duncan was fighting to keep him back. In the gallops he was easier to hold, but out here on the racetrack he sucked in the excitement of the crowd.

The fourth fence came up and they were over it nicely. 'You want to go?' Duncan shouted to his horse. 'You want to go, son?'

Delacroix's ears flicked forward, back, forward.

All right then, thought Duncan, as he put his head down, giving the gelding a squeeze with his thighs. Delacroix spurted to the front, took the next fence and went clean away from the lot of them. It was all over. Duncan and Delacroix streaked away at the front of the field. By the time they had cleared the last but one fence, Duncan had plenty of time to look over his shoulder and see that he had half a dozen lengths in hand. Thank God, a winner at last.

Not that Delacroix was slowing. He was romping home and loving it. Then Duncan picked up a new murmur from the crowd and he realised something was happening behind him. One of the horses had pulled away from the pack and was mounting a late challenge. Duncan spurred Delacroix on and he jumped the last fence beautifully. Then, with only four lengths to the winning post, a black gelding screamed past him, snatching victory from his grasp. Duncan couldn't believe it. Watching the win slip through his fingers was like being hit by a bus.

Stunned, Duncan walked Delacroix back to the enclosure. Petie was there, his eyebrows knitted hard. Duncan jumped down as the stable lad took the reins. 'I'm sorry, boss. I don't know what the hell happened there.'

'You did nothing wrong,' Petie said. 'Neither did yer feller.'

'What was that black horse?'

'A 33-1 outsider. No-hoper. Something wrong there.'

'Like what?'

Petie swept a hand through his thinning hair. 'Forget it. Go and get weighed in.'

Something wrong. When you are beaten in a race you are expecting to win it is all too easy to think *something wrong* when there is nothing wrong at all, except for the fact that you've just been beaten. Sometimes it feels like a slap in the face; sometimes a kick in the arse; and sometimes as if you've been hit over the head with a lead pipe.

Petie, however, was not one to dwell on a defeat. He was the sort of man who, if he tipped over a wheelbarrow of sand, just picked up a shovel and filled the barrow again. If he got beat he moved on. So when he said *something wrong* he got Duncan wondering.

The horse that had just beaten him was called Chania House. Trained by William Osborne.

Osborne's name was no longer mentioned in Duncan's home. There was no more talk of 'Uncle Willy' – Lorna understood his resentment. And though she said she couldn't believe Osborne would have deliberately put Duncan on a dangerous horse, the fact was that he had tried to do so. And in any event, the consequences had been tragic.

Osborne had faced no repercussions following the Royal Enfield affair. As far as the racing community were concerned, Michelle's death was an accident. A tragedy, for sure, but not something that could have been avoided. It made Duncan's blood boil. All the old bitterness that he held for Osborne returned tenfold.

He'd had a disbelieving phone call from Michael after the news had broken.

'I can't believe that bastard is getting away with it,' Michael said down the phone, his voice holding all the bitterness that Duncan felt. 'He put her on that horse, for Christ's sake. If it wasn't for him, she'd be alive right now. Laughing and smiling and . . .' He broke off and took a deep breath. 'It just doesn't seem right, you know? He should pay for what he's done, but instead, he's just living his life as though nothing happened.'

Duncan couldn't agree more about the unfairness of the situation. Even the fact that Osborne had announced he was dropping his breach of contract lawsuit against Duncan and

Lorna didn't make Duncan feel any better. So much for burying the hatchet – he'd plant one in that fox-faced skull if he could. Osborne had intended to harm him. There was no doubt in Duncan's mind. And then, having entered the horse for the race, Osborne was prepared to let any young jockey get on his back rather than scratching. Duncan had tried to mend fences, to accept the proffered hand of friendship, and, as a result, had only made things worse. He couldn't get over the fact that he had recommended Michelle to Osborne. He'd thought he was doing her a good turn but had it led to her being offered that fatal ride on Royal Enfield? It was another stick to beat himself with when he couldn't sleep at night.

Michelle's death lay like a pall of black smoke over the entire racing world. Everyone was hurting. At times like this the racing community responds like a single creature; like a hedgehog rolling itself into a ball. An outsider might say, it's a high-risk sport and there are bound to be casualties. But to be reminded of that truth in such a terrible way shocked everyone to the core. Being aware of the dangers didn't make the consequences of tragedy any easier to take. What's more, Michelle was just a kid, and a well-liked kid at that. It was unbearable.

But a single death didn't stop the big wheel from turning. The jump-racing season was now in full flow and there were fixtures to fulfil. The Quinn yard, however, couldn't even lose its blues on the racetrack. Petie's horses were in a slump, none of them performing up to expectations. One after another, they seemed heavy-legged on the gallops. Duncan found Petie leaning against the door of his mud-spattered Land Rover, stopwatch in hand, shaking his head.

'There's something up,' he said. 'I hope it's not a virus.'

That would be a disaster. If a virus had taken hold in the stables it would probably put paid to the entire season.

'Do you really think so?' Duncan asked. 'None of them are coughing, are they?'

'No. There's no coughs, no fever and they're all eating up. I've got to get it checked out, all the same.'

So a man in a white coat came down to the yard in a mobile laboratory. Over the next few days all the horses were blood-tested and their saliva swabbed. Nothing was found – which was a relief. But the horses still failed to perform at home or on the track. Petie wondered if the introduction of the animals from the Osborne yard had brought with it an infection of some kind. But the Osborne horses had performed better than Petie's, so they didn't seem to be the cause.

Duncan mentioned the problem to Charlie on one of his visits to the Grey Gables. 'Nine times out of ten,' Charlie said, offering Duncan one of Mrs Solanki's samosas. 'It's what's in the feed.'

'Does Mrs Solanki make anything other than samosas?' asked Duncan.

'Oh yes. You should try her curry. '

'You seem quite well at the moment, Dad.'

'It's the spices in this Indian food. She makes it specially for me. What were we talking about?'

'The feed. You said it was likely to be a problem with the feed.'

'There's a good chance. George is your man. Ask him to look at the feed. He'll tell you if there's a problem there or not.'

'George isn't around at the moment. He's in hospital with a hernia.'

'Go and see him anyway.'

Duncan told Petie what Charlie had said.

'I don't mind going to see George,' Petie said, 'but the feed's no different to what we always have. I use Jack Bishop and he makes it up for me the way I like it. I rang him last week and he told me nothing had changed.'

The mystery remained.

'Jesus Christ,' Roisin said as she led The Black 'Un back into his stable. There was a terrific noise coming from the other end of Petie's yard. A hooting and shouting. Duncan swore under his breath – he felt responsible for the racket.

While Duncan had been in Ireland for Michelle's funeral – a magnificent but poignant occasion – Mike Ruddy had called and ended up speaking to Lorna, evidently at some length. The upshot was that she had agreed to his scheme to vacate the house for a City-boy house party and clay-pigeon shoot.

'But I turned him down,' Duncan had protested. He'd told her about it when Mike had first suggested the idea and she'd been as keen as he was to avoid the hassle.

'That was then, when we thought Daddy's dosh was on the way,' she pointed out. 'Now we know it doesn't exist, so we need to raise money where we can. We've still got this house, let's make the most of it.'

Put that way, it made sense. Part of Mike's plan was to bring the stockbrokers to the stables as part of the weekend's fun and games. They seemed to regard it all as high jinx, and had devised a game in which the loser had to fill twelve barrow loads of horse shit and wheel them across the yard. One of them was at it right now. Hence the uproar.

'Where's Petie?' Duncan asked.

'He's disappeared up to the house. He can't take any more of it.'

'So who's looking after them?'

'Kerry and Fee. I just told them to keep the group in one place. Not to let them go wandering off.'

'Where's Mike?'

Roisin shrugged.

Kerry and Fee seemed to be managing pretty well without the agent. They had lined up three horses for the stockbrokers to take a look at, two chestnut mares and bay gelding. It was a job tailor-made for a mouthy fellow like Kerry. He was deep in salesman mode as they lined up the three animals in the yard. By his side, Fee said little but she made an impression all the same. In tight jodhpurs and riding boots, whip in hand, she cut a figure straight out of many a male fantasy. Duncan had no doubt thoughts were on her as much as on the horseflesh on view.

Between them, Kerry and Fee had hatched a plan. While Kerry was talking up the horses, at certain points Fee was going to signal to the stockbrokers, as if tipping them off as to which horse was the best buy. Not that the brokers had even agreed to buy a horse just yet. But these were people who fed off inside information, and tipping them the wink about a horse might persuade them to make a bid.

Kerry held a restless stamping gelding while Fee held the two more placid mares. 'If I can have your full attention, gentlemen,' Kerry said with authority, 'I'd like to let you in on what's involved in owning a high-calibre racehorse.'

The stockbrokers, with one of their number still wheeling barrow-loads of dung in the background, moved a little closer, some nervously eyeing the stamping horse, others distracted by Fee and her riding crop.

'This is not like buying stocks and shares,' Kerry continued. 'Horses are highly sensitive creatures, selectively bred and expertly trained. To us they are like people, part of our family, and we hate selling them. For that reason we are very careful about who we sell to. Obviously, economics come into play. You can't keep an infinite number of horses at a stable, so you ask for investment, which is something you guys know all about.' Kerry's voice, full of Irish charm, rolled on seductively. 'Being a racehorse owner is not all about meeting the sporting heroes or glamorous models you see in the owners' bar, though you do get people in it for that stuff and for the business connections. But that's of no interest to me. Sure enough it's a thrill to own a racehorse, but it's a responsibility. It's up to us to check that this is the right horse for you and you are the right owner for this horse. If there's no match, we simply don't sell. OK?'

This brought nods and murmurs of agreement. 'That gelding looks lively,' one of the men said.

'I'll say he is,' Kerry replied. 'So let me tell you what you have in front of you. You need to be in the know or you can end up with' – and he indicated their colleague returning for another load of dung – 'what your man here has in his barrow – a load of shite.'

It got more laughs than it deserved.

'All the animals we will show you come with their certificated bloodstock pedigree, with the names of sire and dam, some of which you will recognise if you're at all familiar with the sport of kings. We also provide full, recent veterinary certificates, though you'll want to hire your own vet just to be sure your new asset is in perfect health, though these three horses are. So, let me tell you about their pedigree . . .'

Duncan and Roisin watched from a discreet distance. They heard the men laughing. In fact, they could be heard three fields away.

'He's in the wrong business,' Roisin said, a trace of admiration in her voice. 'He's got them eating out of his hand.'

116

Duncan was glad of it. The more he thought about this scheme, the more he needed it to work. Since he and Lorna had heard they were broke, they had managed to sell off some horses, bringing their holding down to twelve – though they hadn't approached Osborne and, Duncan had noted with relief, Lorna had not suggested it. Petie had generously agreed to buy out five of the remaining animals, including The Black 'Un, Destiny's Dream and Ansible. As there was no way Duncan and Lorna could find the stabling and veterinary expenses required to keep the remaining seven, they were looking to sell them off to whoever they could find. These stockbrokers might be the answer to a prayer.

The car collection had also been auctioned off. All the vehicles had been sold, some at knockdown prices, but it had been essential to get the cash together to pay the staff and the bills. The hope was that a buyer for the estate would come along and take on the staff as well as the buildings and the grounds. It was heartbreaking to have to tell loyal and hard-working people like Mary and Len that there may no longer be a future for them on the estate, but Lorna and Duncan had been honest with them. It had been a painful learning experience for both of them. Fortunately, most accepted the news without protest though there had been some tears. No one was surprised. They all knew that Duke Cadogan had been sailing on a fancy yacht, holed below the waterline. Some of the staff took their wages and cleared out. Others stayed on, hoping for the best.

Duncan's days of speeding around in a yellow Lamborghini had come to an end, not that he cared that much. He'd not driven it since the fateful day of Michelle's accident and he would have got rid of it even if he hadn't been forced to. He bought a second-hand Ford Cortina instead and parked it as far away from Sanderson's black Porsche as possible.

Duncan walked up to Petie's tumbledown cottage and found the trainer sipping tea from his favourite chipped mug. 'Have those eejits gone yet?' Petie asked.

'No. Kerry is giving them the hard sell.'

'I thought that damned agent o' yours was going to handle it.'

'He's still not here. Kerry seems to have it all in hand.'

'I just want them off my property. They give me the willies.'

'Yes, off your property and on to mine.' The plan was for Lorna and Duncan to move out of the mansion for the weekend while some of the brokers moved in. 'I appreciate you letting us do this, Petie. I only hope it's worth it.'

The door burst open and they turned to see Kerry in the doorway looking pleased with himself. 'Am I the dog's bollocks or what?' he cried.

'Which one did they go for?' Duncan asked.

'Which one? They've made syndicates to take all three.'

Duncan was gobsmacked. Kerry was a genius. 'Thanks, mate,' he said. 'I owe you.'

'You sure do. Listen, they asked for a discount. I said we don't do discounts but seeing as how you'll be stabling the horses here, I'll ask the guv'nor. So you'll give 'em a discount of fifteen per cent, Petie.'

'Fifteen per cent of what?'

Kerry named a figure and Duncan and Petie nearly fell off their chairs in shock.

Kerry's beam grew broader. 'The dog's bollocks. I told you.'

'Did you tell them that for horses we trade in guineas?' said Petie.

Kerry looked at Duncan and rolled his eyes. 'Can you believe this man? Now listen, they want us to race the three round the gallops so that they can bet against each other. We'll keep it nice and tight, put on a display.'

'No way!' Petie shouted. 'Not on my gallops, you won't.'

'At this price we'll do it all day stark naked if they want us to,' said Kerry. 'You, me and Roisin, Duncan. Come on, let's give these boys a show.'

The brokers were treated to a fine display in the form of a very tight race. Kerry went in front from the off; Duncan moved up on the inside; then Roisin took the lead. Kerry mounted a late challenge but Roisin held on to win by half a length. The betting between the brokers was fast and furious and noisy. It would be impossible to say the race was rigged since the jockeys hadn't actually told anyone what they were doing.

Following the race, the chief broker, a bald-headed chap with a cut-glass accent called Tennyson-Collins, requested a word with Petie. After a lot of bad-tempered grumbling, the trainer stumped off to see him. When he came back after ten minutes, his mood hadn't improved. 'Tried to get me to invest in some new-fangled rubbish,' he complained.

'What sort of rubbish.'

'Something called a mobile phone. I mean, what sort of clown would want to carry his phone with him everywhere he goes? You'd never get a moment's ruddy peace. I sent him away with a flea in his ear.'

Duncan and Kerry agreed. It seemed like a daft idea.

Mike Ruddy finally turned up, accompanied by his two sexy assistants. They'd been delayed on the motorway. For once Mike looked stressed. He looked even more stressed when Kerry told him he'd missed the sale and his commission with it. However, he swiftly took charge, taking the brokers to lunch, followed by an afternoon of clay-pigeon shooting on the Cadogan estate.

'Leave them with us,' he reassured Duncan. 'It will all be fine.'

Duncan wasn't so sure about that. The City lads had been raucous enough when sober on a chilly morning at the yard, he hated to think what they'd be like at night after they'd hit the booze and God knows what else. Mike Ruddy had told him that the stockbrokers had hired a couple of strippers as entertainment and ordered in crates of champagne.

'I hope they don't trash the place completely,' Lorna said that night as they sat down to dinner – a Chinese takeaway – in Kerry's flat, Kerry having volunteered to stay over with Roisin for the weekend.

'What does it matter?' Duncan said. 'We're selling the place anyway.'

They were watching *Dallas* on TV when the phone rang and Duncan picked up. A woman asked for Kerry.

'He's not here right now. Can I take a message?'

'Who was that?' Lorna asked as he replaced the receiver.

'She didn't say. She hung up.'

'Do you think Kerry's seeing someone on the side?'

'Couldn't say.'

'What did she sound like?'

'She sounded female.'

'Young or old?'

'In between.'

'Blonde or brunette?'

'She sounded bald-headed.'

Lorna hit him with a cushion. 'I wouldn't want to be in his shoes if Roisin finds out.'

On Sunday evening they returned to the Cadogan mansion. The stockbrokers had indeed trashed the place. There was a half-eaten buffet in the kitchen. The other half of it seemed to be on the floor and trodden into the lounge carpet. Beer and wine had been spilled. Half-empty champagne bottles had been abandoned all over the house. The curtains in the lounge had been pulled down. There was a man's shirt on the stairs. Upstairs, there was more food and drink debris and a window had been broken.

Lorna went directly to their bedroom. They'd left strict instructions that their room was not to be used and at first glance it looked like their wishes had been respected. Then Lorna found three used condoms on the bedside cabinet.

'Bastards,' she said. 'Oh gosh, look at this.'

A small lacquer box on the cabinet was half full of white powder. They both knew it wasn't talc.

Duncan found a note from Mike Ruddy in the kitchen suggesting that they get in professional cleaners and bill the brokers for setting everything straight. It also said that Mike had taken a message from the estate agent on Saturday afternoon: a prospective purchaser was coming to view the property on Tuesday morning.

'I'm really sorry about all this, Lorna. We'll have to get some cleaners in first thing.'

She surveyed the mess and blew a stray lock of hair from out of her eye. 'No. We can't afford that. We'll do it and then we'll send them the bill just as if we had cleaners in.'

'What? Don't tell me they taught you how to use a mop at those fancy boarding schools you went to?'

'Actually, they did. There's a whole lot of unpleasant shit you learn at boarding school.' She was already rolling up her sleeves.

Duncan looked at his wife with admiration – and concern. 'OK, then. Just so long as you promise you'll stop the moment you get tired.' Her early pregnancy symptoms had receded recently but he constantly worried about her condition.

'I promise. But you can get rid of the condoms.'

They got started straight away. Lorna tracked down cleaning equipment in the kitchen and they went hard at it, scraping, scrubbing and vacuuming. Duncan managed to fix the curtains while Lorna dealt with the carpets. The mess was endless and the work was exhausting. When they'd finished, they soaked in the bath, only to find another condom in the shower. Afterwards, they collapsed into bed.

'How do working people have the energy for sex at the end of the day?' Lorna said.

Before Duncan had thought of a reply she'd drifted off to sleep.

In the morning, while Duncan was out picking up the glass for the broken window, Lorna rang a cleaning agency and glaziers to get quotes. Then, after talking to Mike Ruddy, she called Tennyson-Collins and told him his company would have to foot the bill. She quoted the figures she'd come up with, plus fifty per cent.

'You must be joking. I'm not paying that to get a couple of stains off a carpet.'

Lorna, who'd learned to stand up to her father from an early age, wasn't intimidated. 'Who says I'm joking? You'll pay up or I'll see you in court.'

'Listen here,' said the stockbroker. 'We paid a very handsome sum for the use of your property, which I would expect to in-clude all cleaning services. As far as I'm concerned that's the end of the matter.'

'Very well,' Lorna said. 'But before you hang up, what would you like me to do with the cocaine?'

'I beg your pardon?'

'The cocaine you left behind in the black lacquer box in the front bedroom. Would you like me to post it to you? Or shall I ask the local bobby to come and dispose of it?'

There was a long pause on the other end of the line. 'Just send me the bill. I'll see it's taken care of.'

'Splendid,' said Lorna. 'Let me have your address.'

9

Duncan made it into the yard on Monday afternoon. 'Nice of you to honour us with your presence,' Petie said, despite the fact he'd given Duncan the morning off to fix the house. But he'd insisted Duncan join him in the afternoon to visit Gypsy George in hospital. Petie said he hated hospitals and needed moral support.

George had been kept in after his hernia operation because he'd developed a fever. He'd been at the hospital a few days now and, for a man who only ever resorted to the 'indoors' for the purposes of sleeping, was going out of his mind.

'Thank the Lord,' he said when Duncan and Petie arrived. 'Have you come to get me out of this place?'

'All in good time, George.'

'Come on, lads. I can't stand another night of this. The old boy this side of me keeps telling me he was fit as a fiddle until his ninety-third birthday and wants to know why it all went wrong. The one on the other side thinks he's fighting Mussolini. You've got to spring me.'

'We can't just carry you out in a blanket,' Petie said. 'But I'll see what I can do.'

He went to have a word with the ward matron to find out when George might be able to leave. Meanwhile, Duncan produced a small white paper bag from his pocket. 'I brought something for you,' he said.

It was a bag full of horse feed. George looked at it and wrinkled his nose. 'Look, the food in here may be rubbish but I'm not eating that.'

'It's not for you to eat,' Duncan said. 'I want to know what you think of it. The horses aren't running right and we're out of ideas.'

'Give us it here.' George took the bag, opened it and buried his nose deep into the feed. He inhaled deeply, and quickly held the bag at arm's length. 'Oh that's shite, that is! You've not been giving them that!'

'What's wrong with it?'

'I don't know, but it's crap. Can't you smell it?'

Duncan took the bag back from George and sank his own nose into it, inhaling deeply. He shook his head. 'Smells like ordinary horse feed to me.'

'No, there's something else in it.'

Petie came back. 'What's going on?'

Duncan explained that George had said there was something wrong with the feed.

'Give it back here,' George said. 'I don't know, you boys, I leave you alone for five minutes and you're feeding junk to my horses.' He sighed deeply, took one of the nuts from the bag and put it in his mouth. He sucked at it. 'I know what that is,' he said.

'What?'

George chewed it a little. 'Yes. I know that.'

'What? What is it?' Petie wanted to know.

'Quiet! I'm thinking.'

George ruminated on the horse nut in his mouth. He swished it from one side of his cheek to the other, like a wine connoisseur.

Then like a connoisseur he spat it out, but into his hand. 'Herbicide. It's been sprayed with herbicide or an insecticide of some kind. That'll play havoc with the horses' lungs.'

Duncan and Petie stared down at him, unsure of what to say.

Then the old man with a snowy head of hair woke up in the next bed. Seeing George holding the little bag, he said, 'Are they sherbet lemons? Because if they are, I wouldn't mind one.'

After all the effort they had put in to getting the big house ship-shape to impress a possible buyer, it galled Duncan to realise they needn't have bothered. When he opened the door on Tuesday morning he was confronted by someone who knew the house and its grounds all too well.

At first Duncan was confused to see George Pleasance standing next to the estate agent. He assumed they'd arrived separately but at the same time. 'I'm sorry,' he said to Pleasance, 'this isn't a good time – this gentleman is an estate agent and we're waiting to show someone around.'

'I know that, Duncan.' Pleasance was all smiles. 'That someone is me. I've always admired this place and I'm thinking of buying it.'

In his surprise, all Duncan could manage was a strangled, 'Oh.'

'I believe it is customary,' said Pleasance, 'to invite prospective buyers over the threshold. May we . . .' And the pair of them marched in as Duncan stood aside.

Just then, Lorna appeared, making a planned entrance down the long staircase into the grand reception area. She wore a severe tailored suit of dark navy and a pearl necklace. 'I'm going for the classy businesswoman look,' she'd told Duncan. Given her burgeoning figure she also looked dead sexy which, they had reckoned, wouldn't harm their chances with a male buyer. Now, to Duncan's dismay, it worked like a charm on George Pleasance.

'Lorna, my darling, you look wonderful,' he cried. 'So elegant and grown-up!' He turned to the estate agent, a middle-aged smoothy in pinstripes. 'It seems like only yesterday I was chasing this beautiful young woman up these stairs in her school uniform.'

If Lorna found their effusive laughter as creepy as Duncan did, she didn't let on. Instead she allowed Pleasance to grasp her around the waist and kiss her on the lips. She then led the pair of them into the front sitting room and began offering drinks.

It appeared that Pleasance did not want a guided tour of the house. It was unnecessary, he said. He would just take a stroll around the grounds to refresh his memory then he'd go away to put some figures together. He'd be making an offer very soon, one which he promised they would find satisfactory.

'That's marvellous,' Lorna cried. 'Isn't it, Duncan?'

'Absolutely,' Duncan agreed. He couldn't think of anything worse.

After visiting George in hospital, Petie had spoken to Phil, his head lad, a sixty-year-old cloth-capped veteran with blackened teeth. He'd instructed Phil to quarantine the existing feed supply at the yard and to get an emergency delivery from another source. Petie's outrage at discovering that the feed had been tampered with was tempered with relief that the problem was not viral. It just left the question of how the feed had been contaminated – and by whom.

Petie called Jack Bishop, his usual supplier, and told him that the feed had been adulterated with a toxic substance, probably some kind of herbicide. Bishop was incredulous. The same feed was being supplied to other yards, he said, so calls were made to check that everything was OK elsewhere. No one reported any problems. Petie and Bishop concluded that the feed was either being contaminated on the delivery round between the supply warehouse and the stables, or it was being spiked by someone working at the yard itself. It turned out that a new man had been employed as a driver a few months ago, and the finger of suspicion pointed his way. Bishop promised to check him out. In the meantime, they agreed that nothing was to be said to anyone. George was now out of hospital and he would monitor the feed, using his finely tuned sense of smell to detect if it had been tampered with.

It could just have been a coincidence, but the change in the horses' food supply seemed to bring an immediate improvement to their performance on the track. At Newbury at the weekend, Duncan piloted Billy Blake to victory in the first race. It was a better class of competition than his last outing at Warwick over the same distance, so his win was a surprise.

'Must have been the ground,' said Petie as he led the pair of them towards the winner's enclosure.

Duncan was about to say it might have been because they weren't up against the Monk on Cherry Orchard on this occasion, when he was distracted by a squealing redhead who almost pulled him out of the saddle to smother him with kisses. It was Lorna.

'Surprise!' she whispered in his ear. And a fantastic one it was too. She'd commandeered her friend Sophie, one of the bridesmaids at their wedding, to drive her to the meeting.

Kerry came a close second in the two-and-a-half-mile chase which followed. Then Roisin had a winner in the two-mile novice hurdle, which dispelled the sour face she had worn since seeing Kerry give Sophie an over-enthusiastic welcome.

Lorna was by Petie's side in the ring before Duncan's last ride of the day, clearly enjoying her role as the official owner of his mount, Ansible.

'It's great you're here,' Duncan said, for possibly the third time in as many minutes.

'I could get to like it,' she agreed. 'Especially if you win.'

And, blow me down, that's what he did. Ansible, a disappointing favourite at Towcester two days after their wedding, now discovered the stamina that had deserted him that day. Neck and neck with a rival at the last hurdle, he dug deep on the run-in and claimed victory by ten lengths.

'That's a bit more bloody like it,' Petie proclaimed at the end of the afternoon. 'Four winners and a good place – I'll take that any day.'

Duncan agreed, though the fourth winner for Petie's yard stuck in his throat. Sandy Sanderson had won on Destiny's Dream in the three-mile chase, the top race of the day. It hurt that Sanderson was still the only rider at the yard who could get a tune out of such a difficult horse. And Sanderson's antics in the parade ring before getting legged up were particularly irksome. He'd cupped his hands on either side of the horse's head and then planted a kiss on his forehead. Duncan had not seen him go through this pantomime with any other animal so he was convinced it was the key to Sanderson's understanding with Destiny's Dream. But he'd tried it himself back at Petie's and it had not made any difference to the horse's behaviour. It had amused the lads, however, and made Duncan feel like a right idiot. It also underlined the fact that he still had a distance to travel to match the champion jockey's knowledge of horses.

On Sunday, Duncan drove over to see Charlie at the Grey Gables, taking with him a bottle of single malt. He knew Mrs Solanki wouldn't approve but, as he said to his father, if he laid the bottle on its side on top of the wardrobe there was no way she would ever find out. Charlie seemed in good form, though Duncan never knew from one visit to the next how he would be.

'I've asked Devi if she'll make me samosas on a permanent basis,' Charlie said.

'I thought she did anyway.'

'Keep up, son. I've asked her to marry me. I love the woman. I want to make a life with her!'

A life together. Duncan looked at his father and felt a pang of love for the old man. What kind of a life could he offer at his age and with his mental difficulties? Besides, as far as he was aware, Mrs Solanki already had a husband. It was time to change the subject.

'Someone's been putting weed killer in the feed, Dad. George spotted it.'

Charlie looked gratified. 'Told you so.'

'You did too. You don't get much wrong about horses.'

It was remarkable. At times Charlie could mentally check out and be lost in a fog over the simplest of things. But when his long-term memory was faultless and, when he was lucid, he could be consulted on any subject to do with horses and racing. It wasn't just that he could remember every detail of every horse he'd ever trained and raced – the place, the prize money, the condition of the track and the stitch in the saddle leather – it was the accumulated wisdom that came with it.

'So,' Charlie said after he'd settled down in his armchair with a glass of whisky, 'looks like you've got an enemy in the camp.'

'Sanderson's there, riding Destiny's Dream.'

Charlie shook his head. 'No, it can't be Sanderson. He wouldn't want the dodgy feed going to his horse. In any case, he must know you boys are watching his every move. And if it's Osborne doing it, Sanderson might or might not even know about it. Why is he still riding your horse?'

'He's the only one who can get a performance out of him. With everyone else, Destiny just winds up. I've tried, and one moment he's fine, the next he's out of control.'

'You've tried a hood?'

'Yep. Blinkers, bridles, the lot. Changed everything we could think of in terms of gear.'

'And you've watched how Sanderson goes about it?'

'I've tried copying everything he does, Dad. How he holds his whip, where he holds his hands. All of it. I've made micro-adjustments to try and copy him exactly after he's left the yard. No dice.'

'Then you've got to keep watching.'

'Could it be that he's got the chemistry for this horse?'

'Ha!' Charlie got up and poured himself another whisky. 'He wants you to think that. They always want you to think that, but it's bollocks.'

When Duncan was a lad learning about horses, Charlie had told him that horses were as complex as people. You couldn't treat them all the same. They obviously hadn't found the best way to treat Destiny's Dream yet.

'If someone has the key to a horse,' Charlie said, 'it's there to be imitated. You've just got to keep your eyes open.'

The Monday morning following the Newbury meeting, the senior members of the yard staff were having a post-mortem

131

debrief over breakfast in Petie's hovel. That is to say, Petie, George, Kerry and Roisin were gobbling bacon sandwiches and slurping tea, while Duncan, as ever watching his weight, made do with a piece of dry toast. All major decisions took place over the ritual of tea and bacon butties. The topic under discussion was Sanderson and Destiny's Dream.

'Maybe he just has the magic touch,' Duncan said ruefully.

'There's no magic,' Gypsy George said.

'I agree with George,' Petie said. 'Who do you think he is? A wizard with a pointy stick?'

'I've done everything. I've held my hands to within an inch of how Sanderson holds his hands. I've held the reins the same. I've shortened my stirrups and I've tucked in my heels. I've even blown a bloody kiss on the horse's forelock.'

'That you have,' Roisin said. 'More tea?' She offered a giant, chipped brown teapot with a knitted cosy.

Duncan waved the pot away. The combination of tea and pee-pills was a bit too much.

'Over here,' Kerry said. 'Who's got the sauce?'

'There's a point,' said Gypsy George. 'That thing he does. Blowing on the horse. Did you see him do that on the other horses he rode at Sandown?'

'No. I watched him like you watch a Glasgow taxi meter. He only does it for Destiny's Dream.'

'Come here and show me exactly what he does,' George said, putting his cup aside.

'Well, he holds the horse's head and blows a kiss on the fore-lock. That's all.'

'Don't tell, show me!'

'What? I'm not gonna kiss you, George. No offence but you're really not my type.'

'Kiss him!' shouted Kerry. 'Kiss the man!'

Duncan sighed and put down his cup. He stood up, placed his hands on either side of George's head and kissed the old gypsy on the forehead.

'That's it?' said George.

'That's it.'

'Nothing else?'

'I don't care what promises you make, George,' Duncan said, 'but that's as far as I'm going.'

When the laughter had died down, George was seen to be squinting hard to his left.

'He's thinkin'!' Petie shouted. 'Can you hear them chains and sprockets? That man is thinkin'!'

George stood up. He was already heading for the door. 'Follow me.'

They all put down their cups and filed out after him. When he stopped halfway across the yard on the way to the stables, they all stopped behind him, like a small army. George took Roisin aside, whispered something to her and she went back into the hut. George resumed his march to Destiny's Dream's stable. 'Let's have him out,' he said.

Petie whistled to head lad Philip, who went into the stall and trotted out Destiny's Dream. The horse didn't take too kindly to being surrounded by the laughing and chattering group. He snorted and stamped, tossing his head.

'He's in an arsey mood all right,' Petie said.

'Stand!' Philip barked. 'Just being his normal self.'

Roisin returned and slipped something to George.

'Right then,' George said. He stepped forward, placed his hands on either side of the horse's head and blew a kiss on to his forelock. Destiny's Dream seemed to calm down instantly. He relaxed and nuzzled George contentedly.

'What?' said Duncan. 'I've done that. It didn't make any difference for me.'

'That's because you,' George said, 'didn't do what I just did.'

'Which was?'

'I slipped earplugs into him.'

The others were dumbfounded.

'You didn't see me cos you were too busy watching me blow a kiss on his nose.'

'Earplugs make no difference,' Petie protested. 'I've tried that on other horses in my time.'

'It will on this one. He's obviously got painful hearing.' Destiny's Dream was still nuzzling George like he was lovesick. 'Saddle him up, Duncan. This boy'll do anything you want now.'

Sandy Sanderson was pleased to be asked inside Petie's hovel for a cup of tea and a private chat. Not that he'd been excluded from the inner sanctum on the days that he'd come along to school the troublesome Destiny's Dream, but it was more common for him to arrive, do his work, and then shoot off again back to the Osborne yard. To be asked inside for a brew with Petie would give him the opportunity to raise the question of other horses that he wanted to ride – such as Ansible and The Black 'Un. Since he was the only one capable of riding Destiny's Dream, he reckoned he was in a strong position to argue his case.

Petie, forthright as ever, said, 'Sandy, something has happened here at the yard. It means you'll not be riding for us from now on.'

'What?' Sandy nearly spat tea on the old carpeted floor. He couldn't believe what he'd just heard.

'That's the way it is. It's a bad business.'

'What's a bad business? What the hell happened?'

'I don't like to talk about it, but I owe you the details. It turns out that someone was contaminating the feed for our horses. They were spraying some kind of herbicide on the stuff and it affected the horses' pipes, you know?'

'Herbicide? What's this got to do with me?'

'Nothing. No one is suggesting it has anything to do with you. We've got our ideas about who has been doing it but we're not in a position to prove it. Yet.'

'I don't see how it affects me riding Destiny's Dream.'

'Put yourself in my position. I've got to throw a ring around the place, you understand? Keep things tight while we get proof. Until that time, you've got to stay away and that's how it is.'

Sanderson stared at Petie, trying to control the anger rising within him. But as he looked hard at the gnarled close-cropped head of the Irish trainer, he knew that there would be no changing his mind. It would be like trying to push a bus up a mud slope. 'You realise you'll be left with top horses and no one good enough to ride them.'

'I'll have to take my chances. When things have blown over I might be in a position to ask you back. I'm not just thinking about Destiny's Dream. There's Ansible and The Black 'Un.'

Sanderson assessed Petie's words. Either the trainer was playing with him or he was genuinely holding the door open for a later date. While Sanderson instinctively wanted to say *Stuff you and all your horses, Petie Quinn*, he was too long in the tooth and too much of a professional to do that. He'd burned too many bridges in the past. These days his strike rate was slowing up. If he was going to maintain his position as champion jockey he had to have access to horses like Destiny's Dream and Ansible.

'So that's that,' Petie said. 'Now then, do you want another cup of tea?'

Lorna was waiting for Duncan the moment he stepped in the door. 'I've got some good news,' she said. 'The estate agent rang. George Pleasance has made an offer on the house. He's met the asking price, says he doesn't want to haggle – isn't that fantastic?'

Duncan's heart sank. 'I suppose so.'

'Of course, it is. It solves all our problems.'

'Not all of them, Lorna.'

'You know what I mean. You could sound more enthusiastic. I thought you'd be happy.'

'I am, of course, but we mustn't get carried away. Did you accept the offer?'

'I said I had to talk to you but I did say I was jolly pleased about it.'

He thought frantically. 'If he doesn't want to bargain, don't you think it suggests we didn't ask for enough? Maybe we should keep the house on the market. We might get more.'

'Are you mad? You just don't want to sell to George Pleasance, do you?'

No, he didn't. He had very good reasons but he couldn't exactly tell Lorna what they were.

'Why not?' she demanded, correctly reading his silence. 'He was one of Daddy's oldest friends and he's always been very sweet to me. I suppose, that's it – just because he was a bit familiar with me, you're jealous.'

Duncan saw a way out and took it. 'He practically had his hand on your arse. And he'd have had his tongue halfway down your throat if he'd had the chance.'

She giggled. 'It's true. He is a bit of an old letch but if it helps to keep us out of the bankruptcy court . . .'

'Lorna, that's not funny.'

'Oh, OK, I'm only joking. It's sweet of you to defend my honour, if that's what you're doing. I'll stall the agent and ask him to drum up some other possible buyers. No one else has seen it, after all. I suppose it's fair we test the market all round.'

That was a relief. Duncan had bought himself some time. But he didn't see how he would ever be able to tell Lorna the real reason why he didn't want to sell: he was convinced George Pleasance had murdered her father.

10

Petie was one of those weird creatures who seemed to survive on four hours of sleep a night. And he thought that when he was out of bed, everyone else should be too. He called Duncan at 5.00 a.m.

He was in a chewy mood about something. 'When you come, bring in all the papers you have on those damned flibbets you left with me.'

Petie had a habit of making up words. Duncan knew that 'flibbets' were the Cadogan horses he'd moved from Osborne's stables to Petie's.

'You've had the papers. I gave them to you. Did you know it's the dead of night?'

'There should be more. Bring everything you've got.'

Duncan groaned.

'It was your idea to sell them to those pawnbrokers,' Petie said.

'Stockbrokers.'

'Whatever you call 'em.'

'Is something wrong?'

'Just get over here, will ya?'

Duncan sat on the bed, staring at the carpet and trying to will himself awake. Lorna snoozed happily. He dressed quietly and made himself an instant coffee, which he drank black. He had a slice of dry toast for breakfast, eating it as he went through to the desk in Cadogan's former office. He pulled out a file with papers relating to the horses. They were mostly veterinary invoices and reports. He'd already given the foal identification certificates to Roisin, who was well organised and would keep everything in one place.

At the back of the file were some yellowing pages from the *Sporting Life*. Certain results pages were ringed, and Duncan came fully awake as he realised what connected each of the highlighted races.

'Bastard,' Duncan spat.

They were all races featuring horses trained by Duncan's father. They were from Charlie's best season, his last, in which he had started to mount a serious challenge to William Osborne. This wasn't new information but it was concrete evidence that Cadogan and Osborne had marked Charlie's card before their campaign of dirty tricks.

It was light by the time Duncan got to Petie's place. He went straight up to the house and found Roisin with her father.

'What's up?' Duncan asked. 'Did someone die?'

'It's Daddy,' said Roisin. 'He's in a sweat. He's been up half the night.'

'Why?'

'Did you find any more papers?' Petie demanded.

Duncan handed him the file, minus the newspaper clippings. Petie put it on the table next to a collection of other papers – certificates and photocopies of documents relating to the registration of the horses that had been transferred from Osborne's stables to Petie. Petie picked out some of them and set them in front of Duncan.

The first paper was a foal identification certificate for one of the older Cadogan horses, a mare called And So It Goes. 'What do you see?' Petie growled.

Duncan looked closely at the document but he saw nothing unusual. There were the Weatherbys stud book details indicating sire and dam, plus a separate covering certificate to prove the horse's thoroughbred credentials. There was a vet's certificate too, and a photocopy of the foal identification certificate. It all seemed in order.

'You're blind,' Petie said. 'Look at the photocopy.'

Duncan held the photocopy and the original up side by side. The signature and dates were so tiny they were practically illegible. But not quite. He saw that a date of the original had been changed from a 5 to a 6. It had been changed by the simple expedient of closing the loop. The photocopy stated that And So It Goes had been born in 1975. The identification certificate claimed a birth date of 1976. There were actually two covering certificates, suggesting that the sire of And So It Goes had covered the dam in each of the preceding years.

Roisin spread out on the table some back copies of the *Sporting Life*. Race results had been ringed with biro. 'Daddy's been busy going through the records,' she said.

The records showed that And So It Goes had won or placed in several races over three seasons before dipping in form.

The penny dropped. 'And So It Goes was a three-year-old running as a two-year old,' Duncan said. 'And then as a four-year-old running as a three-year-old. But surely someone should have noticed?'

'Well,' Petie said, 'a vet would have known by looking at the teeth. But it depends if anyone goes to the trouble. And look at the odds. They are never long enough to attract suspicion.'

'But how would you control the odds like that?'

'How? By not telling anyone. And by dropping a race here and there.'

'I don't believe it,' Duncan said.

'Listen to the man,' Petie said to Roisin in disbelief. 'After what they did to his da!'

'What I mean is, I don't believe they could have got away with it.'

'It's damned easy, is what it is,' Petie said. 'So long as you stop the information getting out so that every stable lad in the country isn't backing your horse. Didn't I write to the Jockey Club? Didn't I?'

'You did, Daddy,' Roisin said.

Petie had indeed written – or had got his daughter to write for him – telling the Jockey Club that it was high time it went the American way and introduced proper blood sampling for identification of foals, or lip tattooing, or both. By way of reply, the unelected aristocratic authorities who ran the Jockey Club had begged to differ. Racing had to maintain its integrity as a sport for gentlemen. The occasional bad apple, they said, didn't mean it was necessary to disinfect the whole apple cart. Petie was more enraged by the waffle about apples than he was by the implied criticism that his ideas came from someone who wasn't a 'gentleman'.

'The winner of the Derby in 1844 was a ringer,' he cried. 'It was a big scandal then. It's 1980 now and you can still get away with it!'

Duncan didn't like to point out that they obviously hadn't got away with it in 1844 but he took Petie's point. For all the modern technology available to the racing authorities, it was still easy to run a ringer – that is, a horse with false credentials or one substituted for an inferior horse. Though it required careful preparation, getting away with it was easy too. Profiting from the ruse, on the other hand, was much more difficult. The deception was usually discovered as soon as the ringer triggered unusually large patterns of betting. That in turn would be enough to signal to the stewards to stop any payouts to punters pending an investigation.

'Sure, it's still possible,' said Roisin, 'but it's a fair old amount of trouble to go to if you're not going to make real money. Why would anyone bother?'

Petie fixed her with his beetle-browed stare. 'It can still be worth it if you play the long game. Don't be greedy. Spread lots of small bets around. Stick to little races. You can clean up at point-to-points if you've a mind.'

Duncan pointed at the adulterated certificate for And So It Goes. 'But who's behind this? Was it Osborne or Cadogan?'

'I'd say it would have to be both. Though if it came to light, Cadogan would be the owner with the papers. Osborne would claim he was misled by Cadogan.'

'What are you going to do about it?'

'Nothing,' said Petie. 'I can read your mind, Duncan. You'd love to use it against Osborne, but the blame will always lie with Cadogan. Your wife's late father. You'd best not go there. As for the horse, well, she's not much of a contender any longer. We'll sell her on. I'll send a letter to the Jockey Club expressing my doubts about the horse's age, just to cover my own arse. They won't do anything about it. Meanwhile, we'll have Roisin go through all of the documents, in case anything else turns up.'

'Thanks a bunch, Daddy.'

'Well, you can do that later. Now we've got to get to work. Where's my list for first lot?'

Duncan made his way across the yard to Prince Samson's stall where Nicky, one of Petie's best stable lasses, was getting the big grey ready for him. The perfume of lavender hung in the air around his stall and a bunch of dried flowers was suspended from a beam in the roof. The secret to handling Sammy was a secret no longer. As Duncan had said to Michelle when she'd first let him in on it, 'What happens when you're not around and the horse needs attending to? It's not fair on him.' So they'd spread the word to Phil, the head lad, and now Nicky looked after him day to day because, of course, Michelle was no longer around.

The morning after the fatal accident, Duncan had arrived at the yard before dawn. Petie was up and brooding in his kitchen. Duncan came right out with it.

'What are you going to do about Prince Samson?'

Petie raised a bushy eyebrow. 'I'm thinking of asking Martin to take him away. Not right away, of course, we'll keep him for now, but when the dust has settled. He'll be too much trouble without that wee girl to look after him.'

'I think that would be a mistake. He's got the makings and I reckon he'll be OK. More than OK.'

'I don't know. All that perfume malarkey. This is a training yard not a tart's boudoir.'

'Come on, Petie. Michelle wanted him to race here and so do her family. It's only right.'

The trainer had harrumphed to himself and said nothing further on the matter but Prince Samson had not been removed. Phil and Nicky had taken special care of him and Duncan had worked with him regularly, riding him out on the gallops and schooling him over fences in the yard.

He wondered often whether Sammy missed the brown-eyed girl with the bobbed blonde hair who used to lavish attention on him every day. He was convinced that the horse did. Duncan wasn't sentimental about the animals he worked with. They were tools of his trade, not pets. But there was no denying that you got close to some of them. He'd left racecourses in tears more than once when his mount had suffered an injury bad enough for the screens to surround the fallen body and for the humane killer to do its work.

Sammy was definitely one of those animals who could get under your skin. Once he'd learned to trust Duncan, he was as easy as pie to control and he responded positively to affection. Maybe it was because of the abrupt absence of Michelle, but Duncan felt that Sammy understood loss. On the morning in early December when they'd heard that John Lennon had been shot, Roisin had been in tears in Duncan's arms. Sammy had rubbed up and down her back with his great head, as if he'd understood the depth of her feeling.

Now Nicky legged Duncan up and they joined first lot. After the string of horses circled the yard, warming up and stretching their muscles watched by Gypsy George, they took the lane up to the all-weather gallop where Petie was waiting in his old Land Rover. Duncan's instructions were to canter Sammy at half speed over the four furlongs and to come back at three-quarter pace, then to repeat the process twice again at a greater speed. As they returned, Petie came alongside to ask Duncan's opinion. He noticed that the trainer was wearing a green scarf that had belonged to Michelle. Roisin had found it in her bungalow and Petie would wear it, still smelling of Michelle and her lavender oil, when he wanted to get close to Prince Samson.

'He's nearly ready, boss. You should find him a race.'

'Hmm.' Petie was observing the horse closely. He shut his eyes. Petie was a trainer who appeared not to see anything but, at the same time, missed nothing. Duncan knew he was listening to Sammy's breathing, judging how quickly his heart rate was slowing down after his exertions – it was his way of telling a horse's fitness.

Petie opened his eyes. 'I think you may be right, lad. I'll have a word with Martin Joyce at Sandown.'

For many racing folk, the Sandown Park Oyster Bay Meeting heralded the beginning of Christmas. Its feature race was named after a former champion who had dazzled the Sandown faithful with flamboyant and flawless rounds of jumping over many years. Second only to Cheltenham's Queen Mother Champion Chase, the Oyster Bay Trophy was seen as a traditional test over two miles for horses hoping to go on to glory later in the season – horses such as Destiny's Dream, who Duncan was riding in a race for the first time.

George had been right about Destiny's Dream. Now that the horse had earplugs, he would do anything asked of him. Petie had had him thoroughly checked out and evidence had been found of infection in his ears, which made him particularly sensitive to sudden noises – a bit like having the volume permanently turned up to max was the way the vet put it. It was possible the damage was untreatable but, with careful attention and the use of lambswool earplugs, at least the condition wouldn't be made any worse.

Two miles wasn't Destiny's Dream's best distance. He would have preferred another half a mile but, after three days of rain, his stamina would be an asset in the heavy going. Punters had been thrown into confusion on hearing that Sanderson had been replaced on the horse by Duncan. The pundits enjoyed themselves, speculating about backroom rows and making much of the fact that Sandy had been jocked off by the former owner's husband. The odds drifted at the news, but soon came back in to leave Destiny's Dream as joint favourite, which is where he was before Sanderson was replaced.

*

There was panic in the pre-parade ring where Petie and Roisin were getting Destiny's Dream to stretch his legs.

'Daddy, do you know what I did with those earplugs?'

'Earplugs?'

'I brought a new pair of lambswool plugs. I left them with all the gear and now I can't find them.'

'Have you got any others?'

'No. And I've already started to ask around the other trainers. Nobody's got any.'

'Have you looked in the cabin of the lorry?'

'I have.'

'Have you turned out all your pockets?'

'I have.'

'Where did you last have them?'

'Jesus, why do people always say that? If I knew where they were when I last had them then I'd know where they were now, wouldn't I?'

'Calm down, Roisin!'

'You don't suppose someone could have picked them up? You know? Deliberately?'

'More likely you've lost them.'

'Lost them. Right.'

'Just try and think.'

'Think? Do you not think I'm thinking? Fee is looking. I'm looking. Everyone is looking. Oh for God's sake, Daddy, you're no help.'

Roisin marched away leaving Petie scratching his head.

The rain took pity on the heaving crowd and slackened off. From a look at the bruise-black clouds in the sky, it was unlikely to stay away for long but Duncan took the opportunity to take a breather outside the weighing room. As he was marshalling his thoughts for the contest ahead, he felt a hand on his shoulder.

'Duncan. How fortuitous.'

He turned to find himself staring into the smiling features of George Pleasance. The older man wore a belted trenchcoat and a caramel Burberry scarf, his smooth broad face glowing with an unseasonal tan. He looked brand new, as if he had just been unwrapped. He was the last person on earth Duncan wanted to talk to.

'I'm glad I bumped into you,' said Pleasance. 'I'd like a little chat.'

That sounded ominous. The last time Duncan had enjoyed a little chat on a racecourse with George Pleasance he'd barely escaped with his life. In the event, it had been Duke Cadogan who had ended up dead, as a result of the lies Duncan had told after winning on Duke's horse Ra-Ho-Tep at the Cheltenham Festival.

He tried not to dwell on these matters, but they were not easily dismissed.

'It's the house, Duncan. I made you and the lovely Lorna a very fair offer a few weeks ago and you haven't yet favoured me with a response.'

He had to say something – but what? 'Look, George, we discussed it thoroughly with the estate agent and came to the conclusion that it was still early days – I mean, the house has barely been on the market.' He was squirming.

'Bullshit, Duncan. It's you. You don't want to sell to me, do you?'

'The thing is, the estate agent thinks it might be better if we held off for the moment. Maybe next spring would be a better—'

'Next spring you'll have a newborn baby to look after and you'll be thousands of pounds deeper in the mire than you are at present. I know what you owe on that house.'

And he also knew Lorna was pregnant – how? They'd decided

to keep the news to just a small circle, none of whom had dealings with Pleasance.

'In case you're wondering, Duncan, the lady told me herself. I spoke to her last week and she promised to speed up the house business. But I'm seizing this opportunity to do it myself.'

Lorna had indeed raised the matter again and Duncan had promised to speak to the agent. But he hadn't done anything. He felt paralysed.

'Look,' Pleasance said gently, 'I understand how you feel. There's a residue of resentment because of what happened to poor Duke. But I have a proposition. You agree to the sale and I'll make sure it goes through swiftly. I've earmarked the finance already. That will solve a lot of your immediate money worries. And in return for your cooperation I will do you a favour.'

'What's that?' Duncan had to ask. He was in a hole.

'I'm prepared to let you and Lorna continue to live in the house. At least until after the baby is born. And I wouldn't expect any rent from you because I need to have the place occupied while I decide what I'm going to do with it. I'd say that was pretty handsome, wouldn't you?'

It hurt to agree but he really had no choice.

In the parade ring Duncan was dismayed to find Destiny's Dream up to his old tricks, sweating and spooking at every sudden noise. Sandy Sanderson walked by, grinning at the sight of Fee doing her best to hold the panicking horse. This day was going sour fast.

'You're going to hate me,' Roisin said, 'but I've forgotten to bring his earplugs. We've asked around but no one seems to have any. Nobody uses them much.'

Petie said, 'There's a thing I heard once – we could give it a try.

Listen to me, Roisin. I'll speak straight. Do you have any flying clooties with you?'

'Sorry?'

'You know them thin fellahs?'

'What?'

'You know. Plugs. Wicks. Corks. Them pen-shaped ones.'

'I think,' Duncan said, 'he means what you and I would call a tampon.'

'Daddy, why didn't you say so? Actually, I don't but I can find someone who does. Wait here.'

Within five minutes she was back with a packet and was fashioning them into a pair of earplugs. She gently popped them into Destiny's Dream's ears and they worked a treat. He calmed instantly.

Across the ring, Sanderson had just been legged up on to his mount, the Osborne-trained Punctilious.

'I'm tempted to take them out and walk him round again,' Roisin said. 'Just so that little shit will think we haven't cracked it.'

'I couldn't possibly approve of that,' said her father.

So that's exactly what they did.

Down at the start, Duncan cleared his mind of everything that had gone before. For the next four minutes, all he could allow himself to think about was the two miles and thirteen fences that lay ahead. The crowd was substantial at well over 15,000 and this was the race they had come to see. Duncan surveyed the other horses as they circled, waiting for the starter to call them into line. There were few lightweights among them. Previous winners made for a distinguished list of competitors.

The Penderton yard was represented by the victor of last

year's race, the oak-hearted Mindstar Rising, and Punctilious, Sanderson's mount, had won it the year before that. The Joyce brothers were attempting to scoop the trophy with the beautiful Irish mare Violet Hour. Michael Joyce was in the saddle. He and Duncan had said a quick hello while changing, but nothing more. Now Michael sat motionless, hands held low, deep in concentration. These horses, together with Destiny's Dream, were the top four fancies in a field of nine.

The Monk had once told Duncan that in his opinion the Oyster Bay was the most thrilling race of the season, barring the Grand National, because at only two miles it was as fast as you could go over a fence. Better and more thrilling, even, than the Queen Mother Chase at Cheltenham because of Sandown's railway fences, which come in such quick succession in the back straight. You have to be on a spring-heeled jumper to get over those and, of course, your horse also has to be a fleet-footed flyer if you are going to win the race. That's why only the best were lining up.

They were off to a clean, steady start, all striding out with purpose and clearing the first fence comfortably. The lead was taken by Westlake Soul, a renowned front runner, who soon opened up a five-length lead. Mindstar Rising was travelling in second place, followed by Duncan on Destiny's Dream, who in turn was being tracked on the rail by Violet Hour.

By the fourth fence, the leader was eight lengths in front, with everyone else tightly bunched, but by the water jump that lead was shrinking. Duncan held third position, sensing both the Irishman and Sandy Sanderson breathing down his neck. When they came to the first railway fence, there was a faller at the back but all four favoured horses remained in contention. Mindstar Rising now increased the pace to catch the leader but he blundered at the next fence, shooting his jockey forward in the saddle. He lost ground as both Duncan and Violet Hour made headway, with Westlake Soul beginning to tire on the heavy ground.

At the last of the railway fences, Destiny's Dream produced a spectacular leap, touching down just ahead of Westlake Soul. It signalled the beginning of the real race. There were three fences and four furlongs to go with no place to hide. As they turned into the bend, Punctilious and Violet Hour moved up on Duncan. The duel was on.

A shit-storm of mud was being kicked up and Duncan had to wipe his goggles as Sanderson drew upside of Destiny's Dream. Duncan thought Sanderson had made a mistake and was going too early, but then he saw the champion jockey dip his face towards him and let fly a fearful high-pitched scream into Destiny's Dream's ear.

The ploy would surely have worked if Destiny's Dream hadn't been wearing his improvised earplugs. Duncan looked over at Sanderson in astonishment. What he saw, distorted by mud and goggles, was a look of pure hatred. But the tactic had failed. Duncan grinned, sure he'd got the measure of Sanderson. He knew that the champion jockey must be desperate to try a trick like that, even though Punctilious had edged ahead of him into the lead.

Just behind Duncan, Violet Hour was closing and Mindstar was rallying after his mistake at the first railway fence. Westlake Soul was out of it. The four horses battled on over the churned-up ground, almost in a line as they jumped the legendary pond fence. Duncan touched down neck and neck with Violet Hour and the two of them cruised past Punctilious. A volcanic roar rose from the stands as they charged into the home straight. Sanderson was beaten, left to battle it out with Mindstar for third place.

Just two fences to go and then the uphill battle for the line. Destiny's Dream and Violet Hour took the penultimate obstacle abreast but Duncan's horse met the last fence with a perfect stride, opening up a half-length advantage. Violet Hour tried to launch one last challenge up the home hill but, with a lung-bursting effort, Destiny's Dream held her off and stamped his authority on the flatter ground of the final run-in to win by a length.

In the stands and along the rails the crowd were shouting themselves hoarse but Duncan didn't hear them, any more than he remembered the dramas and anxieties that plagued his life out of the saddle. He'd done it. This was what he lived for. The greatest victory of his career – so far.

11

Petie and Duncan savoured their triumph in the owners' bar at Sandown after the final race, soaking up the plaudits and the backslapping. Dick Sommers from Penderton congratulated them on a great race, as did Martin Joyce, who said to Petie, 'I suppose if I have to lose to some bastard over here I'd rather it was an Irish bastard like yourself.' Petie took that as a compliment. All in all, it was a great start to the Christmas season. The only people who didn't join the celebrations in the bar were Osborne and Sanderson which, from the Quinn yard point of view, made the occasion all the sweeter.

Michael Joyce bought Duncan a festive vodka and tonic. He drew the line at conceding he'd lost to a better horse, however. 'That bloody rain did for us,' he said. 'My girl doesn't like the soft so much. We'll have you next time.' For once Duncan didn't take the bait.

'Maybe you will,' he said. He was glad he'd won but it wouldn't have been so terrible to lose to the Irishman who'd shouldered the burden of his cousin's death so bravely.

'How are you holding up? You know, after what happened,' Duncan asked carefully, not sure he wanted to upset the good mood of the day but wanting to talk about Michelle.

Michael looked away to avoid meeting Duncan's eye. 'I'm all right,' he said, his voice tight. 'It just keeps hitting me, over and over. I can't believe she's gone. And I can't believe that bastard . . .' He trailed off, anger making his eyes narrow.

'Osborne,' Duncan said bitterly.

'He's the reason she's dead.'

'And he's getting off scot-free,' Duncan finished. 'It's not right.'

'No.' Michael took a long sip of his drink. 'It's not. But there isn't a lot we can do about it, it's not like he forced her on to the horse or held a gun to her head. She wanted to ride. We can't prove that Osborne was responsible.'

Duncan thought for a second. 'You know, I bet this isn't the first time he's pulled something like this. He's ruthless and he doesn't care who gets hurt. Maybe, if we can find evidence of other instances where he's put his jockey in harm's way, we can begin to build some kind of case against him.'

Michael looked thoughtful. 'He's clever, Duncan. Man like that won't have left any trace. You know I'd love to see him go down, but I just don't see how it's going to happen.'

Duncan let the subject drop and the two of them quickly resumed their analysis of the day's races, but the more he thought about it, the more he was convinced that investigating Osborne's past was the only way they were going to see any justice for Michelle. Even if they had to take that justice into their own hands.

Petie's totals for the day were good. Two firsts including the Oyster Bay and its substantial prize, and two places, with Kerry landing a third placing in the final race of the day. Petie had been enjoying a drink with several of the other Joyce brothers and having difficulty getting their names straight as the whiskies went down. Now, half of them seemed to be in a competition to chat up Fee and Roisin, who were lapping up the attention with good humour. Only Martin, the gaffer, didn't seem completely happy about something. Duncan walked over to the bar where Petie and Martin stood.

'What is it then? You've got two winner's yourself and second in the Oyster Bay. I'd call that a good day, so why the face?' Duncan asked Martin.

Martin wiped Guinness foam from his lips and looked about to see who was listening.

'Look here,' he whispered, leaning forward. 'It was a good day sure enough. But that last race . . . I had a big feckin' wedge on that, and that race was ours. No messing. Something not right there.'

The last race had been won by an Osborne horse called Ecko – with Sanderson in the saddle, naturally. Duncan considered the words. 'What are you saying, Martin?'

'We've been in control o' that handicap since last year.'

'Don't tell me that,' Duncan said, shooting a look at Petie who pretended not to have heard. When Joyce said he'd been controlling the handicap he implied he had previously stopped the horse from doing its best.

'But I am telling you. I come over here and I have to get my expenses somehow. And we had that in our pockets. I done my homework. That horse Ecko, 33-1, blazing in eight lengths clear and he wasn't even trying. That wasn't the horse it was. Now what d'ye say?'

'That's a serious allegation and you should take it to the stewards.'

'Not my way, Duncan, and you know it.'

Duncan looked at Petie, who appeared uncomfortable. The truth was they'd had similar thoughts about Osborne's horses a couple of times this season. While this wasn't the place to debate the matter further, Duncan's mind began to whir. If Osborne was thowing races . . .

Petie broke through Duncan's thoughts with a change of subject.

'About that grey horse of yours, Martin.'

'Ah yes.' The Irishman's big face darkened. 'You're going to ask me to take him away, aren't ya? I imagine he's a bit of a handful now that—'

'That's not what I'm going to say. Our Duncan reckons I should find a race for him. He's been working him regular.'

'Is that so? I always thought it would be Michelle riding him on one of your fancy English tracks. But Duncan here is a good man.'

'I promised him I'd mention it you,' Petie said. 'And I'm sorry about this, Duncan, but I have to say that I'm not quite of the same mind. I think we should take it slowly, make sure we're not going to be in for any nasty surprises when Sammy is confronted with loud crowds. I don't want to rush him. I think we've got the measure of Prince Samson in the yard now, his little quirks and all. But I want to be sure before I put him out on a track."

'What do you want me to say, Quinn? You're the horse's trainer. I haven't clapped eyes on the beast for months.' The big Irishman sipped his drink and considered the matter. 'But I trust your judgement, I think you should keep Sammy under wraps for now. I'll be over some time in the new year to check him out myself and then we can reassess the situation. Will that do?'

Duncan gave a grudging nod.

'Thanks, Martin.' Petie drained his glass. 'Time to go,' he said to Duncan and turned to the Joyce brothers. 'Fellahs, it's been grand!'

On Sunday, Duncan headed for the Grey Gables. He knew his father would have watched the racing from Sandown and he was dreading a renewal of the row about the colours he'd ridden in. But Charlie had either not noticed or chosen to bury the matter. Instead, he was in ebullient mood, pumped up by Duncan's victory. It seemed he'd made a bit of a song and dance about it the previous afternoon. Now Duncan found himself led around the sitting room of the care home being introduced to a variety of cheerful elderly ladies who were fulsome in their praise – and gratitude.

'We all had a bit of a flutter,' Charlie explained when they had returned to his room.

'Really? I hope you don't make a habit of it, Dad. I don't want that responsibility every time I weigh out.'

'Yes, but I knew you'd do the business once you'd told me about the earplugs.'

Charlie looked as pleased as Punch with his little coup but Duncan wasn't going to let him get away with his gambling so easily.

'Are you sure you should be betting? Don't you remember what you said about it being a disease which nearly destroyed you once?'

Charlie considered the matter. 'It was only a couple of quid. Anyway, I didn't go near the bookies. I couldn't ask Mrs S so I got one of the girls from the kitchen to put the money on. Just for fun, son.'

What could Duncan say? Not much, especially if it cheered the old man up. He resented feeling as if suddenly he was the parent.

Charlie changed the subject. 'Your lot seem to have got over the feed business.'

'Yes. We still haven't found out who was doing it though.'

'Could it just have been one bad delivery? An accident?'

That was a good question but Duncan didn't know the

157

answer. He shrugged. 'Petie and Roisin will get to the bottom of it. There's something else though, Dad. About Osborne.'

'There's always something else where that bastard's concerned.'

'I think Osborne has been ringing.' Duncan had been talking it over with Petie in the light of what Martin Joyce had said to them both the day before. Petie had mentioned a couple of other unexpected victories for Osborne earlier in the season – Spring Moon at Towcester and Chania House at Leicester. And there was also the matter of the forged foal certificate for And So It Goes. He related the details to Charlie, who didn't look in the least surprised.

'He's been doing it for years.'

'So how come he hasn't been caught?'

'Because he's whip-smart, that's why. It's easy to substitute a horse. Some trainers wouldn't even know and your jockey could easily be deceived unless he'd spent time with the animal. The stable lad would spot it, but he's the only one. And Osborne's boys will keep their traps shut – he'll buy them off, I imagine.'

'All the same, Dad, it's a load of trouble.'

'But not much of a risk if you don't bet. Osborne'll put a ringer in every now and then but he'll never bet a penny. He'll pick little races and you'll never see one of his ringers tumbling down the odds. He knows how to do it and not get caught.'

'But what's in it for him if he doesn't make money?'

'Think about it, Duncan. Why is Osborne so successful? Because everyone wants him to train their horses. How does he impress the owners? By keeping up a high strike rate. If his win ratio falls, he gets fewer owners wanting to keep their horses with him. I'm surprised he's been doing it as often as you say though. Maybe it's because you've just pinched a load of his best horses and he knows his owners will be worried if his stats come down.'

'He must get caught at it one day.'

'You'd have to get iron-cast proof. Half the Jockey Club have been in business with him at some time or other. They think he's a gentleman like them. A gentleman.' Charlie laughed. 'Fetch us down the whisky would you, son? I've got a nasty taste in my mouth all of a sudden.'

The Quinn yard's success at Sandown had created a feel-good glow around the place and Petie's phone had been ringing all Monday morning. Roisin had shielded her father from as many well-wishing journalists and owners as she could, but she wasn't in the office all the time. The phone continued to peal out none theless and, exasperated, Petie snatched it up.

'Quinn.' It was Petie's usual gruff way of answering the phone.

'Tennyson-Collins.'

'Who?'

'Tennyson-Collins.'

'I don't know no Tennyson-Collins.'

'You most certainly do, sir.'

'I most certainly don't, *sir*. Now state your purpose.'

'My purpose? I'm enquiring about the fitness and otherwise of my investment with you, that's my purpose.'

'Your investment?'

'If I'm not mistaken, it's a triple investment in three of your livestock.'

'Three of my . . . ? Oh I know who you are! You're that baldy-headed flibbert who tried to get me to underwrite some stupid tin-can-on-a-string scheme, aren't you?'

'Are you referring to the mobile phone research project?'

'That's the one. If you think—'

Petie had the phone suddenly snatched out of his hand. Roisin had returned.

'Hello there, Mr Tennyson-Collins, this is Roisin Quinn. Good to hear from you. Daddy's just having a bit of fun . . . Well, his rudeness is part of his charm, that's what our owners say. All these celebrities and film people are so used to being surrounded by yes men – I'm sure you get a bit of that in your own high-powered world – well, they find Daddy's little ways refreshing and that's why they keep coming back. It's a kind of running joke we have going . . . Ha ha, you're quite right, Daddy doesn't call a spade an implement of husbandry. Now, let me tell you how your horses are getting on today . . .'

The next call was for Duncan, who had just finished riding work with Prince Samson. It was his agent, Mike Ruddy.

'I've got another idea for you, mate.'

Duncan groaned. 'Not more parties at the estate. I couldn't go through that again.'

'Put a bit of money in your pocket though, didn't it? I'm always thinking of ways to help you out. Now, listen, Billy Nation and Danny Webb want to invest in a horse.'

'What, the footballers?' Duncan wasn't a footy fanatic like some in the yard, but he tried to keep up though he never seemed to have time to get to a game. He knew Nation and Webb were England internationals.

'Billy and Danny are mates. They're into racing and like a bet. What do you say?'

Duncan knew Mike intended to expand his agency and was looking to break into the soccer world. Selling a couple of England players a horse wouldn't do his business any harm.

'I don't know, Mike. Those stockbrokers have been a bloody nuisance.'

'These are a completely different kind of customer. Top

sportsmen like yourself. Plus, they are awash with money. After they've bought a Porsche and a doner kebab, they don't know what to do with all the moola. You'll be helping them out. And we'll get Cup Final tickets.'

'We let all the so-so horses go to the stockbrokers.'

'Sell them one of the better ones then. Check it out with Petie.'

Petie was easier to persuade than Duncan anticipated. He'd played a bit of football in his youth and, like a lot of Irishmen, he had a mysterious affiliation to Manchester United. He scratched his head. 'We could give it a go,' he mused. 'But if they turn out like those other crackerjack flibbets I'll boot the pair of them across the back pasture, I will.'

He also needed Lorna's agreement to the idea. They'd managed to reduce the number of horses they owned to four but, even with the house sale now going through, it would be prudent to sell them. He called home and began to explain about Mike's scheme. Her reaction took him by surprise.

'Ooh, Billy Nation!'

'He's a footballer.'

'I know that. He's a Villa player now – he was transferred from Everton. Webb's not so good-looking but he's got a nice bum. He plays for West Brom.'

'Bloody hell, Lorna – how do you know all this?'

'I know loads of stuff. And don't think because I'm married and pregnant means I don't appreciate athletic men.'

'Well, OK.'

'Like you, Duncan. So no need to get jealous.'

He put the phone down with a smile. The house sale and the knowledge that they didn't have to move just yet had cheered her up no end. Perhaps he'd done the right thing in caving in to Pleasance after all.

The two footballers turned up at Petie's yard a couple of days later. They arrived in a soft-top BMW driven by Danny Webb. Before switching the engine off Webb gave it a few angry revs. Petie happened to be crossing the yard at the same time, carrying a bucket of feed and he gave them a mouthful.

'Are you here to frighten the horses?'

'You what?' said Danny.

'You press your foot to the boards like that again and it'll be the last time you set foot in my yard,' Petie growled and then he stomped off.

Kerry and Duncan were on hand to step in.

'Who's that?' said the second footballer in a thick Scouse accent. Billy Nation was a freckle-faced young man with a splendid mane of hair cut short on top and long at the back. He wore a permanent grin. The other footballer had a more old-fashioned, blond perm, a serious overbite and seemed to have trouble making eye contact.

'That's the boss,' said Kerry. 'Quite a character and famous for it. I'm Kerry and this here is Duncan Claymore.'

Duncan offered a hand to shake.

'I know you!' shouted Billy. 'You've won me good money.' He blinked at Duncan with admiration.

'And lost him some,' added Danny.

'If we buy a horse,' Billy said, 'do we get to say who rides him?'

'No,' Duncan said flatly.

'I would have thought,' Danny said, 'that the person who owns the horse would get to choose.'

'Is that how football works? The owner of the club, not the manager, chooses the team?'

'It would likely be me or Duncan riding for you,' Kerry put in quickly.

'I'm happy with that!' Billy was still beaming at them like a lunatic.

'Come on, then, let's give you a tour of the yard and show you the beautiful horse we have in mind for you.'

It turned out that the footballers were easy to please. They gawped at everything and, to Duncan's surprise, were polite and respectful to the stable staff. Duncan made a point of introducing them to Destiny's Dream.

'Don't make any sudden noises,' he warned them. 'This fellow has very sensitive hearing.'

The pair of them looked awestruck to be so close to the Oyster Bay winner. It was certainly an advantage to a stable, Duncan thought, to have a real star to show off.

After that the visitors were falling over themselves to buy. Duncan had selected Parisa, a six-year-old liver chestnut who Duncan had first encountered at Osborne's stable. At the time, Parisa had developed a trick of pretending to jump a fence, only to put on the brakes at the last minute and send his rider sailing over the birch on his own. The horse would then poke his head over the fence to look disdainfully at the jockey who had been dumped. Provided you weren't the unfortunate rider, it was quite amusing. By a regime of incredible patience, Duncan had cured the horse of the habit and taken rather a shine to him. But though Parisa had been placed in a couple of lower class outings he hadn't yet pulled up any trees. However, Duncan felt there was plenty of potential in the animal if his talents could be unlocked.

'He's not the finished article,' Duncan said frankly. 'You boys need to recognise that.'

Oddly it was not the grinning Billy who was at ease with the horse, but the goofy Danny Webb. He stepped in and stroked the horse while his mate hung back. Parisa dipped his head into the footballer's shoulder and nuzzled against him.

'Have you been around horses before?' Duncan asked.

'Never,' said Danny. He looked Duncan in the eye for the first time since they'd arrived almost an hour ago. 'But this is the one we want.'

They all shook hands on it. Duncan felt that the footballers should at least be properly introduced to Petie before they went, so they crossed the yard to seek him out. When called, Petie emerged from one of the stalls. He tipped his cap back on his head and dug his fists into his hips as he accepted the introduction, with Kerry waxing lyrical about the lads' glittering skills on the football pitch.

When Kerry was finished, Petie nodded briefly. 'Well,' he said, 'as long as you boys commit no nuisance you'll be all right. Now, I've a lot of work so I'll leave you with Kerry and Duncan.' With that he ducked back into the stall.

Kerry and Duncan walked the two over to their car.

'Commit no nuisance,' Billy said, still smiling.

'We'll have the papers drawn up through Mike Ruddy,' said Kerry.

'You haven't got a tip for us, have you?' Billy said, sweeping a hand through the long hair on his neck.

'A tip? Yes, sure,' said Kerry. 'Drive very carefully round these country roads. You never know when you're going to encounter a scrumpy-crazed farmer in his old tractor.'

The two footballers climbed into the car and Danny turned the ignition key. Quite unconsciously he revved up the engine, then he wound down the window. 'Sorry,' he said.

The two men, who were about to become known at the yard as 'Mullet and Perm', drove away, proud owners of a thoroughbred steeplechaser.

Duncan arrived late on Friday. Lorna had woken complaining of stomach pains and, despite her urging, he had refused to leave her and she had refused to let him call the doctor. Instead, he'd fussed around her, bringing her hot-water bottles and lemon tea and anything else he thought might help. Finally, she'd said she was feeling a bit better. 'I suppose I shouldn't have eaten all those chocolates last night.'

'What chocolates?' Duncan had been with Charlie.

'It was great.' She was beaming, apparently no longer in pain. 'I had a Caramac, a Marathon and one of those Old Jamaica bars. I used to hate those – so sickly. Don't look at me like that! Just because you can only eat lettuce.'

He left her to it, trying not to dwell on where her food cravings may take her next, and arrived to find the normal routine of the yard had been disrupted. Horses were still in their stalls and the stable staff were gathered in the central courtyard, hands in pockets, blowing misty breath into the air. There was no conversation.

'What's going on?' Duncan whispered to Kerry, who was standing on the fringe, stamping his feet on the frosty ground.

'Petie's doing a search.'

'What do you mean?'

'He's got everyone's keys – lockers, cars, bags. They're going through everyone's stuff.'

Duncan looked around. He could see mutiny in many eyes. This was going down like a lead balloon.

Before he could ask any more questions, Petie, Roisin and George strode into the middle of the yard. The crowd parted to let them through.

Petie began to speak in an unfamiliar, formal tone, projecting his voice over their heads. This was serious.

'I am sorry to have kept you waiting around like this. I am also sorry to have been looking into your personal possessions. It's not the way I want to run my yard but I believe I have had no choice.' He cleared his throat. Duncan realised he was finding this difficult. 'As you all know, a few weeks ago we discovered that our supply of horse feed had become contaminated with herbicide. It explained the poor performance of the animals in our care, both here and at race meetings. Since then – since we replaced the feed – our horses have returned to form and we've had a bit of success, I'm delighted to say. But I would be letting them down – and our owners and all of you who sweat your guts out here day and night – if I just forgot about the bad feed and pretended it hadn't happened. Because it wasn't an accident. It wasn't just one bad batch. Someone deliberately poisoned our horses over a period of weeks. They could have had the yard out of business and all of us out of our jobs.

'So I have been doing some investigating. First with Jack Bishop, our feed supplier, who I've known for years and consider to be above suspicion. He promised to undertake his own enquiry, which he has done exhaustively. He has just reported back to me that he is convinced no contaminated product has been delivered from his vans into this yard. And so, with a heavy heart, I have concluded that someone on these premises is responsible for poisoning the feed. That is why I have taken the liberty of searching the yard this morning.'

He paused and the silence was deafening.

'George,' Petie called.

Gypsy George stepped forward, holding a black plastic bag.

'Show us what you've got there.'

From out of the bag George produced a large white jerry can

and held it up high so all could see. 'A five-gallon can of weed killer,' he announced. 'Empty.'

There was a collective gasp and a few murmured expletives.

'Does this belong to anybody?' Petie said.

There was silence.

'Come on now. We've just found this in the boot of a car. And I know whose. Perhaps that person would like to offer an explanation.'

But no one stepped forward. There was just the commotion of a body pushing through the crowd and the noise of flying feet as a slim figure with a mop of dark curly hair ran for the car park.

Fee Markham.

There was a gasp of shock, shouts, and a couple of lads turned to race after her.

'No!' called Petie. 'Let her go. It's over.'

From the car park came the sound of an engine turning over, then the squeal of wheels as Fee fled the yard for the last time.

'Nobody,' Roisin shouted, 'talks to that bitch ever again.' The staff nodded their heads and murmured agreement. 'Nobody,' she repeated, looking Kerry full in the face.

'Now,' said Petie, 'there's a float behind the bar at the Carpenter's Arms tonight and I hope you'll all join me to toast our little victory at Sandown last week. In the meantime, we've got a lot of work to catch up on and we're a pair of hands short, so let's get on with it.'

Fee's dismissal was the talk of National Hunt yards throughout the country. After the feature in the *Punter* and her televised tussle with Sandy Sanderson at Warwick, she was a well-known figure. In the Quinn yard, the reasons for her betrayal were hotly debated. Why on earth had she done it? Especially after Petie had gone out of his way to promote her talents. One theory pointed at Roisin. It was well known that Fee and Kerry were good mates – maybe too good – so perhaps jealousy was at the root of it. Older hands tended to lay the blame at William Osborne's door – perhaps he'd won Fee over somehow. Hadn't she worked for him for a few months when she was just starting out?

All became clearer when it was reported that Fee had been seen in Osborne's yard. She was working for him now. They said that Sandy Sanderson was pissed off about it and had sworn he'd do all he could to make sure she never got any rides for Osborne, but nevertheless, that seemed to solve the mystery. Fee had been in bed with Osborne all along – quite possibly literally. It was only a matter of time, some said, before she'd be riding regularly for Osborne. It was all anyone needed to hear.

12

January 1981

The Welsh Super National at Chepstow was usually held at the end of December but this year it was postponed because of bad weather. The team from Quinn's yard were not surprised to see Fee Markham among the Osborne people. She appeared to be working simply as a groom, doing all the usual tasks: filling hay nets and water buckets; tacking up and untacking the horses; leading horses out. Presumably the reward for her betrayal would come later. For the moment it looked as if Osborne was making a point of bringing her along to a major meeting. Showing her off like a trophy.

The Quinn team made no contact with her whatsoever. There were no nods of recognition or polite smiles, they just turned their backs and tried to pretend she didn't exist. It was hard to ignore her presence, however, when Tangerine Flake, the horse she had paraded in the ring, romped home first in the National and she led it, beaming in triumph, into the winner's enclosure. By her side was the victorious trainer, William Osborne, and on the horse's back, of course, was the champion jockey, the grinning Sandy Sanderson. 'What a feckin' rogues' gallery,' Petie muttered loudly as he stomped off to the bar for a stiff drink.

Though the beautiful setting of Chepstow was usually a happy hunting ground for Petie's yard, this meeting was not a good one. Riding Destiny's Dream over a longer distance, Duncan had modest hopes in the big race and was still travelling well at the three-mile mark. Then, just when he was revising his prospects, Destiny's Dream jumped straight into a faller ridden by an amateur jockey and Duncan was unseated. He hit the ground like a sack of King Edwards and for a second the lights went out. Then his instinct kicked in to get up and out of the way. Destiny's Dream was still running.

Duncan was moving but he was short of breath, a sign of rib damage. He saw the first-aid man – an old boy with a silvery beard – coming his way and tried to dodge him. But the old boy wasn't having any of it and insisted on prodding him around. As he reached Duncan's ribcage Duncan winced and felt a wave of nausea.

'You look pale,' said the first-aider.

'It's a bruise. I can tell. I've done it before. Now I'd better catch that horse cos it's worth a bob or two.'

The first-aider wasn't fooled but Duncan managed to joke his way out of a fuller examination.

Kerry wasn't riding in the next two and offered to take over but Duncan wasn't having any of that, either. He rode in hidden agony, cursing his luck. It would have made more sense if he'd let Kerry take the reins, because he showed nowhere in both races. Later, a doctor examined him and diagnosed three cracked ribs, saying that Duncan shouldn't ride until they had healed. But that didn't take into account that the next day he had more rides at Cheltenham, so he got Lorna to strap him up and soldiered on. After all, what kind of a jockey would he be if he let three little cracked ribs spoil a day's racing?

William Osborne was having trouble with his new vet. The old boy who had looked after his horses ever since he opened the yard had died and his junior partner, a man in his early thirties, had taken over the practice. Osborne had summoned the vet to perform a practice known as 'firing' that was said to prolong the career of National Hunt horses. It involved inserting red-hot needles through the horse's skin to burn tendons.

The new vet wouldn't do it. He said it was not only barbaric, but there was also not a scrap of evidence that it had any effect. Two grooms stood around waiting for the outcome of the dispute.

'What are you on about?' Osborne said to him. 'It's common practice at every training yard. It's done everywhere.'

'Correction,' said the young vet firmly. 'It's done in some yards. Both the RSPCA and the Royal College of Veterinary Surgeons have condemned the practice. It causes unnecessary suffering and there's no scientific evidence that it helps the horses.'

'Burt never had a problem.'

'I'm not Burt.'

'No. You'll do well if you become half the vet that Burt was.'

'That's as maybe.'

'Listen,' Osborne said, 'the scar tissue tightens the skin around the tendon and gives it some support, see, and that makes future injuries less likely.'

'You believe that if you want to. But it's nonsense. In fact, it's horrendous. It's like something out of a medieval horse-keeping manual.'

'What do you know about training horses? There have been many horses who have won major races after being fired. Just get on with it, will you?'

'You only want to do it because it's what you've always done. Go ahead. But you'll have to get another vet.'

'How much do you want?'

'What?'

'I want it done. What's your price?'

'You don't get it, do you? There are some things I won't do.'

'You know you can't afford to lose a contract this big. You take that attitude and you needn't come back here again.'

But the young vet was already packing his bag. He turned and walked to his car.

'Go on then, sod off!' shouted Osborne. 'You go back to your white mice and your budgerigars.'

The vet waved genially and got into his car.

Osborne turned to his grooms. 'What are you looking at?' Osborne snarled. 'Go and find some work.'

He stormed back to his office, a scruffy little outhouse with a large mahogany desk piled with papers and a telephone. Digging out a battered copy of the Yellow Pages, he found the number of another veterinary practice. That vet also expressed reluctance to perform the operation. 'The whole world had gone raving mad!' Osborne shouted, crashing the phone back on its cradle.

He sat slumped in his chair, brooding. After several minutes, someone knocked on the door timidly. He ignored it. Whoever it was went away.

Finally, Osborne picked up the phone again. This time he phoned the Jockey Club and asked to speak to Sir Darley Lane, former officer in the guards, now a senior administrator.

'Willy! How are things? How is my horse?'

'That's exactly why I'm calling you, Darley. I've got some interesting news for you. We're really very pleased with the way he's been coming on. Very pleased.'

'Splendid!'

'So pleased that with your permission we're thinking about running him at the Cheltenham Festival.'

'With my permission? That's even more splendid, Willy! My cup runneth over!'

'No promises, mind. We won't want to run him if he's not ready.'

'Understood.'

'That's all, Darley. Just wanted to let you know.'

'Well, thank you so much, Willy. That really has made my day. Now I can enjoy my lunch!'

'All right then. Talk to you again soon.'

'Indeed, Willy, indeed. Thank you for the call.'

'Oh, there is one other thing, while I have you.'

'What's that?'

'Not sure whether to mention it really. Might be nothing, but I think the Jockey Club should know what's being said and all that. You're familiar with Petie Quinn?'

'Bolshy little Paddy up in Warwickshire?'

'That's the one. I just heard something and it might be nothing. Something about him using a new stimulant.'

'Indeed?'

'Well, as I say it might be tittle-tattle. But he could be a candidate for a random.'

'Indeed. I'll mention it to the great and the good.'

'Darley, it didn't come from me. You know how easy it is to make enemies in this game.'

'Mum's the word, old chap. And thanks for the splendid news about Cheltenham.'

Duncan did everything he could to disguise his cracked ribs but it became apparent to those around him that he was hiding significant pain. He wasn't winning races and it hurt him just to do riding work at the yard, so he had to admit defeat and take time out of the saddle. There was nothing for it but to try and take it easy, keep his weight under control and rest until his ribs glued themselves back together. If things went well, his doctor told him, he'd be back racing in a few weeks. Meanwhile, Kerry picked up his rides.

Kerry picking up his rides was OK by Duncan, except for the fact that there were one or two little jobs of Kerry's that he had to take over in return. They had come under pressure from Tennyson-Collins to field one of the horses Kerry had smooth-talked the stockbroker syndicate into owning. As a result, one of them had been entered for a low-grade race at Wetherby and someone had to take care of the owners.

'Can't you just tell them the horses aren't ready?' Duncan said. The idea of entertaining Tennyson-Collins and his cronies at Wetherby filled him with dismay.

Petie made it clear he wasn't going to get involved on race day. 'I've told him they're not ready but the fecker is ringing me every other day. It's like he thinks these horses change value every hour. He asked me do I think their stock is growing. I told him the only thing that's growing is the pile of shit they generate and can he send that fellah again to wheel it all away. Well, it got a laugh out of him and then he got all hoity-toity serious on me and said they wanted to see one running. So, Duncan, you're going to have to look after them.'

If Duncan had a choice between dealing with Mullet and Perm or Tennyson-Collins and his mob of stockbrokers, he'd have preferred the footballers. But this was a job like any other and he couldn't pick and choose. Both he and Petie knew perfectly well that they could not have a truly competitive yard unless they attracted owners and that meant a spot of glad-handing and being sociable. Unfortunately, some, like Kerry, had a gift for it, and others didn't – that would be Duncan.

So, on the day, he rendezvoused with Tennyson-Collins and five of his suited cronies in the owners' bar. The stockbrokers ordered champagne and complained that there were no ice buckets. Duncan stuck to a single glass of white wine. The City boys had already been told that Kerry would be riding their horse, Strange Happenings, in the last race of the day, a bumper for geldings over a mile and five furlongs.

'A bumper,' Duncan explained, 'is a flat race run under National Hunt rules.'

'What, no jumps?' Tennyson-Collins asked, puzzled.

'It's for complete novices. The idea is to get them used to running over a distance in race conditions. A lot of it is horse psychology. The crowd can be terrifying for them.'

'Can we go and have a word with Kerry in the weigh station?' another suggested, his eyes already sparkling from the champagne.

'Weighing room,' Duncan said, 'and no. No one gets to go in the weighing room except for the jockeys and their valets.'

'So when, exactly,' Tennyson-Collins said, 'do we brief him on how to ride?'

'You'll get a chance to have a word with your jockey when the horse is in the parade ring.'

'Will it win? Should we have a bit of a flutter?' asked one of the group eagerly.

'Bugger that,' shouted another. 'Where's all the good-looking women? I've only seen two girls so far and they had arses like Red Rum.'

Duncan looked glumly into his glass of wine. He was going to need a few more if he was going to make it through the day.

Duncan spent most of the Wetherby meeting trying to give his stockbrokers the impression that he was available for all their questions and yet dodging them at every turn. If he saw them walking towards him he would duck the other way. If they did manage to buttonhole him, there was always someone he needed to speak to urgently: the head lad, the steward, the starter, or if he'd used them all up, the *billinger*, which was a made-up word. *I need to speak with the billinger before the next race.* He found a quiet spot to watch Kerry land a winner and a second – rides that would have been his had he not been injured.

Before the fourth race of the day, Gypsy George summoned Duncan and Petie to the pre-parade ring to look at their scheduled runner, Round Robin. There was obviously something wrong with the eight-year-old gelding – he was sweating up badly and foaming at the mouth.

'He's normally bombproof,' George said. 'I don't like the look of him.'

Petie spoke to the groom. 'You've been with him all this time?'

'Every minute, Petie. Every minute.'

George said, 'I'm suspicious. I think we're being set up. He's been given something.'

Petie rubbed his chin. Then he came to a decision. 'We'll scratch him. I'll go and tell the stewards. Can someone let Kerry know we're standing down?'

George tried to calm Round Robin who was becoming increasingly agitated. 'I'm going to fetch the vet,' he said. 'I'm worried about this lad.'

When the vet arrived he said he'd seen horses get in the same lather before a race but he agreed with the decision. 'You know the horse and you know how he usually behaves. I'll take a blood test and send it off. See if that tells us anything.'

'I think he may have been doped,' George told the vet.

'That's funny,' the vet said as he was taking a blood sample. 'I was scheduled to run a random blood test on all the horses in this race.'

'Oh really?' George said. 'If you were scheduled, then it wasn't random, was it?'

When it came to the last race of the day, Duncan couldn't avoid the brokers any longer. He'd arranged to meet them in the owners' bar so that he could take them over to see Strange Happenings paraded around the ring and to chat with Kerry before the race.

By now the City boys were all well oiled and gave Duncan a resounding cheer when he walked into the bar. Everyone seemed to stop what they were doing to look at him. His cheeks flamed. He didn't mind the attention when he'd earned it on the track, but this focus for playing minder to half a dozen drunks was something he appreciated a lot less.

Tennyson-Collins tried to press a drink on him. When Duncan declined, Tennyson-Collins said, 'What's "strangles"?'

'Strangles? Who have you been talking to?'

'What is it?'

'It's a bacterial infection. Affects a horse's breathing. Very contagious, especially in young horses. Why do you ask?'

'Well, we were having a few snifters in the bar here and one chap asked us where we kept our horse and so I mentioned old Quinny. And this chap says, "Quinn's yard? Haven't they got a problem with strangles?"'

'Jeez? Who said that?'

Tennyson-Collins gave a slurred description of a tall gent in a cloth cap, who could have been pretty much anyone at the racecourse. But Duncan was barely listening. He knew perfectly well who would have said it. It was William Osborne, or one of his staff, up to his old tricks. It would have been said in a voice loud enough so that other people at the bar might overhear.

Strangles was desperately bad news for any stables. The bacteria is spread by direct contact with infected horses or from horse handlers, buckets, feed, water troughs and tack contaminated with nasal discharges from infected horses. Some horses become carriers of the infection and intermittently discharge the bacteria. Rumour of infectious disease was one of the dirty tricks Osborne had used to engineer the downfall of Duncan's father, and here he was, at it again. Even an unproven rumour of strangles could be disruptive: a yard suspected of carrying the disease might be kept away from racetracks for a period while they were being tested.

From what had happened to his father, Duncan knew that Osborne would be carefully planting the gossip. It wasn't the trainer's style to report a suspicion of infection to the racing authorities. Instead, the careless aside in the men's urinals, the throwaway comment in the bar, the casual remark near the stalls would much more effectively seed the wind.

'It's nonsense,' Duncan said. 'Someone is trying to upset you. Forget it.'

Tennyson-Collins treated Duncan to a ten-minute lecture about how the same tactics were at play in the buying and selling of stocks and shares.

Duncan wasn't surprised. 'There's always some slimy bugger out to do an honest man down,' he said with feeling, thinking of his father. 'Come on, folks, let's go and have a word with your jockey before it's too late.' His head was spinning from the effort of being civil.

Duncan led the stockbrokers down to the parade ring. Petie was there having already saddled up their mare, Strange Happenings. The sun had broken out, shining on Kerry's silks of yellow with purple stripes and an orange cap – a design that had preoccupied the City boys during long evenings in a local wine bar, so Duncan gathered.

'I say you look spiffing, doesn't he, chaps?' cried Tennyson-Collins, as Kerry allowed himself to be clapped heartily on the back and have his hand shaken by each of the excited syndicate of owners. However, their respect for the jockey was nothing compared to the awe with which they gazed at the horse. Her groom, Nicky, had turned her out beautifully with a gleaming coat and a plaited mane.

Tennyson-Collins leaned across and spoke confidentially in Kerry's ear. 'The boys want to know if you're riding to win.'

'What?'

'Should we bet to win? Or to place?'

Kerry looked at Duncan, and Duncan said, 'Well, if we knew the outcome of every race we'd be very rich men, wouldn't we?'

Petie, overhearing the exchange, asked, 'What's that now?'

'They want to know if we have a chance,' Duncan said diplomatically.

Petie turned to the stockbrokers in irritation. 'Look, if it's up it's up, if it's down it's down, and if the day is long then the night is short. So there you go.'

The stockbrokers laughed as a team. 'I told you he's a card!' Tennyson-Collins announced, apparently pleased. Then he whispered to Duncan, 'It's just that the language is not what we're used to. Did he just say that it has a good chance?'

'She,' said Duncan. 'We don't call horses *it*. Does *she* have a good chance.'

'That's right. Does she have a good chance? I mean, it's not fancied is it, at 20-1 on the boards?'

'I'd say, with Kerry riding, well . . .' He rubbed his chin judiciously. The six stockbrokers shuffled towards him, listening intently. This was *information*. 'I'd say there's an each-way chance, but bet very cautiously.'

He felt six pairs of eyes boring into him as they tried to see right to the bottom of his advice. Then they looked at each other and nodded, satisfied enough. Duncan turned to Kerry and with his back to the men he squeezed his eyes tight shut.

'Don't worry, gentlemen,' Kerry shouted, shaking hands with each man in turn all over again. 'I'll be giving it my best shot.'

Petie gave Kerry a leg-up into the saddle. 'Away you go, fellahs,' he said, 'and enjoy the race.'

Duncan led the men out of the paddock. They were quite keen to get a bet on. 'Cautious,' Duncan remind them, 'be cautious.' He reckoned the horse didn't stand a chance.

They went up in the stand to watch. Duncan stood next to Petie behind the men, who grew violently agitated as the action unfolded in front of them. Their excitement almost blew the roof off the stand as Strange Happenings bolted up like an express train and won by a clear ten lengths.

'Jesus,' Petie said to Duncan. 'D'ye think they doped her as well?'

'We make a right pair, don't we?'

Duncan was sitting with his father in his room at the Grey Gables. Charlie refused to have more than one dingy sidelight on and the pair of them sat in silence staring at the fading flowers on the wallpaper, both nursing their various ills. For Duncan, it was the pain in his chest. He'd had to dose himself up with painkillers to get through the day at Wetherby but now they had worn off.

Charlie's pains were not physical. Mrs Solanki had taken an extended holiday over Christmas and the New Year to visit family in India and she had not yet returned. This did not sit well with Charlie. He was morose and rude to the staff who had replaced her and not exactly pleasant to everyone else. Gypsy George and Petie had reported to Duncan that his dad had been on the glum side during their recent visit.

Duncan tried another conversational gambit. With his father so down, Duncan hadn't intended to talk about William Osborne, it not being a topic likely to cheer him up, but he was desperate.

'We reckon Osborne was up to his old tricks today.'

'Another ringer?'

'No, Dad. We think he doped one of our runners. We had to scratch to be on the safe side.'

'You'd think it would be difficult running a ringer, but it's not.'

'Then suddenly there's a rumour going round that the yard's got strangles. It's what he did to you, isn't it?'

But Charlie didn't appear to be listening. He was fumbling in the back of the bedside cabinet and after a moment, produced a bottle of whisky. He seemed to have acquired a number over the festive period. Duncan was going to object but thought the better of it. What else did the poor old sod have to get excited about sitting in an old folks' home in the dark? Besides, though he didn't care for the taste of Scotch, a quick belt might ease his hurting body.

'I'll join you for once, Dad.'

Charlie found two glasses and poured generously. 'Now,' he said, after an appreciative sip, 'you want to know about ringing.'

Duncan allowed the fiery liquid to slide down his gullet, spreading its glow throughout his chest. It helped. If he just sat still and took little sips he might be able to get his mind off his bloody ribs.

'The thing is,' Charlie was suddenly talkative, 'you need an expert. A dab hand with the paint brush. I knew a feller once.'

Why was Dad talking about painting? Duncan wasn't sure. The old boy was losing it more frequently these days. The sooner Mrs S got back, the better – though he'd better not mention her.

'Eddie – that was his name. Bloomin' magician.'

'If you say so, Dad.'

Give it another half-hour, thought Duncan, and then he could in all conscience go home to Lorna. Better not drink too much, he thought, as he let his father travel back down memory lane.

The following morning, Petie was about ready to rip the phone out of the wall. He'd had a number of unwanted calls. The first two were from other trainers – not unfriendly towards Petie – who just wanted to check to see if there was any truth in what they'd heard about strangles at the yard. Duncan had tipped him off and Petie was quick to reassure the callers. But when he asked where they'd heard the news, they weren't able to say exactly. Nothing had been officially reported, but the rumour was hanging in the air like a bad smell. Like Duncan, Petie was convinced it bore the hallmark of an Osborne plot.

Petie was already in an agitated mood therefore, when Tennyson-Collins rang to congratulate him on his horse's victory. He also wanted to know when the members of the syndicate could expect to receive their prize money. As it happened, the purse for that race was not large. And, as Petie took some pleasure in pointing out, as trainer he kept a percentage and the jockey was due an additional ten per cent on top of his jockey fee. Furthermore, it was accepted practice for the owners to tip the head lad and the team who looked after the horse. Thus the prize money, modest to begin with, was considerably reduced before it reached the syndicate. Divided among its members,

Petie guessed each man could blow his share on a couple of pints and a packet of cheese and onion.

Nevertheless, Tennyson-Collins was not easily dismayed. It turned out that the City boys had not taken Duncan's advice to bet cautiously and had walked off the course deliriously happy, their wallets stuffed with notes. Now the chaps wanted to know when Strange Happenings would be running again – and whether Petie had given any thought to Ascot next month.

Petie carefully laid the telephone receiver down on the table and bellowed through the house, 'Kerry! Roisin! Anyone, before the pope shits in his hat!! Will somebody come and talk to this crackerjack flibbert?'

Roisin took over negotiations.

Duncan and Lorna were in bed. Making love with cracked ribs was not comfortable but some pains were worth enduring. Now, though, they were lying apart.

'What are you thinking?'

'Just about when I can get back in the saddle.'

She turned to him and kissed him softly on the mouth. 'Liar,' she said.

'Why do you say that?'

'Because you're miles away. It's like you've got something else on your mind.'

It was true. He was thinking about William Osborne and his latest plot to damage Petie the way he had Charlie – the doping of Round Robin and the strangles rumour. But most of all, he thought about Michelle.

After his conversation with Michael in the owners' bar, he'd been using his time off to do a bit more digging. He'd been correct in his assumption that this wasn't the first suspicious death that had occurred on one of Osborne's horses. It wasn't just Royal Enfield who had been a liability in Osborne's yard. Nine years ago, Darren Webster, a conditional jockey, had been buried on the gallops under an Osborne-trained steeplechaser called Golden Heels. The lad had never recovered consciousness and died in hospital ten days later – that's what a friend of Philip's, one of Osborne's former employees, had told him. Golden Heels, said Philip's pal, was a 'twenty-four-carat nutter' and all the lads avoided him. But Darren had been promised a ride on him at Fontwell if he impressed while working with the horse. The result had been tragic. Another young and keen jockey lost to Osborne's greed. And Duncan was sure there would be others.

This discovery simply reinforced Duncan's opinion of William Osborne. He was a ruthless, self-serving bastard who cared for nothing but his own interests. He'd been getting away with this for too long. He was ruining lives, destroying careers, damaging horses and businesses and no one was trying to stop him.

Duncan's hands clenched by his sides as he thought about everything the man had done. He couldn't tell Lorna his thoughts – she wouldn't understand. But Duncan had resolved to take Osborne down, whatever it took.

He would avenge the deaths of Michelle and Darren Webster, and all the other people that Osborne had trampled on his way to the top of the racing world, including Duncan's father.

'You're planning something,' Lorna said.

Jesus, she could read his mind already and they'd only been married four months. 'No,' said Duncan. 'It's just these ribs. It's so frustrating.'

'Do you think I don't know you? You're planning something.'

'Rubbish, Lorna.'

'Let me in on it.'

Much as he was tempted, that was one thing he couldn't do.

Duncan's enforced leisure meant that he spent more time hanging around the house. It was a huge place for just the two of them, now Duke's staff had gone. He'd often wondered what they did all day but now he found out. Houses, especially large old ones, needed daily attention, and even in January the grounds had to be maintained. When he saw Lorna traipsing round the five bathrooms with a mop and a bucket of bleach and cleaning stuff, he got on the phone to Mary, their old housekeeper, and organised some part-time help. For all Lorna's willingness, he wasn't happy with his pregnant wife keeping the place in shape. Although he could help out for the moment, soon he'd be racing again and she'd be getting bigger and more weary.

He was on the phone in the drawing room, trying to find a gardener to put in a couple of days a week, when he spotted a Mercedes-Benz S-Class sedan purring up the drive. He knew that car. He quickly cut short the call and went to greet his unwelcome guest. Lorna had told him that George Pleasance had the disturbing habit of turning up unannounced 'whenever I'm in the area'. Much as he wanted to, Duncan didn't see how he could object. The property now belonged to Pleasance and they lived here on his gift – which could be swiftly reversed. Duncan hated it but he was loath to move Lorna out of the luxurious house she had grown up in, especially in her condition.

The fact was, he was supping with the devil but he had no choice. So he intended to make the most of it.

Pleasance wore a cashmere coat draped over his shoulders like a cloak. He proceeded into the drawing room, as if he owned the place, which he did. As Lorna went off to make tea, he asked after Duncan's health. 'How's the injury?'

'Not so great.' Duncan heard himself waxing on about his

ribs, wondering how he could raise the one issue he wanted to discuss with Pleasance. As it happened the other man did it for him.

'So you'll be riding again in a couple of weeks?'

'Yes.'

'That's good, Duncan. Because I'm going to want something from you.'

Duncan felt he should make his point early – he knew Pleasance's reputation. 'George, I'm not going to take a fall.' There were jockeys who would fix a race – not try or deliberately make a mistake – but Duncan wasn't one of them.

Pleasance wagged a finger at him. 'Now, now, Duncan. I never ask anyone to do anything they don't want to do. I'm only suggesting that, considering how I'm letting you stay on here, there might be some way you could do me a favour by way of return.'

Duncan hesitated. 'OK.' He didn't like what he was about to do but he reckoned he had no choice. From down the hall he could hear the chink of china being arranged. Lorna would be back soon with the tea and this was his chance. 'It's like this, George,' he said.

And he made his pitch.

Petie had fielded enough calls about the strangles rumour to know that the Jockey Club would soon be on the phone. Either Osborne would have sown his rumour so well that it would trigger a response from the racing authorities, or he would have gone directly to one of his cronies on the board. Osborne had plenty of contacts in high places. Petie himself had little respect for the self-appointed toffs who governed the sport, but he knew that if they said jump he would have to ask 'How high?'

So he'd decided to get the jump in ahead of them. He'd

arranged for his horses to be tested in advance of any official request. That way when the Jockey Club called he could avoid being shut down for a couple of weeks.

Meanwhile, the results of the blood test on Round Robin confirmed that some unidentified stimulant had been found in his sample. No action would be taken against Petie because he had done the right thing and scratched the horse from the race, but he agreed to have all his animals tested for the substance at the same time as they were being tested for strangles.

He was waiting for the vet to arrive when a soft-top BMW turned into the yard. Danny Webb, one of the footballer owners, got out holding a plastic carrier bag.

'Jaysus,' Petie muttered, 'it's Mullet and Perm.'

Except that Perm was on his own, and alone he looked smaller. Petie wondered if footballers came in reduced packages these days.

Danny approached Petie sheepishly. 'I didn't rev the engine. All the way here I was telling myself not to rev the engine.'

Petie was puzzled. 'What the feck are you talking about?'

'Frightening the horses.'

Petie was even more perplexed. He ground his teeth. 'Shouldn't you be training? Practising falling over and what have you?'

'Sore foot.'

'I've got the vet coming in a minute. Want him to take a look?'

'No need. I've had the physio on it.'

'I'm joking with you, son. What can I do for you?'

Danny blew out his cheeks and looked around nervously. 'Parisa.'

'What about Parisa?'

'He's my horse, right?'

'Sure he is.'

Danny fumbled in his plastic carrier bag and brought out a handful of carrots. 'Can I just give him these?'

Just off junction 12 on the M40 was a small country park known mainly to local dog-walkers. Waiting in the car park, leaning against his car, was a slender young man, well muffled against the January evening. So well muffled, with his collar turned up and woollen bobble hat pulled down and scarf wrapped round his neck, that it would not be possible to say with any certainty who he was. Although a look in the boot of his car, at the riding boots, saddle and whip, might lead an observer to assume he had some professional association with horses.

Headlights lit up the clearing and a car turned into the entrance. He looked up hopefully but it was not the vehicle he was waiting for. The car parked up and a middle-aged man liberated a large Labrador from the back seat. Dog and master set off down a wooded path.

Finally, after another ten minutes, a small, knocked-about Ford Fiesta arrived and a young woman with a mop of dark curls wound down the window. Fee Markham.

The man opened the Fiesta's passenger door and got in. The couple exchanged a hug of welcome and began an earnest discussion. There was plenty to talk about. The irony was that they could have held their conversation in greater comfort and considerably more convenience earlier that afternoon when they had both been present at Warwick racecourse. Not that they had spoken to each other at that time or even acknowledged each other's presence. For fear of the consequences.

13

Roisin had finally recovered from the shoulder injury she had sustained at Chepstow and she had two races lined up at Southwell. Kerry also had two at the same meeting. What with Strange Happenings having done so well at Wetherby, Petie was keen to find out if her performance there had been a fluke. He had also scheduled a first outing for Parisa under the new ownership of Mullet and Perm.

The appearance of these two horses gave Duncan, who was still sidelined, the task not just of babysitting the stockbrokers but also the two footballers. It seemed as though both sets of owners had no trouble getting time off work to visit a modest racecourse in the East Midlands on a weekday afternoon. Duncan, in the comfort of the owners' bar, had intended to pair them off so they could entertain each other for the afternoon. But it was like asking a pair of geese to get along with a hive of bees. After a quick discussion of recent football results, they had nothing left to say to each other.

But both parties had the same question to put to Duncan: 'Is our horse going to win?'

Roisin was scheduled to ride Strange Happenings in the third race on the card. If the stockbrokers had any misgivings about having a female jockey on their horse they kept it to themselves. After all, so far Petie had a one hundred per cent success record, so who were they to question his call?

But before that, Roisin was riding in the opening race of the day. Her mount, Flapdoodle, was the horse that had unseated her at Chepstow. Despite that, Roisin had been working hard with the animal and she was convinced he had a bright future.

The going was soft and the weather squally, with gusts of wind unnerving some of the horses. The starter had a tricky job getting the runners in order, but when he did, Flapdoodle jumped off to a decent start. He met the first hurdle with a perfect stride and winged it, with Roisin positioned nicely on the rail behind the front runners. At the second there was a faller. All Roisin saw was a flurry of silk ahead of her. She negotiated the fallen jockey and was running on well – when disaster struck.

Out of control, the loose horse veered wildly across her, leaving no room for manoeuvre and forcing Flapdoodle to run off the track at the third hurdle. She was out of the race early and, after all the preparation for her comeback, it was an inglorious result. But no jockey could have done anything about it. All she could do was swallow her disappointment and hack back ignominiously, past the winning post towards the paddock.

As she approached the spectators she was met with a chorus of whistles and jeers. The spectators at the far end hadn't actually seen the incident and seemed to think that she'd simply gone the wrong way. Some of the men in the crowd pelted her with paper cups and plastic bottles.

'Bloody lady jockeys!' she heard one yell at her through the chorus of boos.

'Get off home and mop the floor!' bellowed another.

Roisin was shocked.

'Daddy, they think I went the wrong way!'

'They didn't see darlin'. These things happen. Don't worry. Come on, let the lad take care of the horse.'

Petie walked back with her, steering her by the elbow, but she shrugged him off. She was livid. And there in the paddock she walked slap into William Osborne.

'That's the second time,' Osborne said, 'that you've not watched where you were going.'

Roisin could curse like a sailor on the *Ark Royal* when she wanted to, but right then she was speechless.

'Not exactly a good day for you female jockeys, is it?' he smirked.

'Hold your head high and keep walking,' Petie said in her ear.

She couldn't even march back to the weighing room and wash off her shame with a hot shower. She had to go back to the grotty, damp caravan parked near the stables. At least she could slam the door behind her and get ready for the third race. And if she shed a tear, then at least no one would see it.

Things went better for Kerry in the next race, where he came in a close second. Duncan was standing next to him in the winner's enclosure when he saw a deputation of stockbrokers heading towards him.

'Here we go,' he said to Kerry. He had a pretty good idea what their sudden appearance was about.

'I'll see you later,' Kerry said, swiftly heading for the weighing room.

Duncan left the enclosure to intercept the posse walking across the grass towards him. It was Tennyson-Collins, brows knitted, leading his band of suits – three of them on this occasion. They all looked like men on a mission. 'Duncan,' Tennyson-Collins said, 'a word in your shell-like if I may?'

'Sure. What's on your mind?'

'I'll get straight to the point without beating around the bush.

191

We, that is, the chaps and I, the syndicate if you like, as owners of the horse—'

Duncan interrupted him. 'You don't want Roisin to ride Strange Happenings in the next race.'

'It's that obvious, eh?'

Duncan said nothing in return. He simply gazed back, unblinking, into Tennyson-Collins's eyes.

'Well,' the stockbroker said, 'if it's plain to you then you must agree with us.'

'Why?'

'You saw what happened in her last race. It was a joke.'

'What happened?'

'She didn't even remember the bloody course!'

'First, you're wrong. She was run out by a loose horse. It wouldn't have mattered if it was me, Kerry or the Duke of Albuquerque riding, there was nothing to be done and if you knew about racing you'd know that. Second, Roisin is scheduled to ride and the stewards don't allow last-minute switching for no reason.'

'Don't shit us,' said one of the suits. 'We know you can cry off injured.'

Another said, 'Look, are we the owners of this horse or not?'

Duncan ignored these remarks. 'Third, she's been schooling that horse for weeks. She's got the touch for it, better even than Kerry. Trust me.'

'I don't feel happy at all about it,' Tennyson-Collins said. 'I want a word with the top man.'

'You mean Petie Quinn?'

'Yes.'

'You know Roisin is his daughter, don't you?'

This information silenced Tennyson-Collins. Duncan decided to appeal to his better nature. 'Look we know what we're doing.

We're not going to put someone up who can't do the job. We need to see if the horse fluked it last time out. Come on, you're here to enjoy the day out. Relax, have a cautious each-way bet and trust me, Roisin will get the best out of that horse today.'

'We'll see,' Tennyson-Collins said, shaking his head and turning away. 'We'll see.'

'I'm betting she'll go backwards,' muttered one of the men.

In fact, when they reached the bookies' stands they found that the odds on Strange Happenings had shortened after her easy win last time out. They interpreted this as ignorance on the part of Joe Public and they all ignored Roisin and bet on the favourite instead.

As it turned out, the race was the most dramatic event on the card. With eight starting, a faller at the first hurdle brought down the favourite. The remaining six stayed tightly bunched for the rest of the course until the second last. With everyone squeezed tight going into the hurdle, Strange Happenings touched her nose to the turf on landing and had to be picked off the floor by Roisin. Instead of being thrown out of her stride, she rallied and, with Roisin asking for maximum effort, pressed hard on the charge towards the final obstacle, battling to get back on terms with the two front runners, Call That A Hat and Black Static. Coming up to the final hurdle they were locked in a blood-and-thunder set-to with Call That A Hat perhaps half a length clear.

At the last hurdle, all three of them rose and landed together, but Call That A Hat stumbled, unseating his jockey, leaving Roisin to slug it out with Black Static on the run-in. Both horses stayed on, mud flying everywhere, neither surrendering an inch to the other. Somehow Strange Happenings found a surge at the last and, though the judge called for a photo, Duncan reckoned she'd got it by a short head.

This time Roisin received a hearty round of applause as she walked the winner alongside the spectators.

'Don't you want to throw those cups and plastic bottles back at 'em?' Duncan asked her.

'Don't be putting ideas in her head,' Petie said.

The photo confirmed her victory. In the winner's enclosure, everyone now wanted Roisin's autograph.

It turned out to be a very good day at Southwell. Kerry won the biggest race of the day on Parisa, which meant two winners and a second for the Quinn yard. Everyone was having to look over their shoulders at the strike rate for this feisty, eccentric, medium-sized yard in the Midlands.

The stockbrokers were good enough to eat humble pie over Roisin's victory, though, secretly, Petie, Duncan and Kerry were astonished at the performance of Strange Happenings, a little horse they'd practically written off. They were going to have to move her up a class to see if she could compete in more exalted company. Mullet and Perm, meanwhile, were cock-a-hoop. With Mullet pestering Duncan all day long about whether he'd got any tips for them – any 'certs' – they'd bet recklessly on their own horse and had won at decent odds.

Danny Webb in particular followed the horse around everywhere after his victory, patting him, holding the reins, getting in the stable lad's way. In the winner's enclosure, journalists and cameramen went wild for him pressing his cheek against the horse's noseband. Both he and Billy Nation were interviewed about owning a horse and their relationship with Petie, notwithstanding the fact that they knew precious little about either.

Duncan was approached by Bernard Bacon, a freelance photographer predictably known as Burnt Bacon. He had a bad stammer and could sometimes be a bit of a pest, always trying to hustle extra or unusual photographs to flog to the tabloids or the racing journals. But he'd been kind to Duncan when he was a struggling conditional and so when he asked if he could do some special shots of the football stars with the horse, Duncan smoothed the way for him.

Bacon was very happy with his shots. 'I owe you, Duncan!'

'I'll remember that,' Duncan said.

Webb followed the horse back from the winner's enclosure to the stalls, tripping over everyone there, asking to help. He was given an empty bucket to hold and that kept him quiet until the time to box Parisa up for the drive home.

They all said their goodbyes and Kerry went home with Roisin in the horsebox. Duncan drove back with Petie. As they turned into the driveway of the yard they saw another car already parked there. Danny Webb was leaning against the driver's door with his collar up against the wind. Duncan parked alongside the BMW and Petie got out.

'What's this about now, son?' Petie said. 'We've only just said goodbye at the races.'

'I just thought to get a couple of carrots,' Danny said. 'For Parisa. You know.'

'For pity's sake, son, haven't you got a home to go to?'

'Of course.'

'They're not even back yet with the horses. It'll be another half-hour before they get here.'

Danny shrugged.

Petie sighed deeply and tipped his cloth cap further back on his head. 'Two carrots. When he gets back you can give him two carrots. Then you've got to go home. You hear me, son?'

*

Eddie Merryweather was seventy-nine years old. Born the year Queen Victoria died, he was raised in the Black Country near Dudley, where his father worked in a nail factory. When he was sixteen he enlisted, underage, with the British Army. He found it ridiculously easy to lie about his age in order to go to war. He had a notion that the recruiting sergeant at the Wolverhampton drill hall knew perfectly well that he wasn't telling him the truth. He'd arrived with some badly forged papers but he wasn't even asked to produce them.

Like all the other recruits, he was put in the infantry. After several weeks of square-bashing and basic training, Eddie, a willing and capable lad, was assigned to help his training officer with an even newer group of recruits. Then one night his officer disappeared, simply did a bunk. Eddie just carried on doing what he was doing before and assumed responsibility for training the new recruits himself. This went on for some days without any question. When one of his superiors asked what had happened to his officer he truthfully replied that he didn't know. He was told to 'carry on'.

That same superior was shipped out to the front line in France a few days later and was replaced by a younger man. After a few weeks the new superior made the assumption that Eddie was a non-commissioned officer and it was as such that Eddie was himself posted to France. He collected a new uniform before leaving for France, all the time expecting the quartermaster to feel his collar but it didn't happen. Somehow, in a matter of months, he had progressed from being an underage private to a non-commissioned officer, complete with a set of British Army records.

He was sent to Ypres in November 1917 towards the end of the battle of Passchendaele and what he saw there shocked him to the core. He soon realised that the young officers – the commissioned officers ranking above him – were only pretending to know what they were doing and, in fact, knew even less than he did. He did his best and was shot in the leg by a sniper when he went into no-man's-land to bring back one of the lads under his command. He was shipped home with hundreds of other wounded soldiers. His injury left him with a pronounced limp, which remained with him for the rest of his life.

When Eddie returned to England he felt resentful about the way that commissioned officers were so much better treated than NCOs. They were decorated with medals denied to most of the men who had suffered the hell of Ypres and they were given facilities – tearooms, billiard halls, recreation rooms – closed to the ordinary enlisted men. While in London, and almost as a dare to himself, he stole an officer's coat and hat and went into a tearoom reserved for commissioned officers. He disguised his Black Country accent, kept himself to himself and was served tea and cakes by a very pretty waitress.

He started to make a habit of it. All you had to do was straighten your back and talk as if you had a hot potato in your mouth. For good measure, and to give him an extra moment to think, he added a slight stammer. If anyone pressed hard on awkward details he looked into the middle distance as if he saw ghosts there and people backed off. It turned out to be all too easy to pass himself off as someone he was not. Many doors and facilities became open to him this way.

After the war ended, men were quick to throw off their uniforms and so Eddie went back to the Black Country to look for work. Because of his disability he could find nothing steady. He looked up some of his comrades in the hope of finding decent employment but a lot of them were in the same boat. He spent a lot of days killing time. Then one of his old comrades introduced him to horse racing by taking him to Gatwick racecourse, where the Grand National was run during the war. It was there that Eddie first heard the term 'ringer'.

'What's a ringer?' he asked his former comrade-at-arms.

'Well, for example, it's a decent three-year-old in a race for only moderate two-year-olds.'

Eddie was fascinated. It seemed to him that if he could pass himself off as another person altogether and disguise himself as an officer, it shouldn't be too difficult to pass off one horse as another. And so began his lifelong career as a prolific and highly skilled ringer of horses.

The whole business of setting up a ringing operation was complex and involved stables and betting gangs, but he soon found that the most in-demand job was that of a painter. It became his particular skill. That way he could do the job, release the painted horse to the ringer gang and get out of the way of the repercussions. He'd previously known nothing about horses so he got a job as a lowly stable lad just so he knew how to be around them. He practised painting without anyone knowing.

He started by working on horses' legs, disguising a coronet, a pastern or a sock, simply reducing the white marking to see if anyone at the stable would notice. No one did. Then he got bolder and worked on a face stripe and a star. He wasn't stupid enough to be obvious. He was just developing his skills. He found out which materials washed off after a shower of rain and which didn't.

It wasn't long before he could take a bay mare into a barn and, within a day, bring her out as jet black or as a grey. More easily, he could give a black horse white feet or change a star into a blaze at short notice. Twenty-four hours later he could return the horse to her original colour. He put his skills on the market and soon found plenty of potential employers.

At that time there were hardly any rules regarding horse

identification and the game was wide open. Eddie earned a reputation as a craftsman. When the long arm of the law began to reach in his direction he used some winnings to buy a passage on an Atlantic liner to the United States. There he offered the same skills to horse-owning bootleggers, who were very appreciative. So appreciative that the US Jockey Club, well ahead of its British counterpart, started to introduce a more accurate identification system for horses.

All the same, Eddie enjoyed almost a decade as a master ringer in America. He married and lost his wife in tragic circumstances when a fire burned down his apartment. Not long after that the famous Pinkerton national detective agency had him in their sights and once again he slipped out of the country by sea, this time to Australia.

There he expanded his repertoire to include the skill of horse doping. He knew how to dope a horse to win and how to dope a horse to lose. He famously distracted the team around one favourite for a big race while a skilful farrier quickly changed all the horse's shoes, substituting weighted shoes in place of racing shoes all in time for the race.

He did well for a number of years on the Australian circuit but where the British and American law had failed to catch up with him, the Brisbane police force succeeded. With a number of similar offences taken into consideration, he served a prison stretch of almost two years.

On his release he sailed back to England where he passed himself off as a gentleman farmer with horses competing mainly in point-to-point races. He was still painting horses, but after his prison stretch in Australia he was more inclined to run a one-man ringing operation if he could. The fewer people who worked with him, the less chance he had of ending up in prison again; and this way he could ensure that the betting differentials were managed in ways that might not alert the racing authorities. But that wasn't always an option.

Once, he'd disguised a horse for a trainer but it was the trainer himself who bungled the substitution of the horse and, fearing capture, had scratched the horse from the event at the last minute. Because the deception hadn't been carried through, the trainer failed to pay Eddie for his work.

That up-and-coming young trainer was William Osborne.

On a windy evening that January of 1981, Eddie was sitting in front of his coal fire with a blanket over his knees, watching television, when he heard a knock at the door. He rarely had visitors. He had a daughter who lived at some distance and he wasn't expecting her. There was a neighbour down the road who occasionally looked in on him during the day, but never in the evenings.

He got stiffly to his feet and picked up the fireside poker, holding it behind his back. He'd heard stories of the ne'er-do-wells who went around preying on the elderly. He shuffled across the carpet and opened the front door.

It took a moment, but Eddie recognised the man standing before him very well.

'Hell's bells,' he said. 'I never expected to see you again. You'd better come in.'

14

By the end of January, Duncan was back at work riding and schooling horses at Petie's yard and by the third week of February he had returned to race riding. Not before time, he thought. The jumps season was in full swing and thoughts were already turning towards the Cheltenham Festival in mid-March, the highlight of the National Hunt calendar. February was the time to fine-tune and show off some of the Cheltenham contenders but there were also plenty of bread-and-butter races to be contested. After his injury, Duncan was determined to build on his strike rate. Even if he was a long way from a numerical race for the title of champion jockey this season, an impressive strike rate could still enhance his reputation.

He started to fixate on the racing schedule, working out with Petie which extra races they might squeeze into the calendar, especially at some of the smaller meetings. Whether the venues were the cream of the racecourses, like Ascot in the middle of the month, or cold, distant, rain-beaten gaff tracks, it was all good business as far as Duncan was concerned. It strained Petie's energy, if not his resources, but the trainer went along with it as Duncan produced a list.

Petie rubbed his chin. He liked the idea of this one, wasn't sure about that one, was hot against this other one. He took up a pencil and started to cross some of them out, arguing for preferences elsewhere. He came to Hexham racecourse with a low-level meeting scheduled for the first week in March and put a line through it.

'Put that one back in,' Duncan said.

'Have you ever been to Hexham on a filthy March afternoon?'

'I've been there a few times. It's all right. Put it back in.'

'I don't want to go all the way up to Northumberland for that meeting. There's not a single race there with a decent prize. Look, if you want something on that date what about Fakenham? I don't mind driving there.'

'Leave Hexham in.'

'Why? The damn place is further north than you think it is. You think you're about there when you get near Wetherby, and you're not. You see every other damn racecourse in the north of England signposted before you get to Hexham, and probably Scotland too, and then back down again as you try to find it. And when you get there it's an up and down of a course in the middle of nowhere. If I'd wanted windswept moorland I'd've stayed in Ireland.'

'Shame on you, Petie. The scenery is magnificent and the people there are very friendly. Chalk it back in.'

'Are we talking about the same place? I'll not be going.'

'We'll go without you.'

'Are you sure you know it?'

'Hexham. I know it well.'

Duncan did indeed know it well. In truth he'd thought about the location a great deal lately. He'd been over every brick of the place in his mind's eye. He'd thought about the trailer park where the horseboxes and trailers arrive; the stalls where the horses were transferred after arrival; the cinder track where the horses were walked from the stables to the paddock; the proximity of the paddock to the steward's room; the location of the bar;

the distance between the bar and the paddock; and every stone in between.

It was the right place. It was also the right time. A low-level mid-week meeting at the most northern track in England in early March was guaranteed to attract little interest and only a small crowd.

And it was the right time because William Osborne was running two of his horses there that day.

Duncan was setting out his chess pieces on the board.

'All right, if you insist,' Petie said. 'I suppose I might come along. What about entries?'

'Let's give Parisa a run out in the four-mile chase – that should be a bit of tester and it'll keep Mullet and Perm happy. And the stockbrokers are pestering us about their other two horses. We could put the four-year-old Blink Of An Eye, in the three-mile novice hurdle. And the other one, Misty Mountain, for the first race, the two-mile novice chase. Give those boys a feel for real racing in the north of England when the wind is blowing. They'll love it.'

Petie stared at him. 'I don't know what kind of bird you're cookin',' Petie said finally, 'but I smell it all right.'

Selecting a ringer is not difficult. A number of horses of the same colour together in a field can look the same even to their owner. Closer up you will be able to tell by particular markings, but even then a blaze down the front of a horse can look like a stripe, which is after all another word for a thin blaze. Stars can be small or large and, depending on the time of the season, can appear to be a little smaller or a little larger. If two horses, say a two-year-old and a three-year-old, look identical, then it would take an expert such as a vet to examine its teeth to tell the difference. And a vet isn't going to do that until it's too late.

Of course, a groom or leisure owner who works every day with the horse will be able to tell the difference, because their relationship is a very close one. The jockey will only be able to tell if he or she has done plenty of schooling with the horse, and then only if it starts behaving in a way that is completely at odds with its usual performance. Professional trainers have often been caught out, especially if they work with a considerable number of animals. As for the owner – the kind of owner who comes and looks at the horse over the stable door once a month – well, forget it.

It should be added that many cases of mistaken identity have occurred in racing as a result of genuine mix-ups, cock-ups, incompetence, idiocy or misunderstandings, rather than cleverly planned plots.

Bless the punter, then, who lays down a crisp ten-pound note trusting that Moonlight Serenade running in the Biggleswade Brewery novices hurdle is the horse it says it is on the card. Ringing horses is as old as the business of racing itself. Of course, the practice is not common by any means. But by the same token it is only just this side of rare.

In 1981 Eddie Merryweather had no microchips or lip tattoos to worry about. Each horse had a passport containing details of the horse's pedigree, colour and individual markings. The passport was an essential document. Passing off one lookalike horse as another was hardly difficult as long as you had the passport and a horse that conformed to its description.

Eddie's job was made infinitely easier by the commercial provision of hair dyes not for horses but for people. All he had to do was walk into a chemist and lift his materials off the shelf and put them into the basket. Back in the days when Eddie had first learned his craft, he had had to experiment with talcum powder, chalk dust, diluted bleach and peroxide. In those early days, a heavy downpour of rain could expose his work in a few minutes. In comparison, his job nowadays was relatively simple.

This particular job was made simpler by the fact that the ringer horse had already been identified for him. In the past, he would often have to source the ringer, perhaps by travelling to France or to Ireland. But in this case the horse would be provided. It was always easier to disguise a light-coloured horse and the animal in question was dun-coloured. All Eddie had to do was disguise the star and the stripe on the horse's head and deal with the horse's socks: the white markings extending just above the fetlock. Bizarrely, he was asked to paint out only three of the four socks. It made little sense but it wasn't his job to ask questions.

He'd agreed to come out of retirement for this one job, not for a fee or even for the name of a winner on race day. He'd agreed in payment of a debt he'd incurred several years ago. His terms were simply that no one would ever know that Eddie Merryweather was involved in any way.

Eddie did his shopping in Boots the chemist on the high street. If anyone thought it unusual that a bald-headed eighty-year-old man had filled his basket with large quantities of hair-colour products, no one said anything. And just in case, Eddie also bought a bottle of Lucozade.

While Eddie Merryweather was out shopping, Duncan was in the sauna at his health club. He used the sauna every day, if he could, to help keep his weight down. It was also a quiet place to go and think things through. He'd found that if he turned the dial up high enough he'd often have the sauna to himself.

Unlike most people, Duncan had trained himself to take long stretches in high temperatures.

Kerry would often join him in the hotbox. If the sauna was otherwise empty they could chat about their business without being overheard. Part of the problem with being a recognised jockey was that there was always someone flapping their ears in the hope of getting insider information.

The sauna door opened and Kerry walked in, closing the door behind him with a gentle click. He spread his towel on the pine bench. 'Have you seen that new girl on the reception. Jeez, a man could go mad. Shouldn't be allowed to wear a skirt that short.'

'That why you're late? Chatting her up?'

'All good fun, Duncan, all good fun. You could do with a bit of fun yourself from time to time.'

'I've got plenty of fun like that at home.'

'I'm sure you have. But you shouldn't close your eyes to the world around you.'

The two men fell into silence. Kerry turned over the glass timer and the sand started running. He breathed out heavily.

After a while Duncan said, 'What do you mean I could do with a bit of fun?'

'Well, you've been a bit heavy of late, that's all I'm saying. It's like you've always got two thick lines between your eyebrows.'

'Two thick lines?'

'Yes, two thick lines.'

Duncan sighed.

The door opened and a huge man came in causing the two jockeys to fall silent again. The man seemed to take up half the sauna. He sweated up quickly, and every couple of minutes he tried to flick perspiration beads from his forehead, but without success. He lasted about ten minutes before leaving them to it.

When he'd gone, Duncan said, 'Kerry, I want to ask you a direct question.'

'Fire away.'

'Are you shagging Fee Markham?'

'Ah, that kind of direct question? Why do you ask me that? And why now?'

'I'm asking you because you couldn't keep your dick in your pants if your life depended on it.'

'That's not fair. I mean, if my life depended on it, I'm sure I could. I mean, I'd make a pretty good effort.'

'You haven't answered me.'

'No, I haven't answered you.'

'Well?'

'You haven't told me why you're asking.'

'Because if you were, you Irish pillock, it could complicate a lot of things.'

'I'm sure you're right. Jeez, you've no faith in me.'

'Well then. Are you or aren't you?'

Kerry turned and looked at him. 'No, I'm not. There. Are you happy now?'

'Yes.' Duncan supposed he was. He'd be happier still if he truly believed him but he guessed this was as close to the truth of the matter as he was going to get.

It was late afternoon and darkness was beginning to fall on Petie's ramshackle cottage. The trainer sat morosely in the gloom and glared at Roisin. 'Is he still there?'

Roisin went to the window and peeped out at the yard. 'He's still there.'

'Oh for pity's sake. What's he doing?'

'He's just leaning against his car, with his hands in his pockets.'

About forty minutes earlier, Danny Webb had drawn up in his BMW. It was his third visit with carrots in three days. Petie had patiently explained to him that he couldn't keep turning up and that he was getting in the way of all their careful preparations and the work they had to do.

'You don't get people just turning up to watch you train, do you?' Petie had asked.

'Yeh. All the time.'

But Danny hadn't taken any hints and had persisted in returning. Around the horse he was like a lovestruck teenager. He brought carrots and apples to give to Parisa and when, on one occasion, he was allowed to hold Parisa's reins, he had broken into a grin a mile wide. He looked so blissfully happy that no one had the heart to stand him down.

Now he was back again. He'd exchanged a few words with Gypsy George and George had come up to the house to tell them Danny was there. But they'd made George go back and tell the footballer that no one was at home. 'Please yourself,' George had said, 'but I'm away now to my caravan. I'm not looking after him.'

So Danny had waited out there in the cold for forty minutes. Any moment now they would have to turn on a light and reveal their presence.

'For God's sake, Daddy, let's put the kettle on and invite the poor lad in. He's going to catch his death.'

Petie groaned. 'So this is what my life has come to since I got into finding owners. I've got crackerjack stockbrokers to the right of me and eejit footballers to the left. You'd better go and get him, I suppose.'

Roisin fetched the footballer in with some fib about having just got back from across the field. He looked frozen to the bone. She sat him down in one of Petie's broken old armchairs and gave him a cup of tea.

'Would you like a slice of bread and jam with that?' Petie said.

'Yes please,' said Danny.

'Roisin, cut the lad a slice from that loaf. Danny, you must have a hundred and one places to be of an evening, a young fellow with all of your money.'

'Not really.'

'Pubs? Clubs? Discos?'

'I don't drink.'

'A footballer who doesn't drink? Isn't that like a bear that doesn't shite?'

Danny shrugged. 'Can I have riding lessons?' he said.

'What?'

'Riding lessons.'

'What d'ye think I'm running here, son? This isn't the Donkey Derby on Skegness beach.'

'What Daddy means,' Roisin said kindly, 'is that racehorses aren't like the horses that people keep for hacking out. They just go the one way, very fast.'

'Oh,' Danny said. He looked crestfallen.

'If you wanted lessons,' she added, 'you could just go to a riding centre and they'd fix you up and have you riding in no time.'

'I doubt that,' Petie said. 'If his club knew he was asking about getting up on a horse, I reckon they'd have a fit. Isn't that right, son?'

Danny's head dropped and he looked away.

'Those legs of his,' Petie said to Roisin, 'are probably insured for a small fortune. His club isn't going to risk him on the back of an old nag any more than they'd let him jump a fence on Parisa!'

Roisin couldn't bear to see the young footballer's sad face any longer. 'Look, Daddy, what if we just let him walk around the menage for a minute or two?'

'On Parisa? You're feckin' jokin'!'

'Not on Parisa. Something very quiet. Just for a circuit or two.'

'Sure, darlin'!' Petie framed a headline with his large, leathery hands. '"England Striker Comes Cropper At Petie Quinn's Yard". That will look lovely on the front page of the *Sporting Life*. I absolutely forbid it.'

'Just a circuit, Daddy.'

George Pleasance's favourite London nightclub was Tramp on Jermyn Street in Mayfair. The entrance to the club was modest, framed by a simple awning and squeezed between rows of swanky tailors' shops. But inside it was an exclusive playground for celebrities, middle-aged rock stars and the chronically rich.

It had a surprisingly unfashionable vibe and some described it as resembling an old-fashioned gentleman's club with an added disco. But if you could afford the price of the champagne you were considered to be a VIP and you were welcome, whatever your age, to dance with women in tiny skirts. The venue was therefore well out of the range of most jockeys and certainly beyond the means of apprentice and conditional jockeys. Which is why Richard 'Rikki' Piper, a nineteen-year-old conditional beginning to make a name for himself, couldn't believe his luck when he was invited to the club and told that his name would be on the door on Valentine's Day evening. All he had to do was mention George Pleasance.

Rikki had heard about Pleasance, knew he was one of racing's shadier characters, a man who was reputed to have pulled off a variety of gambling coups and who wielded influence among the industry's backroom players. He knew too that Pleasance had an eye to the future and liked to get jockeys on side on their way up – which was why he assumed the gambler had taken a sudden interest in him. So no one could say that Rikki hadn't been warned that to play with George Pleasance was to play with fire. But, like most young jockeys – and like Duncan Claymore before him – he thought he could flirt with Pleasance's generosity without getting in too deep. Jockeys are by definition thrill-seekers and risk-takers. The air of adventure, dark glamour and danger in George Pleasance's invitation appealed to Rikki, not unlike the way the perils of National Hunt racing itself appealed. Not to mention that it was Valentine's evening, and being without a girlfriend of his own, where else was he going to go?

Giving his name on the door made Rikki blush to his scalp. Five feet seven in his socks, Rikki had pretty bad acne and was still young enough to feel self-conscious every time he spoke his own name.

'Are you with George Pleasance?' he was asked by the man on the door.

'Yes.' He wondered how the doorman knew that.

Then he saw a large hand with a gold ring holding a lit cigar waving at him from a table in the corner. George Pleasance was sitting next to a bald-headed man. Also seated at the table were two drop-dead gorgeous females – really, two of the most beautiful women Rikki had ever seen in his life. The bald-headed man looked bored stiff and sat with his arms folded.

'Rikki, dear boy, take a seat,' Pleasance drawled. 'Really, I'm so thrilled you could make it. We love jockeys, don't we, girls? This is Judith and Selina.'

'Oh yes, we do love jockeys,' said Judith.

'Hi-eee!' said Selina and she lifted a hand to wiggle her fingers at him.

'What are you drinking?' Pleasance asked. Before Rikki could reply, he added, 'Have some bubbly. Makes it easier, doesn't it?' Pleasance signalled to a waiter who produced a glass and filled it with champagne. Pleasance stared at Rikki as if fascinated, as if jockeys were a species of leprechaun and Rikki was the first real one he had ever seen.

'Forgive my bad manners, Rikki,' Pleasance said, 'but I want you to meet my business associate, Norman.'

Norman was the bald man. The disco-light bounced off his shiny pate. Rikki offered a handshake, but Norman kept his arms folded. He nodded, minimally. Rikki blushed and took a drink.

'You can shake my hand,' said Judith. She was a brunette with flashing eyes and flawless ivory skin. Her fingernails were painted flamingo-pink. She crossed and uncrossed her legs in a hiss of hosiery.

'Me, too,' said Selina, a lithe, tanned blonde. She had an Australian accent and eyelashes that fluttered. Just like Judith, she wore black stockings and impossibly high heels.

'The thing is,' Pleasance said, 'having got you here I've just been told that something's come up that I've got to deal with. So Norman and I are going to have to leave you with the girls. Is that all right?'

'Er, yes, sure,' said Rikki.

'I've put a tab behind the bar. Just ask the waiters for anything you want.' Pleasance stood up and so did Norman. 'Take good care of him, girls.'

Pleasance offered Rikki a parting handshake, but held on to his hand rather too long, still staring at him as if the leprechaun might grant him a wish.

After he'd gone, Selina said, 'I think jockeys are so brave. You must be fearless to go charging at those great fences on some big brute of a horse.'

'Gosh yes,' said Judith. 'But they aren't great at everything. Like drinking. I bet you can't keep up with us two, Rikki.'

'Oh, I bet I can,' said Rikki.

'Better order another bottle then,' said Selina.

Three and a half hours later, Rikki had to be helped down Jermyn Street by his two beautiful minders. He had an arm around each of them. He was singing. He thought he had fallen off a horse and landed in heaven. When they came to the Cavendish Hotel on the corner of Jermyn Street and Duke Street and they asked him inside, he thought he had ascended even higher. In fact he was travelling the other way but was too drunk to notice.

'What is it about jockeys that makes them so sexy?' A voice cooed in his ear.

When Selina and Judith told him, more than once, that he was irresistible he believed them. He was too young, too stupid and too sloshed to think anything else. Once they had got him up to the room and deposited him on the bed they took off their coats and went into action, chopping up white powder with a credit card. Judith went first, rolling up a ten-pound note as a straw to snort the cocaine. She put a hand to the side of her face.

'God, that's much better,' she said. 'Now I can do anything.'

Selina was next.

'What's that?' Rikki said. He'd smoked a joint before but had never tried cocaine. The room was spinning. He thought he might pass out.

Judith unzipped her dress and hung it over the back of a chair. She was wearing self-supporting stockings and a matching set of pink underwear decorated with little white daisies. She reached behind her back and unclipped her bra, letting her small creamy breasts spring free. Hooking her thumbs in the waistband of her knickers she pulled them off too and stepped boldly towards Rikki.

The jockey couldn't take his eyes off her. Even when he heard the whisper of Selina's clothes being removed, he remained mesmerised. A few seconds later, Selina, now also dressed only in stockings and high heels, knelt on the bed beside him.

'Who's going first?' Judith giggled.

'Want to flip a coin?' Selina said.

Rikki was speechless. He tried to sit up but Selina pressed a hand on his breastbone and pushed him back on to the bed. She started to undo the buttons on his shirt. Judith meanwhile reached for his belt. Within a minute they had the young jockey stark naked.

'Looks like he's not in the mood,' Selina said. 'Too much champagne.'

'We'll have to fix that,' said Judith. 'Lie on your front. Not you!' she added as a bemused Rikki tried to turn over.

Selina lay face down next to Rikki who stared in stupefaction at the smooth cheeks of her pert bottom.

Judith got up and fetched the cocaine. 'You know the little hollow at the base of a girl's spine, just above her bum?'

Regrettably, Rikki was little acquainted with that delectable portion of female anatomy, though it looked as if he may be about to rectify his lack of knowledge.

'They say it's best if you snort it from there.' Judith poured some of the white powder into the smooth cavity of Selina's back, and then with the credit card she began gently chopping it. She divided it into two lines. She handed Rikki the rolled-up banknote. 'Here you go, lover boy.'

'What?' said Rikki.

'Put it up your nose. This is better than winning the Grand National.'

Rikki seemed to think about it for a few seconds. Then he took the banknote and snorted one of the lines. 'Crikey!' he said. 'Crikey!'

Judith took the second line for herself. Then the two women rolled Rikki on to his back.

'Any action?' said Judith.

'Yes, I think something might be happening.'

Rikki could do nothing more than gasp as the two women went to work.

'Happy Valentine's!' one of them said.

The best ever, he thought.

When Rikki came to in the morning, someone was opening the curtains. He had a cracking headache and a dry mouth. The girls had gone. Standing over him and looking less than amused was Norman, the bald man George Pleasance had introduced as his 'business associate'.

'Check-out time,' said Norman. He was holding a camera.

Rikki scrambled out of bed and picked his underpants off the carpet. As he began to pull them on he looked around for signs of Judith and Selina, but the only other person in the room was the very large man opening the windows. He had a pudding-basin haircut and black-framed spectacles held together with a bit of masking tape.

'Where are—?'

'Your girlfriends have gone,' said Norman. 'No, they didn't leave a note. They said you weren't the marrying type.'

'Har-har!' said the bespectacled man. He had a pink face and when he laughed it flushed a bright scarlet.

'Hurry up and getcha clothes on. I've told you, it's check-out time.'

Rikki pulled on his shirt and underpants. He had to hunt for his trousers. Before putting them on he took his wallet out of the pocket and looked inside.

'No, they haven't rolled you, you muppet,' said Norman. 'What do you think they are?'

'Respectable girls, those two,' said the bespectacled man, his huge gut quivering with mirth. He seemed to be enjoying himself immensely.

'Right,' Rikki said, 'I'll be going then.'

'That's the idea,' said Norman. 'Now then, about the bill.'

'The bill?'

'Yes, the bill for the room, the champagne, the coke, and for any other services rendered.'

'Har har!'

'Well, never mind about it,' Norman went on, 'because Mr Pleasance will take care of it all. There's just one thing.'

'What's that?' said Rikki.

'You're racing at Hexham in the last race. Horse called I Am Legend.'

'Yes.'

'Well, you ain't.'

'Not now anyway,' laughed the man with glasses. 'Not now you ain't!'

'You have to cry off. But late. Like the morning of the race.'

'I can't do that!'

Norman held up the camera. 'I've got some pictures here says you might wanna 'ave a think about that. You with your little pink jockey bum in the air, snorting white powder off a girl who seems to 'ave mislaid her clothes. 'Ow would you like your mum to see that? Or your Auntie Madge?'

Rikki blinked in bewilderment.

Norman grinned for the first time. 'But don't you worry, I'll keep those pictures safe. Now, suppose you 'ad an injury on the day of that race. Just supposin' you had a broken arm. What would you do?'

'But I haven't got a broken arm.'

'Stop!' said the bespectacled man, laughing. 'You're killing me, you are!'

'Just supposin' you did 'ave. What would you do?'

'I'd phone . . . and tell them that I couldn't make it.'

'That's right. You phone and tell them. You tell them you've got a dicky stomach and you've got the runs or anything you like. Unless you really want a broken arm. Do you want a broken arm?'

The truth about the last twenty-fours suddenly dawned on Rikki. It finally occurred to him that glamorous and sexy girls in expensive London nightclubs didn't find him irresistible just because he was a jockey. 'No,' he said, struggling to keep the tremor out of the voice. 'No.'

'That's the spirit,' said Norman. 'Now then. Check-out time.'

15

On the same morning that Rikki Piper was getting an education in harsh reality, Duncan was heading to Ascot. The Ascot Trophy, this year sponsored by Solaris Vodka, was one of the course's best-established steeplechases, offering serious prize money to the winner. Run over two miles and five furlongs, it was seen by many trainers as a final outing before the big Cheltenham races.

Not that Duncan or Petie expected to land the prize. The odds-on favourite was Alchemy, a bay gelding of grace and beauty trained by William Osborne. Over the season, Alchemy hadn't just been beating his rivals, he'd been obliterating them. However, Petie had entered a horse that he fancied could at least give the favourite a race, namely The Black 'Un, the small horse with a big heart who had surprised them at Towcester last autumn. Duncan was looking forward to racing him again. He'd be up against Sandy Sanderson on Alchemy and racing pundits were describing it as something of a grudge match between Osborne and Quinn. They weren't wrong to do so.

Of the six races on the card, Roisin was riding in the first and last, a two-mile novice hurdle and the bumper. Roisin had a disappointing opening to the day's racing. Billy Blake was still entitled to race as a novice since his win at Newbury, his first ever, had been in the current season. As they set off in a field of just five horses, they had high hopes for him. But halfway round the course, after staying well and jumping smoothly, Roisin felt one of the horse's muscles go on landing, just as if it had been her own. Maybe she could have carried on but that wasn't her philosophy or that of anyone connected with the Quinn stables. They thought too much of their animals ever to put them at unnecessary risk. Though it was hugely frustrating there was nothing to do but walk Billy Blake back and let the vet take a look.

In the second race, a three-mile chase, Duncan rode Cantabulous, a horse who had triumphed last season at Punchestown in Ireland. He'd hardly raced since then after suffering from carpitis, an arthritis-like inflammation of the knee joint. Gypsy George had steadily nursed him back to full fitness and, though he was much fancied, his lack of form over the season had raised a few question marks. But he stayed well and proved his quality by squeaking home first by half a length.

With no ride in the third, Duncan took an interest in William Osborne's pre-race habits. He wanted to confirm what he already suspected: that Osborne usually – but not always – went to the owners' bar where he liked a drink between races. And that he usually – but not always – went into the parade ring to give a final briefing to his jockey just ahead of the race. Duncan's observations also told him that Osborne had a weak bladder and that, along with his drinking between races, caused him to make frequent visits to the toilet.

At the start of the Ascot Trophy, Alchemy and The Black 'Un deliberately hung towards the back of the field as they made their way up the hill for the first time. Someone up front had taken a five-length lead but both Duncan and Sanderson knew that whoever it was was already out of it. Duncan thought that Alchemy looked slower over the fences than some but they stayed together – and moved up together after the open ditch. Duncan took up fourth position on the inside as they made the turn.

The pace had quickened now and the field was grouping together. When they hit the fifth fence there wasn't much daylight between them. The front runner had dropped back to two lengths clear and everyone else was making good progress. Duncan was practically scraping the white paint on the inside rail while Sanderson had gone on the outside and was giving it up to no one.

They went into the turn at the top of the Ascot hill, fearfully bunched, and at that moment in the race, all seven jockeys thought they might be able to take it. The Black 'Un got right into the roots of the next fence as they nudged and niggled for advantage, each rider looking for an edge.

By the time they hit the sixth from home, some of the runners were feeling the pinch. Duncan was lying in third now, with Alchemy inches ahead and both of them within two lengths of the leader. Over the final ditch, Alchemy made ground and then put his nose in front for the first time, The Black 'Un staying with him, muscling through.

After the second to last jump, and with nothing between them, Alchemy conjured an aggressive, sweeping move to the front. Duncan asked The Black 'Un for more and he gave it. Alchemy went ahead by half a length but The Black 'Un wasn't done. He came back and pressed on at the final fence. The spectators were going insane with excitement in the stands as they cheered on the two favourites.

They jumped the final fence together, both spring-heeled. The rest of the field was receding, leaving the pair of them to slug it out right to the winning post, receiving a wonderful reception from the Ascot crowd. Each horse had put in a magnificent shift, but the day could only go to one of them. Alchemy, the favourite, found a final surge on the line to snatch victory and cap a magnificent contest.

Duncan bent to murmur his congratulations into his horse's ear. It may be a daft gesture but the big-hearted horse deserved every accolade going. The Black 'Un may not have won this time, but he had let everyone know he was a genuine contender.

Ahead, Sanderson had slowed his horse and was patting Alchemy's shoulder in appreciation. Even a cold-hearted bastard like Sanderson knew when credit was due. Duncan softened. Despite his animosity towards the other man he knew that the right thing to do was to go up to him and congratulate him on a great race. Sanderson was an odious figure, but he wasn't champion jockey for nothing and he had managed to squeeze that last drop of juice out of his horse when it really counted.

Duncan walked The Black 'Un over and offered his hand. 'Well done. You rode a great race.'

Sanderson ignored him and turned his horse away.

Duncan shrugged. 'Please yourself.' He walked The Black 'Un to the enclosure.

Petie intercepted him. 'Fantastic!' The trainer was overjoyed. 'This horse owes us nothing! My God, he gave him a scare!'

In the winner's enclosure, Burnt Bacon was jostling to get pictures again and Sanderson was ignoring his request to pose with the winner. The photographer turned to Duncan. 'Any chance of getting Petie Quinn?' he asked.

Petie was notoriously camera shy, but he was in such high spirits after that performance that he let Duncan call him into the enclosure, where he stood holding The Black 'Un's reins trying to choke back an oafish smile as Bacon snapped away. 'That's your lot!' Petie shouted, fleeing when a second photographer took an interest.

'I can use these,' said Bacon, plainly delighted. 'Rarity value!'

'Hey, listen, Bernard,' Duncan said to him confidentially. 'Will you be up at Hexham on 5th March?'

The photographer wrinkled his nose. 'I doubt it. Too bloody far and too bloody cold.'

'There's a horse running we're interested in buying. I need a pro to get some action shots. So we can study the horse, you know? Before buying. Professional rates.'

Bernard unzipped a pocket and pulled out a grubby diary. He flicked through it. 'Well, seeing as it's you, Duncan, I could do it.'

'Brilliant.' Duncan shook hands with him. 'See you there, Bernard.'

Duncan had been thinking about what Kerry had said to him in the sauna. It had irritated him at the time but, on reflection – and though he'd never say so to his face – the Irishman had been right. Duncan hadn't been much fun recently. Of course, he had good reason to be serious and reflective, but not to take it out on the people he was closest to. So he organised a dinner, inviting Petie, Kerry and Roisin, and Charlie and Mrs Solanki, thankfully now returned from India.

They met at a country pub called the Last From Home, owned by Josh Cody, a former flat-racing jockey. Josh could have been one of the all-time greats had he not let boozing do all the talking for him. As time went by they'd had to pour him into the saddle before a race, and he faded from the scene, a cautionary tale to young jockeys on the dangers of drink. However, during his short-lived time at the top he'd had the sense to put some of his money into the pub he now ran. Of course, to say that he 'ran' the pub was a bit of a stretch, unless you called running it sitting behind the bar reading the *Sporting Life* while young girls hurried around serving, cooking and keeping the customers happy. But the Last From Home was a cosy place with a warm welcome and a reliable menu.

Josh had a face that was so lined it looked like a bit of saddle leather that been left out in the rain for twenty years, but it crinkled nicely when he smiled. 'You fellows had a decent day at Ascot,' he said, coming from behind the bar to greet them. This was true. Duncan had enjoyed a win and a fine second in the big race and Roisin had romped home in the bumper.

'Not bad,' said Duncan.

'Not bad he says! And you,' Josh said, pointing to Roisin, 'are fantastic. Better than that Irishman you hang out with.'

'I haven't even taken off my coat!' Kerry protested. 'Do you want me to stay or not?'

Josh, a pint-sized fellow, reached up to clap a welcoming arm round Kerry's shoulder and then turned to do the same to Duncan's father. He well remembered Charlie from his training days.

'Your table is ready, ladies and gentlemen. Follow me.'

He settled them in a cosy corner by the fire and his eager young staff took drink and food orders. They ordered steaks even though Duncan would give most of his away. Being vegetarian, Mrs Solanki had a quiche. Petie wanted to know when, exactly, egg and cheese flan had started to be called quiche. Kerry said it had happened in the summer of 1974 and Petie said he must have missed the announcement.

'So,' asked Josh as he poured the wine, the role of sommelier being the one he took seriously, 'what are you folk celebrating? The royal engagement?'

'What do you mean?' asked Duncan.

Roisin burst out laughing and Lorna rolled her eyes. 'Really, Duncan,' she said, 'that's priceless even for you.'

Duncan was bemused. 'Honestly, I don't know what you're talking about.'

Lorna grinned. She was enjoying his ignorance. 'I'm always telling him to take his eyes out of the form book. If she had four legs and a tail he'd know all about her.'

'You bet,' Kerry piled in. 'Her dam, her sire and whether she likes firm going.'

Roisin hooted with laughter and dug Kerry in the ribs with an elbow. Even Petie's eyes were twinkling with merriment.

Mrs Solanki reached across the table and patted Duncan's arm. 'Prince Charles announced his engagement yesterday, to that nice Diana Spencer.'

'Oh.' The penny finally dropped and he felt foolish. It was true, sometimes his concentration on racing was so fierce that the world outside passed him by. He looked around with a grin. His wife, his father, his friends were all laughing, having a good time. This was exactly what he had wanted.

He lifted a glass. 'I propose a toast then. To Lady Di. And to all of you. Lorna and I are very happy you could come out tonight. There's no special reason.'

They all drank to that and suddenly Charlie said, 'Yes, there is a reason.' All eyes turned to him. 'I've decided to go racing again.'

This was a significant announcement. It had been some years since Charlie had been on a racetrack, not since he'd lost his reputation and been warned off. He hadn't even been able to look in at Quinn's yard. The game just bought back too much bile and anger.

'Ooh, that's exciting,' cried Lorna. 'Are you going to Chelten-ham, Charlie?'

Mrs Solanki smiled benignly but she didn't have any knowledge of the racing business. The others looked uncertain because they all knew Charlie had been banned by the Jockey Club – 'warned off' all racetracks for a period of nine years. The notion of Charlie showing his face at the Cheltenham Festival, which would be crawling with press, officials and racing insiders with encyclopedic memories, made no sense.

'No,' Charlie said, 'I'm not going to Cheltenham.'

'Hexham,' said Duncan soberly. 'Dad is coming to Hexham next week. He can slip in quietly and no one will notice.'

'But, Charlie,' said Lorna, 'isn't Hexham almost in Scotland? Why would you want to go all the way up there?'

'Because,' the old man said, 'I'm feeling lucky. A little bird has put me on to a winner.'

There was an awkward silence as the guests digested this information.

'Well,' said Mrs Solanki, 'I think Charles and Di are going to be very happy, don't you?'

A couple of days later, two horseboxes left Petie Quinn's yard. Roison was at the wheel of the big blue one, with three horses and grooms on board. They were headed south-west for Somerset and Wincanton racecourse, where they would rendezvous with Petie and Kerry who were travelling by car. The second, smaller box, painted a dull olive-green, was aimed east, though its destination was closer to home, Huntingdon racecourse in the featureless flat of East Anglia. Gypsy George was at the wheel with Duncan and the stable lass Nicky for company; in the back was Prince Samson, heading for his first experience of an English racetrack. The sweet pungent smell of lavender permeated the enclosed space. 'I don't mind it, you know,' said George. 'Reminds me of fields around Frome when I was growin' up.'

Duncan was aware from conversations with Michelle that, despite his neuroses, Sammy had survived a couple of outings on Irish tracks, at Galway and Leopardstown, where he'd won a two-and-a-half-mile novice chase. He'd be racing over a shorter distance today in a two-mile handicap. It was part of a plan cooked up by Petie and Martin Joyce back in January, when the Irish owner had watched Roisin ride on the big grey, Duncan being sidelined at the time with his rib injury. Joyce had been impressed and at once proposed entering Sammy for Cheltenham. He mentioned the Arnold Lane, a two-mile chase sponsored by a leading bookmaker and run on the first afternoon of the Festival.

Petie had looked at Joyce in alarm. 'For God's sake, man, he's as nervous as a sack of kittens, he's never been near an English track and you want to chuck him into all that crazy Cheltenham malarkey!'

Joyce had nodded. 'You're right, Quinn, it's crazy. But listen to me. We're all still bleeding for Michelle. Her mother cries herself to sleep every night. My heart aches for that poor girl and this is a decision made in my heart. Michelle wanted that horse to race at Cheltenham. I don't care if he comes in five minutes after every other animal, I want him there in her memory.'

Petie had tipped his cap back on his head and given the matter some thought. 'I hear you, Martin. How about this then?' And he had proposed a trial run ahead of the Festival. If that turned out to be a disaster they could always scratch Sammy from Cheltenham. 'Duncan can ride him at Huntingdon for you at the end of February – he should be fit by then.'

Duncan, a witness to this conversation, had enthusiastically endorsed the plan and here they were, some six weeks later, driving to the East Anglian course for Prince Samson's English debut. For once Duncan's principal concern was not whether or not he would win, but whether he could even get his horse to take part.

Martin Joyce met them in the parade ring where Nicky was proudly showing off the grey horse. If anyone noticed the odour of lavender that enveloped Prince Samson and his connections, they were too polite to comment.

'He's a fine-looking animal, all right, and that girl's turned him out just dandy,' said Martin appreciatively. 'I must say, George, whatever happens, your stable have done your damnedest for that horse. Don't think I don't know it.'

Gypsy George grunted noncommittally but Duncan knew that he would be relaying the compliment to Petie the moment they got back to the yard.

Duncan looked at George and Martin expectantly. 'Any instructions?' he asked.

The two veterans of the turf looked at one another and both shook their heads. 'You know what Sammy's like these days,' said Martin. 'I think we're in your hands, son.'

So the race tactics were up to him. Duncan was happy enough with that, though if it all went tits up then he could expect the lion's share of the criticism.

As it turned out, his biggest problem was getting Sammy safely to the start, because the horse pulled hard and threatened to run away with him, but Duncan hung on tight and got him into line. Once they were off, however, Sammy settled easily and jumped as well over these fences as he did back home. Duncan hid him in the pack for the first mile, with his jumping getting sweeter all the time. In fact, he realised that the horse's jumping rhythm was taking him into contention. As they turned for home, with just two fences left, Prince Samson was lying third. The horse in the lead made a mistake at the penultimate fence and almost unseated his rider. Whether or not that disturbed the second runner, Duncan wasn't sure, but he didn't care – Sammy flew the fence and cruised past both his rivals. They leapt the last obstacle with feet to spare and won by an easy three lengths.

In the winner's enclosure, Nicky was in tears as she fawned over the horse, George wore a grin of benign stupidity and Martin clasped Duncan so tightly to his great barrel chest that he feared his ribs would crack again. At last the big Irishman let him go. 'Next stop Cheltenham,' he said with triumph.

'Actually, Martin,' Duncan said, catching his breath, 'we've got a date at Hexham first. I hope you've not forgotten.'

Joyce beamed at him. 'Don't you worry, son. I'm very much looking forward to it.'

16

Fee Markham was up early on 5th March, the day of Hexham races. She was in charge of two horses and she had a lot to do. The journey to Northumberland was over four hours long and it was prudent to factor in extra time for possible delays. In horse racing there were no prizes for latecomers.

At Osborne's yard the policy was to give the horses very light exercise on the morning of a race, no more than to stretch their legs. Then they had to be washed, brushed and shined up. Fee also liked to plait the manes of her horses and as a result her animals were always in the running for the 'best turned-out' prizes. Before loading up, the horses' legs were padded in case of sustaining a knock while travelling. Then the animals were loaded into the horsebox side by side.

The two horses Osborne had running at Hexham were I Am Legend and Amnesia Moon, two very different prospects. A seven-year-old grey gelding, Amnesia Moon had been on good form and was expected to start as favourite in the top race of the day, the four-mile chase, up against Parisa. By contrast, the four-year-old I Am Legend had disappointed in his first season. Osborne still had hopes that he could come good and had entered him in the last race of the afternoon, the Hadrian's handicap hurdle in the hope of him getting more accustomed to racetrack conditions. I Am Legend was bay-coloured with a distinctive white star between his eyes, such a distinguishing feature that it was entered on his passport.

Fee was travelling in the horsebox alongside regular driver Jim Pitts. Jim had been working for Osborne for over twelve years. Before they could set off, they had to wait for William Osborne to come and make his last-minute check, something he did before any of his boxes or trailers left. He could never entirely trust his staff after one of his horses had been thrown about en route to Fakenham years ago, before he had employed Jim as his regular driver. Osborne wordlessly made his inspection and then gave them the nod to leave.

When travelling to a race, Jim always liked to make two stops. The first for a breakfast of bacon sandwiches and a cup of tea and the second – assuming they'd made good time – at a pub for a couple of pints before delivering the horses to the racetrack. As a seasoned driver he knew his routes and had his favourite pitstops, revisited many times over the years. When driving north beyond Leeds, regardless of which track he was heading for, Jim liked to patronise the Saracen's Head on the A1. They had a good, roomy car park in which to turn the horsebox and a pint of bitter that had stayed reliable in over ten years. Having made good time, he announced to Fee that he needed a 'toilet break', which Fee had come to realise was Jim's code for feeling thirsty, and they turned into the pub car park.

Fee looked at her watch. 'OK, we're in good time. Look, I reckon the sun might come out. You'd better park up under those trees.'

'If there's any sun coming out I'm a Dutchman,' Jim said. But he parked where she'd told him anyway.

They both jumped down from the cab and Jim locked the door. 'Give me the keys,' Fee said. 'I'll just check the back. Can you get me a shandy, please? I'll be right with you.'

Jim crunched over the gravel and disappeared into the pub. Fee waited a moment and then went to the back of the horse box to make sure that the securing pin was loose and that the box was unlocked. Then she followed Jim inside. He was still at the bar being served.

'I'll find us a nice table,' she said, and so she did. A nice table with no view to the rear of the pub where the horsebox was parked.

Eddie Merryweather's employers had been waiting for him in an olive-green horsebox when he pulled into the lay-by off the A1. He did a neat job, working in the horsebox, his own car parked to the rear. The men who had commissioned him sat in the cab up front, patiently waiting for him to complete the task they'd set for him. He asked no questions and did exactly what he was told to do.

The horse whose appearance he was altering did have a name – More Tomorrow – but Eddie hadn't been told what it was and he didn't want or need to know. Without looking at the horse's teeth, he guessed that the animal was four or five years old, a bay with a pronounced white blaze on his face. Eddie had been instructed to turn the blaze into a star and he'd been given a photograph of another horse so that he could get the star in exactly the right position. He'd been asked to get rid of three of the horse's white socks, leaving just one sock visible on the left foreleg.

Eddie had also been instructed to make the dye semi-permanent. It was important that a shower of rain didn't wash the new markings away at the time of the race; but it seemed the intention was to return the horse to his natural colour later on. He was pleased to think that the ringers intended to wash the dye off as it meant that the horse would not be killed. Too many times in the past, with the deception having been successfully accomplished, horses run as ringers had simply vanished. As a rule the animal was quickly put down and the carcass given to the local hunt so that the evidence would be eaten by the hounds.

Using the materials he had bought in Boots, Eddie worked methodically. He was pleased to find he had lost none of his old touch. He wore an apron and a pair of rubber gloves to stop the dye from colouring his own hands. First, he soaked the horse's hair in the spot where he was to work and dried it thoroughly with a towel. Then he brushed it and began working in thick amounts of dye, starting with the lower reaches of the blaze and moving up. The horse hair soaked up the colour easily. He left the dye to set and started on the socks. As he worked he chuckled to himself, thinking about how much more difficult it had been in the old days, messing around with powders and bleaches and peroxides.

The only tricky thing was to estimate the amount of time to leave the dye in for, because the longer it was left, the darker it would get. The skill lay in making sure that the result didn't look patchy against the natural bay colour of the horse. It was better to leave it on for less time and then add more, than to go too dark and struggle to lighten it all again.

Eddie had never expected to get pulled back into this game. But a debt of honour is a debt of honour and when his unex-pected visitor had turned up at his door that night he had agreed to pay that debt. After all, the man had kept him out of jail.

Eddie had come out of prison in the late 1960s having served time for being part of a crooked betting syndicate. His involvement had been in doping horses. Now in his sixties, he'd thought that a life of crime was no way for a man to live out his later years so he'd resolved to go straight. But with a criminal record, getting a job proved impossible. Prospective employers simply didn't want to know him. It all seemed too familiar, like his experiences after the First World War, which had steered him towards a criminal career in the first place. He could have made money by continuing to shop around his skills as a fixer and counterfeiter but he genuinely wanted to put all that behind him.

The problem was that his talents lay in dyeing, doping and ringing – which didn't leave him too many options to use his skills legitimately. He concluded that he knew plenty about horses and still liked to be around them, so his best bet was to find work as a stable lad, just as he had done many years ago before he went crooked. But everyone in the racing world knew his name and his history. No yard would give him the time of day. No yard would dare be associated with him.

Except for one, a small stables where the owner was setting up as a trainer. He was working all hours with not much help. He'd heard of Eddie and knew of his disreputable past in the racing world. He listened to Eddie's story with cool, unblinking blue eyes, then asked Eddie to come clean about his recent misdemeanours and for some reason Eddie did. He saw in those blue eyes what the trainer was seeing in him: a tired and beaten man.

'All right,' the trainer had said, 'I'll take you on.'

Eddie worked hard for him. Together they established a decent training yard and Eddie never used his doping or ringing skills again. Instead, he turned his cosmetic skills to showing off the horses in his charge. He was expert at plaiting, shining and turning out a horse. If an animal had a scar or a coat with unsightly whorls, Eddie could fix it. They even made quite a bit of money for the yard by winning showing events, and that money went towards building up the stock.

Shortly afterwards, the police came looking for Eddie on an unrelated charge – something he had had nothing to do with. It was easy, however, for the police to 'round up the usual suspects' – and Eddie fitted the bill. He was arrested and charged. His new employer had been outraged and gone to bat for him. He had remonstrated with the police and told them he could vouch for Eddie's activities since he'd started working for him. He said he was prepared to stand up for him court if necessary. Eventually, the charges were dropped. There was no doubt in Eddie's mind that his new employer's faith in him had kept him out of prison.

Eddie continued to work for the trainer until he retired. He often wondered why the trainer had taken him on when everyone else had said no. Eddie had come to the conclusion that it was because he was a decent and kind man who listened to his heart as well as his head. A man who knew what it was to make mistakes in life and to put them behind him. So, when that same man had come knocking at his door asking for a favour, Eddie couldn't turn him away.

When he was satisfied with his work, he shampooed the horse in the dyed areas to get rid of any excess colour and dried the coat off with a towel. Then gathered up all his tools and chemicals and stowed them in a leather bag. He took off his rubber apron, wiped his hands on the wet towel and put both of these things inside the bag. There was nothing left in the horsebox to indicate that he had been working there.

When the road was clear of traffic he emerged from the box and tapped on the cabin door. His employer got out of the passenger seat and a younger man from the driver's side. For the first time, Eddie got a proper look at the younger man and realised that he had met him many years ago, when he was a lad.

'All done?' said the older man.

Eddie nodded. The two men went to inspect his work while Eddie lit up a cigarette and stood by the side of the road.

When the two men reappeared the younger man said, 'Bloody brilliant.'

'Is that it then?' Eddie asked.

'It is, Eddie.'

'And you won't be coming back to ask me again?'

'No. I promise. I shan't ask you again.'

'You and me, Charlie, we go back a long way.'

'We do indeed. You remember Duncan here, don't you?'

'Of course. But you've grown up a bit since I saw you last.'

'Eddie, we need to get going,' said Charlie. 'I'm going to shake your hand and get out of here.'

'Right you are. When you want the colour out, crush up some vitamin C tablets and make a paste with water. Dampen the coat and let the paste sit for half an hour. Then shampoo it and the dye will come out. You need to do this in the next couple of days or it'll be harder to get the colour out. Don't try to dye on top of dye.'

'I hear you.'

'Do I get a name? Just for a flutter, like?'

Duncan spoke, 'I Am Legend. Last one at Hexham.'

'Today?'

'That's right. I Am Legend. Today.'

Jim Pitts was still on his first pint when the second horsebox pulled up in the car park at the rear of the Saracen's Head and cruised to a halt alongside the first. Not that Jim or Fee could see it because their table looked out of the pub towards the front.

The switch was executed quickly. The horseboxes were opened simultaneously. I Am Legend was trotted out of Osborne's box and directly into the vacated second box. Then More Tomorrow was trotted into Osborne's box alongside Amnesia Moon. The rear doors were closed and pinned shut on both boxes.

This part of the exercise took less than a minute. Then the second box was driven away. It was as if it had never been there.

The next thing to do was to stop at a telephone box. Duncan made one short call. To George Pleasance. 'It's on,' Duncan said and replaced the receiver.

On arrival at Hexham, Fee and Jim unloaded Amnesia Moon and the horse that was to race under the name I Am Legend. The usual formalities applied and Jim produced the passports for both animals. In each case the passport description corresponded with the horse's appearance, right down to the star on I Am Legend's nose. Fee asked the official to confirm that I Am Legend's vaccination certificate was all in date and after checking he confirmed that it was fine. The man quickly lost interest and moved on.

Fee and Jim walked the two horses in the pre-parade ring to loosen them up after the long drive and to make sure there were no last-minute niggles. As Amnesia Moon wasn't running until the fourth race, Fee wasn't expecting to see Osborne just yet but he surprised her by turning up before the first race. He wasn't in the best of moods.

'That little shit has cried off,' he said. 'That's the last time I'm giving that spotty jerk a chance on one of my horses.'

'Who are we talking about?' said Fee.

'Rikki shitting Piper, that's who. He left a message – a message, I ask you – saying he's been taken ill. Diarrhoea. He can't be that ill – he was riding at Warwick yesterday.'

'Well, if he's got the runs—'

'Whose side are you on?' He glared at her. 'Anyway, it occurred to me – how would you like to ride?'

Fee went white. This hadn't been part of the plan. 'What? On I Am Legend?'

'Well, you don't think I'd put you up on Amnesia Moon, do you? But you probably can't do worse on I Am Legend than that little twit Piper. '

So far Osborne had shown no support for her career as a jockey. In fact, he'd made his contempt for women jockeys pretty clear.

'I'm not prepared,' Fee said. 'I've no kit. Nothing.'

'Well, forget it then. Just don't come begging me for rides in the future. You've had your chance. I'll ask around. There'll be some other conditional knocking about who'll jump at it.'

Osborne stalked off. He hadn't even glanced at his two horses.

'That's put him in a nice mood,' said Jim.

'For a change,' she said and they both laughed.

Petie and his team were looking out for Charlie's arrival at the course. As a banned person, it was important that no nosy official or member of the racing press spotted him. They'd taken the precaution of booking an executive box and the distinguished old man with a trilby pulled over his forehead was whisked out of sight as soon as the coast was judged to be clear.

'Executive box' was a rather fancy name for a hut perched above the winning post near the owners' bar, but it was comfortable. A spectator had a fine view over the course and the rolling Northumberland countryside and drinks and sandwiches could be ordered throughout the afternoon's racing. Duncan ensconced his father by the window with a pair of binoculars.

'Do you think you'll be all right here, Dad?'

'I'm grand,' Charlie said. 'I've got everything I need.'

'I'll ask Roisin to look in on you,' Petie said. 'And I'll come up here while the races are run.'

'I tell you I'm fine! Off with you! You've got work to do.'

Duncan hung back to have another word. So far, Charlie had been in excellent form. His conversation on the journey, the way he had spoken to Eddie, his handling of the horses – it was as if Duncan had been with his father of old. But it had been a long day already and a lot of it remained. He couldn't stay with Charlie all afternoon but it was imperative his father remained where he was. Duncan didn't know what the precise consequences would be if Charlie was discovered at a racecourse in defiance of his ban – the Jockey Club could hardly warn him off again – but there might be nasty ramifications for himself and Petie. And given the other circumstances of the day, the last thing he needed was for an inquiry to be set in motion.

'Dad, listen to me – you do know how important it is that you stay in here, don't you?'

His father fixed him with an icy glare. 'Of course.'

'Seriously. Stay here, OK?'

Charlie suddenly smiled. It was as if the sun had come out. 'Duncan, my boy, don't worry about a thing.'

With Parisa on the card, naturally Mullet and Perm had made the trip and they seemed to have brought half the professional footballers in the north of England along with them. The place was heaving with athletic young men displaying their own variations of mullets and perms. The small number of local reporters and press stringers were cock-a-hoop at the opportunity to work up some additional copy.

Also in attendance were representatives of the stockbroker syndicate who had travelled all the way to the remote latitudes of the north to see their other two horses, Misty Mountain and Blink Of An Eye. This time they had no objection to Roisin being in the saddle as she took Misty Mountain down to the start of the first race, a two-mile novice chase. It was just as well they had no objection as she'd also picked up the ride on Blink Of An Eye after Kerry twisted an ankle and found himself on official 'keep the lads smiling' duty.

'You can't win 'em all,' he told the syndicate after Misty Mountain came in fourth.

Duncan was on hand when Kerry made similar noises after Blink Of An Eye's third place in the second race, the three-mile novice hurdle.

He stepped in and said cryptically, 'Save a pound for the last. I've heard something.' Then he walked away, leaving the stock-brokers staring after him.

Duncan had been keeping an eye on the televised odds for the last race. I Am Legend had started at 33-1 but now the odds were tumbling and currently stood at 15-1. Money was pouring on to the horse and Duncan knew that was from somewhere in the south.

It was all a matter of timing.

Duncan figured just after the second race would do it. He found Mullet and Perm in the bar and asked them to step outside.

'You know you've always been after me for a tip?' he said to Billy Nation.

'Yes.' The Scouser's broad smile got even broader.

Duncan put a finger to his lips. 'Have you noticed the money going on I Am Legend in the last?'

'No.'

Duncan looked round, very careful not to be overheard. 'The odds are dropping like a stone. Clever money somewhere.'

Billy widened his eyes. 'Gotcha! Should have brought more cash.'

'Not a word to anyone else, mind. You too, Danny.'

'Not a word. Thanks, mate,' said Danny.

Duncan patted Billy on the shoulder. 'Benefits of ownership. You didn't hear it from me. I'll leave you to it.'

The two footballers moved off to a corner of the bar and put their heads together, whispering.

It's started, thought Duncan.

Then he found Tennyson-Collins and told him the same thing. 'Not a word to anyone.'

'Absolutely.'

'And you didn't hear it from me.'

'Mum's the word.'

Duncan knew that Tennyson-Collins would be obliged to tell everyone in his syndicate. And he knew that Danny and Billy wouldn't be able to resist spilling the beans to all their footballing mates. And both the stockbrokers and the footballers would be well stoked with cash.

Let nature take its course, he thought.

In the corridor between the owners' bar and the executive boxes where Charlie sat, there was a bank of three pay phones. After a few minutes Duncan popped his head round the corner. All three phones were occupied. Billy Nation was talking on one of them and two of the stockbrokers were busy on the others. Out in Tattersalls and alongside the brick-built grandstand was another bank of pay phones. A quick glance established that these were also busy with footballers and stockbrokers.

Every one of the Quinn connections would be phoning either their brother or their father or their best buddies. And all of those people – equally sworn to secrecy, of course – would be making their own calls. Within the hour everyone's grandmother would know I Am Legend was a good thing in the last at Hexham. Because racing information travels faster than rumour itself.

17

Michael Joyce was riding the Irish raiders' gelding See What Happens in the fourth race, a four-mile chase and a considerable test for a horse over twenty-three obstacles. It was an ambitious distance for Parisa as well, Duncan's mount, but Petie was keen to find out how the horse would handle the challenge. It had been Duncan's idea to enter him in the first place but Petie had bought into the idea. 'We know he can jump,' he'd said to Duncan, 'and we know he's got a bit of pace but will he stay? We've got a real prospect if he can.' Duncan was amused that Petie was now so enthusiastic about a race and a venue he'd been so keen to deride but he was also delighted. He'd felt a bit guilty about forcing Petie to come this far north.

Aside from the Irish horse, who was a guaranteed threat in Duncan's book, he was conscious of Amnesia Moon, the Osborne entry and clear favourite. Sandy Sanderson had not deigned to make the journey and so the animal was due to be ridden by Tim Devany, a jockey Duncan knew and liked. Tim usually rode for the Penderton stables where Duncan had cut his teeth in the early days.

'You're riding for the enemy today,' Duncan said to Tim in the weighing room.

'I don't mind who I ride for, Duncan, so long as it gives me a chance to drive you into the ground.'

'Good luck with that. I'll see you in the winner's enclosure. You'll be on my left.'

'No, you'll be on *my* left.'

'You're a master of wit and repartee, Tim, did you know that?'

Before the start, Duncan walked Parisa up to the first fence. He was a horse who liked to take a look at what he was going to do and Duncan knew well that if he got a good stride on the first fence he'd jump confidently for the remainder of the race. Duncan sat for a while and allowed the animal to have a long look. He heard the starter calling him in but only when he thought the horse was good and ready did he turn Parisa round.

'Waiting for someone to photograph you there, Duncan?' shouted Michael Joyce in the pink silks.

'When you're as good-looking as me you'll do the same.'

'Good-looking!' shouted Tim Devany. 'I've seen better-looking things on the end of a bog brush!'

'Watch out for that open ditch, Tim. You got wet last time you were here.'

The banter wasn't subtle but they all enjoyed it – it took the edge off whatever nerves were flying around. The starter called them to order and sent them away. Amnesia Moon dwelt a bit at the off; See What Happens was one of the first to show; and Parisa tucked in behind the front runners. With sixteen horses it was a crowded field and Duncan didn't want to get stuck too far back in case of fallers or errors in front of him.

The four-mile course started at the bottom of the back straight and sent them on over two and a half circuits before concluding on a separate finishing spur in front of the stand and the spectators along the rails. It was a race for the one-paced plodder who would never give up. Duncan rated Parisa as a bit more than a plodder but as for stamina – he wasn't sure. That was what they were going to find out.

The most testing section of the course was the long climb up the back straight followed by an innocuous-looking fence at the top. But the climb took it out of an animal and there were fallers on the first circuit and the second. Coming down the hill to the water jump for the second time, Parisa made a mistake in his stride and lost ground to the four horses ahead, who included Amnesia Moon and See What Happens. Duncan fought to get back on terms and was just making progress as they took the turn which led them out into the country for the final time. However, he was grateful for the breathing space as, at the first fence in the back straight, Amnesia Moon and the Irish horse came to grief when a loose horse ran across them out of nowhere.

Tim Devany and Michael Joyce were both pitched from the saddle. Joyce got his foot caught in the stirrup and he was dragged along for twenty yards before he managed to kick himself free. Devany came off even worse as Amnesia Moon fell on top of him, crushing his body into the turf.

Duncan saw the carnage ahead of him almost too late, but Parisa executed a neat side step and rounded the fallers. There was no time for Duncan to dwell on the disaster behind him. His job was to get on terms with the two remaining front runners who were now a dozen lengths ahead of him up the back straight. He recognised one of them, Calendar Girl, a renowned stayer who would run till Doomsday; the other horse seemed to be of the same mould.

Parisa gamely toiled after them, over the open ditch and up the hill to the danger fence. The two ahead jumped it clumsily but safely and Parisa, to Duncan's delight, skipped over it as smartly as he had the first time around. Duncan glanced behind him. The rest of the field were strung out far in the distance. His third place was safe anyhow. But, as Parisa galloped down the slope and turned into the finishing straight with one fence left to clear, he realised he could do better. Calendar Girl seemed to be wading through treacle and the other animal was making similarly heavy weather of it.

Parisa jumped the last cleanly and set off after the other two on the long run-in, eating up the ground as they came back to him. He ran out a winner by five lengths.

Petie gave him the thumbs-up as he grabbed the horse. They would have plenty to discuss about the unexpected victory and the horse's prospects but now was not the moment. Duncan let Petie take Parisa over to the winner's enclosure and got weighed in quickly. Then he went to find how his fallen comrades were faring.

Though bruised, Michael Joyce wasn't seriously hurt. His face was white, making the crop of freckles stand out across his brow. He knew he'd had a lucky escape. 'Tim's off to hospital,' he said.

Duncan found the other jockey in the race-track ambulance. He stuck his head inside and forced a grin on to his face. 'Were you that desperate to get away from me?' he said.

'Don't be daft. You'd just have been looking at my arse if it hadn't been for that loose horse.' Despite the jokey response Tim looked in considerable pain. The medic attending to him was already administering morphine.

'You'll be a lot more comfortable in a moment,' the medic said. He indicated to Duncan that he wanted to close the door and get under way. To Duncan he said in a whisper, 'Crushed pelvis.'

There could be no elation for Duncan at winning the race. No one liked to see a rider badly hurt, even though it had happened to all of them at one time or another. They knew the risks. No one made anyone do this crazy job. But it cut deep to see another jockey – particularly a friend – in agony.

Duncan watched the ambulance drive off the course and then returned to the winner's enclosure. Danny and Billy were there but they knew what had happened and asked after the fallen jockeys. As fellow professional sportsmen they fully understood the implications of sustaining a bad injury.

Petie made an attempt to lift the air of gloom. 'Don't you worry – they'll patch young Devany up and he'll be back soon enough. And look at it this way, this fellow,' he said, laying a hand on Parisa's shoulder, 'has done enough today to make me think of him for the National in a year or two.'

'The Grand National!'

'Not yet. But give it a couple of seasons. He's a fine jumper and now we know he stays.'

It was enough to lift the mood. Burnt Bacon was on hand to take pictures of the celebrity footballers on either side of Parisa, and they continued to smile even when some wag among the spectators kept shouting, 'Which one's the 'orse?'

The photographer was delighted. 'You didn't tell me they were coming,' he said.

'Bonus for you,' said Duncan. 'You got those pictures for us?'

'Oh yes.'

Duncan had given him a list of nine horses in which the Quinn yard supposedly had a purchasing interest. Buried in that list was the name I Am Legend. 'Don't forget the two in the last race.'

'You can rely on me,' said Bernard.

Duncan showered and changed. His racing was done for the day. In the changing room Michael Joyce had regained his colour and his spirits. A valet had produced an ice pack for his swollen ankle. Apart from his ankle, Michael was fine and would be racing again in two days.

'Where's the clan?' Duncan said.

'Where d'ye expect?' said Michael.

Duncan knew perfectly well that he'd find the Joyces in the bar. 'I'll go up there and tell 'em you're still breathing.'

'I think they've guessed as much. But thanks anyway.'

Duncan made his way up to the owners' bar. The Joyce clan, as promised, was over from Ireland. All five of the remaining brothers had made the trip. Duncan had met the Joyce boys a few times and they now embraced him one by one as if he were a member of the clan. They were sparky and on form as ever but, to Duncan's eyes, they were still carrying Michelle O'Brien's coffin. Wariness had settled on them and they all seemed to be looking over their shoulders, waiting for fate's next blow.

News of Michael's progress was gratefully received and Duncan was assailed by offers of drinks from all sides, together with en-quiries about how he'd managed to cheat them out of victory in the chase. 'Admit it – that loose horse was from Quinn's stable, wasn't he? That's the only way you boys know how to beat us.'

Martin Joyce pulled out a seat for him but Duncan didn't take it. His gaze was on a table on the far side of the room. 'Can I have a word in private?' he said to Martin.

The two men stepped outside the bar into the empty corridor.

'He's the foxy-faced bloke in the cap sitting with a gent in a Barbour jacket,' Duncan said.

'Yes, I know the feller. So, it's on?'

'It certainly is.'

'Right then. You can rely on me and the boys.'

*

Crazy money had been flying on to I Am Legend for the last race. The bookmakers on the course were in touch with their home bases through runners scrambling for the latest information by telephone. Tic-tac men were signalling from ring to ring, their white gloves flying. No sooner had the bookies chalked their boards with new odds than they were rubbing them out and chalking up fresh prices. I Am Legend, having started the day at 33-1, had dropped to 14-1 then 10-1 and was now at 11-2.

Everyone could see what was happening.

The news was further compounded by the announcement that the horse's original jockey for the race, Rikki Piper, had been replaced at the last moment by another conditional jockey, Gerry Pardew.

William Osborne was having a quiet drink with one of his cronies in the owners' lounge bemoaning the unreliability of jockeys when a pint of his favourite ale was placed in front of him by a large paw. Osborne looked up and saw Martin Joyce standing over him, a large, intimidating figure. He knew who Martin Joyce was among the Irish raiders though he'd never met him in person. 'What's this?'

The Irishman was smiling. 'That's for all the leads you've given me over the years,' said Martin.

'I don't recall giving you any leads.'

'Not in so many words. But I've studied you. And you're the top.' Martin turned his attention to Osborne's companion. 'This man is outstanding. Brilliant. I've learned all I know about training horses from this man by observing from a distance. Did you know you're sitting next to one of the greats?'

'Well, yes,' said the man.

'That's going it a bit,' Osborne said. 'But thank you for the drink.'

'I watched you,' Martin said, 'bring Eat The Evidence back up after she'd broken down. Everyone else said she was finished. You brought her back and got two more great seasons out of the girl. What a horse and what a trainer. I salute you, Mr Osborne.'

'William,' said Osborne, 'please call me William.' And seeing that Martin wasn't going anywhere, he said, 'Pull up a seat.'

Martin sat down.

'Listen,' Osborne said. 'That was a bad business with Michelle O'Brien. Related to you, wasn't she?'

'We play a dangerous game, William. A very dangerous game. Things happen to the very best.'

'Do you know if Michelle's family got that cheque I sent them?'

'Oh, I'm sure they did.'

Martin continued to wax lyrical about Osborne's remarkable abilities as a trainer. He laid it on thick, but with blarney and unstoppable charm. Osborne occasionally pulled his lips back in a tight smile, pretending to modesty, but in fact it was music to his ears. It was nice for once to bask in an honest assessment of his work. Because, frankly, he had achieved a heck of a lot in this game. Sometimes it took an outsider, like this oafish but well-meaning Irishman, to point it out.

When the man in the Barbour jacket excused himself and got up to leave, Martin took the opportunity to call over his brother Patrick and insist on introducing him to Osborne. Patrick sat down and echoed his big brother's honeyed words. It was an honour and a privilege to take a drink with a man who'd made the title of champion trainer his own. At which Martin shouted over to Stevie Joyce to bring another pint for yer man and then there were three Joyces sitting around and asking Osborne questions, as if he was the number one racing guru of the age.

A third pint was quickly produced and before anyone knew it all five Joyces were around the table quizzing Osborne and hanging on to his every word. It was an odd thing, because even Osborne himself would concede that he wasn't known for his sense of humour, but everything he said elicited appreciative chuckles as if it were a quip worthy of Oscar Wilde. He must, he thought, be on good form this afternoon.

'I have to be away shortly,' Osborne said. 'I need to be in the parade ring for the last race.'

'Get him one for the road,' Martin commanded and one of the boys jumped up and, ignoring Osborne's protestations, headed for to the bar. Martin asked him how he'd handle a scopey horse who was losing energy on the jumps. Osborne trotted out some noncommittal reply about careful training as another drink was put before him.

'You hear that, lads? That's experience talking. Listen and learn. Mr Osborne didn't get where he is today without experience. Look at that expensive watch he wears. That doesn't come from backing losers. Is that a Rolex you're wearing? I'll bet it's no fake.'

'It's no fake.'

'Would you let me see it? I've not seen a real one before!'

Osborne slipped the Rolex off his wrist and handed it to Martin. Martin held it out in front of him with both hands. 'That's a thing of beauty. Look, boys, see how the hand sweeps instead of stutters? That's how you tell a real Rolex from a fake, isn't that right? Sweeps instead of stutters?'

'That's correct,' said Osborne.

'What d'ye mean?' said Stevie.

Martin held it up in front of Stevie's face. 'Look for yourself.'

'I get ya!' said Stevie. 'At least, I think I do.'

'You remember that, Stevie,' he said with a wink to Osborne, 'next time some dodgy punter wants to sell you one.' Martin handed the watch back and Osborne put it back safely on his wrist.

'Been caught on that game, has he?' said Osborne.

'Listen now,' Martin said, 'what's the story with this last race? I've noticed money coming on I Am Legend.'

'Silly money. He hasn't much of a chance at all. I'm just giving him a run out.'

'Are you sure? The odds are dropping like crazy out there.'

'I'm telling you, it's silly money. I've seen it before. Someone in London has a daft bet and for some reason it snowballs and everyone jumps on it. Save your money, boys.'

'There you have it,' Martin said.

'Well, thanks for the drinks, lads. I need to get down to the ring to see what all the fuss is about this horse of mine.'

'Sure, but you've not finished your drink. And you've loads of time.'

Osborne looked at his Rolex. It was true. He still had a quarter of an hour. And Martin Joyce seemed to have another question.

Charlie had enjoyed his time in the executive box, but it was an experience tinged with sadness, regret and anger. It had never been his experience to be at a racetrack and to watch events from behind a plate-glass window. Might as well be at home watching it on TV. He thought more than once of abandoning the box and wandering down to the track, but Duncan had made him promise to sit tight. He understood the lad was worried about him. For some reason he was supposed to stay where he was. People weren't supposed to see him or it would upset their plans.

But, for a horrible moment, he couldn't remember exactly

what those plans were. The world tilted sideways for a second. Then it came back to him. It all hung on the last race. He looked at the runners listed in the race programme and saw Osborne's name. He felt the usual bubble of rage swell within him. He looked for Cadogan's name and then realised that of course it wouldn't be there because Cadogan was dead. The names of his enemies were enough to upset him and if he dwelt on them he was right back there in the thick of it, fighting off false accusations and dirty tricks and taking on the Jockey Club who had supported Osborne. He could fight any one of them singly, he knew that, but all of them ranged against him had been too much.

He sighed and held his head in his hands. He looked through the plate glass and he could see the jockeys in the parade ring. One of them was already in the saddle, getting ready to canter down to the start line. Charlie figured he'd just got time to visit the gents before the start of the race.

To get to the toilets, he had to walk down the corridor and pass the open door of the bar. There was a lot of noise and laughter from within and Charlie wished he could just relax and join in. When he got to the toilet, a man in a suit with a pink shirt and a sky-blue tie was writing something on a piece of cardboard. The man stepped out of his way. 'Away you go,' he said with a smile and an Irish accent.

On his way back to his box, Charlie looked in at the bar. A huddle of men in suits surrounded a fellow in a cloth cap who had his back to the door. The men were laughing and joking and the man in the cap seemed to be holding court. There was something in his voice that Charlie recognised.

It was William Osborne. Sitting back in his chair and soaking up the laughs. The corridor swam. Charlie steadied himself against the wall. A young lady from the bar staff came by and asked him if he was OK. He said he was fine, just catching his breath.

Charlie looked around him, only vaguely familiar with the surroundings. He knew he was at a racetrack but he wasn't sure which one. Then he heard Osborne's voice again and it occurred to him that he was at Newbury. He tried to remember what had happened last time he was at Newbury. Captain Pugwash, that was it. Charlie had had a fancied horse called Captain Pugwash going well in the third race when one of Osborne's jockeys stole his line while coming up to a jump. Captain Pugwash landed badly and was pulled up. Osborne's horse won the race. Afterwards, Charlie was inspecting Captain Pugwash and he'd looked up to see Osborne in the winner's enclosure, smirking at him.

Charlie remembered going into the enclosure as if he was offering to shake the hand of the winning trainer. Osborne had gone to accept the handshake, but Charlie had used the grip to pull Osborne's face on to the bunched fist of his other hand. The trainer had gone down as if he'd been shot.

But now Charlie couldn't remember if this had actually happened or if it was just a wishful fantasy. For there was Osborne, larger than life, enjoying a drink with his fawning acolytes. It was too much to take. Charlie raised himself to his full height. He decided it was time to reacquaint Osborne with his fist.

He stepped into the bar.

'Before you go,' Martin Joyce said to Osborne, 'have you thought about giving a ride out to our lad Michael?'

'Ah! So that's what this is all about!'

'No, not at all. It just occurred to me this very moment.'

'Ha!'

'It's true enough. Michael's a busy boy. He spends half his time in Ireland but he's been racing here a lot this season. Got a good strike rate too. But it just occurred to me we might be able to build an alliance.'

Just at that moment, Martin looked up and saw the elderly man he'd encountered in the gents bearing down on Osborne with murder in his eye. He realised with horror that it was Charlie Claymore. Duncan had asked him to keep an eye out for the old man.

Martin started to get to his feet but luckily his brother Patrick was a step ahead of him. Patrick intercepted Charlie and steered the now distracted old man in the direction of the bar.

Osborne hadn't noticed the drama. 'I'm not against the idea,' he was saying, 'but what advantage is it to me? I already have my pick of riders.' By now he'd had enough. He stood up. 'I have to go. I'll pop to the gents and then get myself to the paddock. All the best, lads.'

Each of the Joyces wanted to shake Osborne's hand in turn and the trainer had the odd sensation that he was being detained. Finally, he extricated himself and made his way to the toilet. When he got there he found a hand-written scruffy bit of cardboard propped on the shelf over the urinals. It said Out of Order, so he went instead into one of the stalls. It was while relieving himself he heard an announcement saying that the horses had gone down to the start. It couldn't be right. He checked his watch. According to that, he still had several minutes in hand. Then he heard the stall door close behind him and the whisper of the lock being manipulated from the outside.

I Am Legend was the 2-1 favourite at the start of the race. Though to call it a race was something of a misrepresentation, 'procession' would have been a more accurate description. I Am Legend rocketed to the front from the start, jumped cleanly, led by fifteen lengths all the way round and cantered home an easy winner. Jockey Gerry Pardew couldn't believe his luck and walked the horse back to the winner's enclosure with a smile as big as a slice of pizza.

Fee was waiting for him but there was no sign of the trainer. 'Where's Mr Osborne?' he said, jumping down from the saddle.

'No idea. Go and get weighed in.'

'What's the hurry?'

'No hurry. Just get weighed in, I'll see you in the enclosure.'

Pardew walked off happily with his saddle while Fee loosened the horse's girth and adjusted the bandage on the horse's left foreleg. Fee needed it to come undone just a little, which it now did, partially revealing a white sock as she walked I Am Legend into the winner's enclosure. Bernard Bacon was on hand, already getting lots of shots of the winner. He was a conscientious photographer and made sure he got pictures of the horse from all angles.

Gerry Pardew came out for his moment of glory but after a couple of photos, Fee whisked the horse away. William Osborne still hadn't made an appearance and Gerry was a little put out, he'd been planning a small speech in which he would ask Osborne to put him up on I Am Legend next time out. However, he guessed the trainer was keen to get on the road for the long drive home and had probably left already. It was a bit rude but then Mr Osborne wasn't renowned for his good manners.

But something strange was happening around the racecourse. The word 'ringer' was overheard in whispered conversations. In a section of Tattersalls a small group of half a dozen men began to chant, 'Ringer! Ringer!' Then the chanting died out.

As many spectators seemed amused as seemed concerned. There was plenty of animated discussion going on.

The result of the race was announced. In first place: I Am Legend.

The bookies started to pay out.

18

After hammering on the door for most of the race, Osborne was finally heard by a race-goer who had just watched the contest.

'Hang on!' he'd shouted as he relieved himself. 'You'll have to wait a minute!'

But it wasn't easy to get the door open. The lock was jammed. 'I'll get some help!' shouted the race-goer.

Eventually, a racecourse attendant turned up to take a look at the lock. Then he went away to find his box of tools. Finally, he produced a screwdriver and Osborne was set free. The trainer was livid. He shouldered the attendant aside and bustled his way out, not stopping to thank his liberators. By the time he got down to the enclosure all the horses had been taken away.

He found Fee. 'What's going on? Where's the horse?'

'I've cooled him down and put him in the stall. Why?'

'He won?'

'By a country mile. Where were you?'

'None of your bloody business,' he snapped.

'Pardon me, I'm sure,' Fee said.

A stranger came up and shouted in his face, 'You're a disgrace,' before walking away briskly.

Osborne was taken aback. Then another man, white-haired and lean, stepped in front of him, blocking his path. The man doffed his trilby politely. He looked familiar but his face was in shadow. The shadow, however, could not hide the sparkle in the man's eyes. 'Thank you for the last race, sir. A very satisfactory result.'

The man stepped back and melted away into the spectators. Osborne was sure he knew him from somewhere. It suddenly occurred to him that it had been Charlie Claymore. It was like seeing a ghost. A chill ran down his spine. But it couldn't have been Claymore. The man had been warned off and surely wouldn't dare show his face on a racecourse.

Someone was calling Osborne's name. 'Mr Osborne! Mr Osborne! There you are!' It was a course official with a walrus moustache. 'I've been looking for you everywhere. The stewards would like a word.'

Osborne looked angrily at the official and then at Fee, as if it were her fault. Then he stormed off in the direction of the stewards' room.

The stewards' committee at Hexham hadn't actually been on hand at the end of the race. They should have been but they weren't and it took a while to gather the three of them together.

The stewards were appointed by the Jockey Club. It was an honorary position, much like that of a magistrate. The system of appointment, the necessary qualifications, the vetting proced-ure, the interviews and all the rest of it was a mysterious process which made the Freemasons look like a model of transparency. Stewards seemed to arrive at their positions of authority in the same way that landowners in the Middle Ages became feudal barons. The racing world afforded them unquestioning author-ity. It didn't matter if most of the racing world thought that stewards were idiots, you doffed your cap all the same.

To become a steward you had to have money. That much was clear. You also had to be a gentleman of leisure because if you worked for a living there was no chance of you casually taking off several days throughout the year to travel for a pleasant afternoon's racing. It was often said that stewards were invariably drunkards. This was unfair because some of them were not.

As far as horse riding went, you were expected to know which end of a saddle faced the front of a horse and which the back. The stewards operated without certification, accreditation, training or testing. There had been calls for stipendiary stewards to introduce a bit more professionalism into the judging of the sport, though so far the Jockey Club hadn't deemed that necessary.

So, on the panel at Hexham on this afternoon sat three enthusiastic amateurs. Luckily, each of them was very experienced, as stewards go. Brigadier John Carrington had had his hearing severely damaged in the First World War. For a ninety-two-year-old man everyone agreed he was quite splendid. Piers Croft-Llandor, thirty-third in line to the throne, was famously teetotal and the most upstanding of the three stewards. He'd been a decent amateur jockey but had retired the previous year at the age of twenty-four because he didn't like falling off. The third steward was another ex-military man, Lord Peter Bleeching, a chap in his sixties who was responding well to his treatment for dipsomania. Unfortunately, Bleeching had other matters on his mind. Just the day before, he'd been arrested for soliciting rent boys in Piccadilly and was doing his best to activate his contacts to influence the decision of the Metropolitan police about whether to prosecute.

Shortly after I Am Legend was officially announced as the winner of the last race, Croft-Llandor became aware of the rumour that had swept the track at Hexham and had even heard the cry of 'Ringer!' Seeing the queues at the bookies' stands waiting to be paid out, he was pretty sure the stewards should at least discuss it, but he was having trouble locating both Brigadier and the lord. Having had nothing to do all day, and believing that the real business of the afternoon was over before the insignificant final race, they had left their station – the Brigadier to get a drink and his lordship was God alone knew where.

It occurred to Croft-Llandor that he might announce an inquiry on his own simply to buy time in order to locate the other two. But he was the least experienced of the three and didn't know if it was in his power to do so. So he carried on looking.

He didn't get very far. Every few steps he took on his way over to the bar to find the Brigadier, he was buttonholed by some cross race-goer suggesting he as a steward should do something about what had just happened. He was about to do exactly that, he explained, and was on his way to confer with the other stewards. If only he could get to them. No sooner had he disentangled himself from one irate fellow than he was accosted by another and his basic good nature didn't allow him to simply brush them off.

Another fifteen minutes had gone before he managed to reach the Brigadier and get his message across in the commotion of the bar.

'What?' said the Brigadier.

'We need to reconvene.'

'What?'

'The stewards' committee.'

'What?'

'You, Peter and I. Oh, for God's sake.'

Finally, Bleeching was found behind the stands making a telephone call in hushed tones. He seemed very cross to be interrupted but at last he was persuaded to return to join the other two. At last they sat down at a table in the stewards' room. Piers closed the door.

'There's talk of a ringer,' he said firmly.

'What?' said the Brigadier.

'A ringer.'

'Who?' said Peter Bleeching.

'The last race. I Am Legend came home by a country mile.'

'William Osborne's horse?' said Bleeching.

'Yes.'

'Ridiculous,' said Bleeching.

'What?' said the Brigadier.

'Is it?' said Piers.

It so happened that Peter Bleeching owned the land on which William Osborne trained his horses. Bleeching had been renting it to Osborne for more than twelve years. He'd also had several horses with Osborne over the years. 'It's nonsense. We all know Willy. It's ridiculous.'

'Willy Osborne?' said the Brigadier. 'Fine trainer.'

'I'll vouch for him.' said Bleeching.

'That's all very well,' said Piers, 'but I'm minded to call an inquiry.'

'We don't want a bloody inquiry,' Bleeching said.

'Good Lord!' said the Brigadier.

'It's quite hairy out there,' Piers said. 'You must have noticed.'

'Can't say I did,' Bleeching said. 'And anyway, it's a bit bloody late to call an inquiry now. The bookmakers have paid and pulled down their tents, haven't they?'

'Well, whose fault is that?'

'Fault? Are you saying it's my fault?'

'I'm saying,' Piers said, 'that we should act now. Better late than not at all.'

'You're both getting a little red in the face,' said the Brigadier, 'and there's no need. No need at all.'

'Well, where do you stand?'

'Let's get Willy in here. Have a quiet chat before doing anything rash.'

'What's going on?' Osborne wanted to know. Osborne, not long
freed from the embarrassment of being stuck in the toilet, had
been bombarded by people either congratulating him on winning the last race or hurling abuse at him, sometimes both at the
same time. He was still unsure of exactly what had happened.
When the stewards wanted a word, it always felt as if you were
a schoolboy summoned by the headmaster. Osborne was determined he wasn't going to take any nonsense.

'Have a seat,' said Bleeching.

'Why? I've got things to do, you know.'

'That's right, dear chap,' the Brigadier said, 'have a seat.'

'Tell me why and I'll sit down. I can't get any sense out of
anyone and I've got to find my grooms.'

'Best if you sit down, old chap, and we get this cleared up,'
said Piers Croft-Llandor.

'Don't old chap me, you young pup!'

'Steady!' said the Brigadier. 'Steady!'

'Why are you getting so hot under the collar?' Croft-Llandor
demanded. 'We just want a quiet word. This isn't official at the
moment.'

'At the moment?'

'Willy,' Bleeching said in a reasonable voice, 'sit down a
minute. Things are being said. We need some information. Then
we can calm everyone down and go home.'

Reluctantly Osborne took a seat. He looked at his watch and
then he looked at the clock on the wall. His Rolex was fifteen
minutes slow.

'All it is,' Croft-Llandor said, 'is that we need to clear up a couple of things.'

'Just so we're fully informed,' Bleeching put in.

'Did you know anything about this money going on I Am Legend? The odds came tumbling rather spectacularly.'

'Not until before the race. I saw it happening but didn't think too much of it.'

'You thought nothing of it?'

'It was just silly money as far as I was concerned. I've seen it before. Stampede money.'

'Did you have a bet yourself?' the Brigadier said.

'No, I didn't. Where's this leading?'

'No one is accusing you of anything,' said Bleeching

'Well, you know we have to ask,' said Croft-Llandor. 'Money starts falling out of the sky and then I Am Legend goes and wins at a canter. You saw the race for yourself.'

'No, I bloody didn't!'

'You didn't?'

'No. I saw none of it.'

'So where were you when the race was run?'

Osborne stood up and shouted, 'I was locked in the bloody khazi of this godforsaken racecourse. Trying to get out of the bloody thing.'

'Good Lord!' said the Brigadier.

When they'd managed to calm Osborne down they asked him if he would object to the racetrack vet inspecting the horse. The clear implication was that the horse might have been doped and Osborne objected strenuously. Finally, he agreed to the inspection. The vet was summoned and Osborne and the three stewards walked down to the stables. What with the Brigadier's bad leg and his cane, it took a while. Dusk was falling across the racetrack. The crowd had gone home and only dead betting slips swirled across the terraces. The stables were half empty, most trainers having packed up their horses and begun the long drive back to their respective yards. The roads heading away from the course were packed with horseboxes, one of them a dull olive green.

Osborne stormed over to Jim Pitts.

'There's hell on, boss,' Pitts said.

'You think I don't know that? Where's the groom.'

'Fee? She's upset.'

'Upset?'

'Yes, they were shouting at her. She's gone off somewhere.'

'For God's sake, turn out Legend. There's a bloody silly fool of a vet somewhere who wants to take a look.'

'The bloody silly fool of a vet,' said a voice at Osborne's shoulder, 'is standing right behind you.'

Jim trotted out I Am Legend. The vet asked for the horse's papers and Jim produced them.

The vet made a thorough inspection of the animal before him. After he'd completed his examination he turned to Osborne, Pitts and the three stewards who were waiting with expectant faces.

'Well,' said the vet. 'There is no doubt in my mind that this is the horse it purports to be. This is I Am Legend.'

'Of course it bloody well is,' Osborne snarled.

'There is also no doubt in my mind,' the vet continued, 'that this horse has not been in a race all day.'

The fall-out following the last race at Hexham stretched over the next few days. After the inspection of the horse, the stewards made a very late decision that an official inquiry would have to be launched, although in typically muddled style, the Jockey

Club were not given a full report until the middle of the following day. Piers Croft-Llandor had been responsible for writing the report and when he was asked if the bookmakers had been informed, he said that he didn't know it was his responsibility. The Jockey Club took charge and notified the bookmakers' associations who in turn notified their affiliates that they should stop paying out until after the inquiry had concluded its investigations.

Unsurprisingly, this was too late in most cases.

The tabloids went into action the following day and their creative sub-editors went to town on the sports pages. William Osborne suddenly became known as 'Ozzy' for the purposes of an eye-catching headline, most of which took the form of denials. *'I'm No Ringer,' Cries Ozzy* trumpeted one of the redtops. This 'quote' was somewhat inaccurate. It had been obtained on the telephone by a journalist pretending to be someone else and it was a loose translation for such filthy language from Osborne that it made the journalist's ears tingle despite his thirty years experience of the trade. Another paper trailed the headline *Ozzy the Ring Master?* One redtop got the booby prize for *I Am Legend Rings Bell.*

Meanwhile, the Jockey Club collected betting evidence. The reports from bookmakers indicated a sudden flood of wagers, starting with some large stakes in London then in the Home Counties and the North-East. There were also a significant number of more modest bets clustered within twenty-five miles of Osborne's yard. The incompetent Hexham stewards were backed out of the inquiry as senior figures at the Jockey Club took over.

Much to his rage, Osborne was summoned before the official inquiry. He maintained his position angrily. He knew nothing about any ringer or any betting. Fee Markham was also summoned. She was able to say, quite truthfully, that she hadn't been working for Osborne for very long and was still finding her way around the yard. She said that if anyone had switched the horse they would have had plenty of opportunity to do so in the pre-race enclosure. There was no security. She added that when she led the horse back after the race was run it looked exactly like I Am Legend. In any event the board of inquiry were not terribly interested in anything she had to say.

The board requested photographers who were working that day at Hexham to supply any relevant photos. Luckily, Bernard Bacon had a ready supply of clear images. In particular, he had an incriminating shot of the winning horse walking into the winner's enclosure. One of the horse's leg bandages had come slightly loose and it revealed a white sock. Other photographs taken days later showed that I Am Legend had no such sock and the bandage had clearly been used to disguise it.

The conclusion was inescapable. Another horse had run that day under the name I Am Legend.

The question for the inquiry was: how far was William Osborne implicated? The difficulty for the Jockey Club board of inquiry was that Osborne was almost a member of the National Hunt establishment. He had been champion trainer over recent seasons, even though this season his supremacy was being challenged. And he'd always been careful to mend his fences with senior figures at the Jockey Club.

However, Osborne was arrogant and his weakness lay in his belief that he was untouchable. Like every good criminal his story was that he didn't know anything about the offence. If the horse had been substituted, he maintained, then it had been done behind his back.

But he was the trainer, the board of inquiry pointed out. He was responsible at every step of the way to make sure things like this couldn't happen. Where was he before the race and, indeed, when the race was being run?

It was alleged that he had been locked in a toilet. Was he locked in the toilet by someone else or was it a mechanical fault? He didn't know. He had his suspicions. He named them. These names were investigated with bookmakers to see if they could be linked to any betting advantage. These investigations took several days.

The newspapers got hold of the tale of Osborne locked in the toilet. *How Convenient!* ran one of the back-page headlines. And that was exactly the trouble. Osborne's explanation of his absence was all too convenient. He wasn't there. He saw nothing. It must have been someone else. The newspaper debates were followed with interest by racing fans everywhere. Considering that almost everyone thinks the sport is rigged even when it isn't, here was confirmation of what everyone knew to be the case.

While the investigations with the bookies' chains took place, the story disappeared off the sports pages. But someone knew exactly how to put it back on again. Duncan remembered a trick or two from the way Duke Cadogan had kept the pressure on Charlie. He went on record as saying that he didn't believe William Osborne was a ringer.

The sports page headlines rang out again: *Ozzy No Ring Master Says Claymore*. 'I've worked with him before and we've had our differences,' Duncan said generously in an interview. 'He runs a tight ship. I find it hard to believe he would do this. If he's found guilty I fear for the future of the sport.'

The interview had exactly the right effect. If the board found Osborne guilty then Duncan feared for the future of the sport. But as every racing commentator said, if Osborne was *not* found guilty in the face of the evidence then there might as well be no sport.

Somewhere in all of this, Fee Markham quit her job. She wrote a short letter admitting that, in failing to spot the substitution of I Am Legend, she had not acted as a diligent groom and as such she couldn't be expected to carry on working for the yard when they were under such a cloud.

The investigation with the bookmakers confirmed what the board already knew, that very large sums of money had been shovelled on to I Am Legend immediately prior to the race. This factor was considered along with all photographic evidence and personal testimony.

The inquiry announced its findings in a press conference. The journalists present listened to a long and formal account of proceedings.

On 6th March 1981 a disciplinary panel of the Jockey Club commenced an inquiry into allegations arising from the alleged substitution of a runner in the Hadrian's handicap hurdle at Hexham racecourse on 5th March 1981. The allegations concerned an attempt to run I Am Legend, a four-year-old gelding.

I Am Legend is owned by Mr Robert Abercrombie and trained by Mr William Osborne and stabled at Mr Osborne's yard near Newbury. Mr Richard Piper, a conditional jockey, was due to ride I Am Legend but was replaced at the last minute by another conditional jockey, Mr Gerald Pardew.

Some days after the race, Mr Osborne and his grooms were interviewed by investigators from the Jockey Club. A number of different accounts were provided to the investigators regarding the events that had occurred prior to the race.

Subsequently, Mr Osborne was charged with being guilty of or conspiring to commit a corrupt or fraudulent practice in relation to racing by the deliberate substitution of another horse for I Am Legend contrary to Jockey Club regulations. Mr Piper and Mr

Pardew were also charged with being in breach of regulations by aiding or abetting in the commission of a breach of regulations.

Throughout the hearing, when considering the evidence in this case, the panel was mindful that the charges were serious and would require cogent and credible evidence to be found proved.

The report included personal racing histories of everyone involved, full accounts of all versions of events, the testimony of racetrack and veterinary officials, evidence of betting patterns around the country and photographic evidence of the horses involved.

Eventually the panel officially announced their decision.

Having carefully considered all the evidence the panel has made the following findings. That the four-year-old gelding I Am Legend was substituted by an unknown horse by persons unknown for the clear purpose of benefiting from a gambling coup.

On the charge of aiding or abetting in the commission of a breach of regulations, Mr Piper and Mr Pardew are found to be innocent and we thank them for their full cooperation with the inquiry.

In the case of Mr Osborne, the panel find Mr Osborne not guilty of conspiring to commit a corrupt or fraudulent practice in relation to racing by the deliberate substitution of another horse for I Am Legend.

In the neglect of his responsibilities, however, the panel does find that Mr Osborne acted in breach of regulations and is guilty of aiding or abetting in the commission of a breach of regulations.

In view of this conclusion, Mr Osborne shall be unable to attend any race meeting or set foot on Jockey Club property until the period of exclusion has ended, and that for a period of seven years.

So that was it. William Osborne was warned off. It had been impossible for the Jockey Club to reach any other decision. Failure to find someone guilty would have been tantamount to accepting that the sport was universally corrupt. The lesser charge of aiding and abetting was a concession to his contacts and his record in the sport.

Pending an appeal that had little chance of success, William Osborne, champion trainer for the last eight seasons, was banned from racing for seven years. It may as well have been seventy.

Osborne was out of the game.

19

Jump racing is the most life-encompassing of sports. It involves man in competition with beast, the elements, a complex set of rules – and money. It is a sport of life and death. And the racing world moves on fast. It has a busy calendar of events and the organisation required in order to meet that calendar leaves little time for anyone to look over their shoulder. There are always races large and small to be run. Horses always need to be prepared, exercised and fed, and stables always need mucking out.

The affair of William Osborne and I Am Legend was history. Just three days after the Jockey Club ban on Osborne had been announced the mighty Cheltenham Festival was due to begin. Cheltenham, of course, was the summit of the jump-racing calendar, a three-day cauldron of top-class racing in which reputations would be made and lost. With Osborne out of the way, all that had happened was that the field had been narrowed.

At the Quinn yard and in every top training establishment up and down the country it was all shoulders to the wheel. Destiny's Dream, Drap D'Or, The Black 'Un and the other contenders had to be treated like animal gods, trained carefully and handled cautiously in the run-up to the big event. Petie had entries in more than half the races; Duncan, Kerry and Roisin had important rides. And after Cheltenham was over there would be the Grand National to think about.

The racing world moves on fast.

Two days before Cheltenham, first thing in the morning when the staff at the Quinn yard had reported for duty, Petie called them into the courtyard. There was some irritation; everyone had tasks they were eager to get on with.

'I know you're all busy,' Petie said to the company, 'but this is important. I promise it will only take two minutes. I called you together like this before Christmas, if you remember, and I announced the result of our investigation into the poisoning of the horse feed. Since then I've had further conversations with Bishop, our feed merchant, and he has told me some interesting things. After a tip-off, he discovered that one of his drivers had been paid to spoil the feed delivered into our yard. That man has since been fired. I don't know who paid him but I have my suspicions – though that's all they are and they no longer matter much. But what does matter is that I put right the mistake I made in unjustly accusing a valued employee in front of you all without giving her a chance to hear my accusations in private and explain why she had weed killer in her car. I was too hasty in my judgement and I am sorry for that. I want you to welcome back to the yard a brilliant young lady who I reckon has been much missed. Come on out, Fee Markham.'

And from a stall behind Petie emerged a familiar slim figure with a shock of black curly hair and a beam on her face bright enough to light up the dull March morning.

There were hoots of delight and a spontaneous round of applause as Fee hugged and kissed her old friends, starting with Petie and Gypsy George.

In the event, Petie did not stick to his promise. Fee's welcome back took a good deal longer than two minutes but it sent everyone off to work in great heart.

Duncan, Petie and Fee had met the night before.

'You deserve a medal or something,' Duncan told her.

'It was quite exciting going undercover. The worst thing was working in that miserable yard. Osborne might have been successful but he treated everyone like dirt.'

'It was a brave thing you did,' Petie said. 'You had your reputation trashed all over the place.'

Fee shrugged. 'I did it for Michelle. Men like Osborne think girls don't count. I'm very happy he's got seven years to stew on it.'

Duncan looked at her with respect. He and Petie had been discussing ways of rewarding her for her invaluable efforts. He'd made one suggestion which, though appropriate, also worried him. But looking at her now and considering her steely determination in recent weeks, he dismissed those misgivings. This was a strong woman.

He looked at Petie who gave him a quick nod. 'Ask her, Duncan.'

'Ask me what?'

'Are you partial to the smell of lavender?'

She laughed. 'That's a weird question.'

'Let me put it another way – how would you like to ride in the Arnold Lane at Cheltenham?'

Her mouth opened but no sound came out. Duncan ploughed on.

'Martin Joyce has entered Prince Samson. In honour of Michelle, really, and he says he doesn't care how Sammy goes.

273

But I rode him the other day at Huntingdon and he hacked up. He's going to be a serious horse.'

'But—' She'd found her voice. 'Won't Mr Joyce want you to ride him? If you've just won on him and you know him?'

'Martin's OK with it,' said Petie. 'In fact, he thinks you'd be grand. He's seen you ride, you know. On Hotandcold at Towcester.'

'Anyway,' Duncan added, 'Martin wants Sammy to run in Michelle's memory and he thinks a female jockey would be appropriate. And, like I said, he doesn't actually care if Sammy comes last.'

'Sod you, Duncan Claymore.' Her dark eyes flashed with anger. 'If I'm riding him then we're not coming in last.'

Duncan grinned at Petie. 'See – I told you she was the woman for the job.'

Just before Cheltenham Duncan called on Charlie at the Grey Gables.

'How do you feel?' Duncan said.

Charlie considered the matter. Duncan wasn't asking about his health and they both knew it. He was giving his father a chance to air his thoughts on Osborne's fall.

Finally, Charlie said, 'I'm content,' and that was all the discussion they gave the matter. It was just another race that had been run.

Neither mentioned Eddie Merryweather or the operation to field a ringer at Hexham. The horse substituted for I Am Legend was now happily resting in a paddock in Wales. Pretty soon the last traces of dye would have vanished. Neither of them had bet on the horse. They hadn't wanted any trace back to them and in that regard they were spotless.

'You know what would make me even more content?' Charlie said.

'What's that, Dad?'

'If I could just get Mrs Solanki to agree to marry me. That would put the tin hat on it.'

Duncan laughed. 'That's not going to happen. She's already married.'

'Are you sure about that?'

'She's *Mrs* Solanki, isn't she?'

'So? She could have been married once. She might be a widow. Have you ever seen her husband?'

'Dad, this is silly. All you've got to do is ask her.'

Charlie pulled a face. 'I don't want to upset her. Or be too obvious.'

'I'll ask about her husband, if you like.'

'No, don't you dare. Just leave it with me. I'm working on it. Now then, are you going to bring home that Gold Cup?'

Duncan watched Prince Samson's race from one of the many bars on the course. It was the quietest spot he could find for his heavily pregnant wife – though a quiet spot does not exist at the Cheltenham Festival. At least it was somewhere Lorna could sit down though she'd had to make a display of her bump before a couple of tweedy Irish punters had taken the hint and yielded their seats. They'd then recognised Duncan and flapped around offering to bring Lorna drinks and snacks, in between importuning Duncan for a tip. He'd got rid of them by suggesting they consider a certain Irish contender in the next owned by Mr M. Joyce.

If he'd had his way, Lorna would be nowhere near the scrum of the Festival and he himself would be in the privacy of the changing room. But at Christmas Lorna had surprised him by expressing a wish to attend. More to the point, she'd been nostalgic about previous Christmases and the lavish entertainment her father had always laid on. It was only natural that she should feel the pang of her father's loss at such a time of year. And only natural that Duncan should feel the guilt he carried with him like a knot in his guts. Would it ever, he wondered, go away? Lorna had gone on to reminisce about the times in the year when Duke's absence would be most painful. Aside from Christmas, it turned out, the hardest time was the Cheltenham Festival.

'That was one meeting I always went to,' she'd said. 'Daddy made sure he had at least one runner and it was always such fun swanking around the parade ring.'

'You can have a runner at Cheltenham, if you want.' Duncan had said it before he'd thought it through, in particular the size Lorna might be at seven months pregnant and how she may be feeling. On the other hand, it had been rather splendid seeing her sail around the ring looking glorious in a suit of aquamarine with enormous shoulder pads and a ridiculous half hat, like a black spider, perched on her rich red auburn hair.

'Well, they're all looking at you, my darlin',' Petie had said. Even he was gussied up in his best suit for the occasion. Duncan, on the other hand, was in the white and red Cadogan silks.

The animal who had made the event possible was one of the three remaining Cadogan horses that Lorna and Duncan had not yet sold, All That Jazz, a small but well-built chestnut gelding who had shown promise as a four-year-old before injury sidelined him. But he'd come back to health this season and had won in mid-February at Folkestone.

There were twenty runners in the opening race and though All That Jazz was better than most of them on the day, he wasn't quite good enough to finish in the frame. Still, as Duncan and Lorna took refuge in the bar, they were happy enough with the outcome. A fourth place in such a competitive event was not to be sniffed at.

'Is Fee going to be all right?' Lorna had her eyes on one of the screens in the bar on which the runners for the two-mile Arnold Lane Steeplechase could be seen heading down to the start. 'I mean, she looks so small on that big horse.'

'Don't worry, Sammy makes every rider look small.'

Secretly, Duncan was worried. Fee had had little time to get to know Sammy and his quirks. As Duncan had told her, the chief difficulty was making sure the horse didn't run away with his rider. He was such a strong beast that there would be no holding him if he decided to take off. Now Duncan could see Fee on the screen working hard to keep the horse's enthusiasm in check. But she had assured Duncan she could handle the horse as well as he could and, as far as he could see, she was being as good as her word.

There were fewer runners in this race, fourteen, but all the same it took time for the starter to get them under control and lined up behind the tape. The vast crowd howled as they finally got under way. Fee managed to drop Prince Samson into the middle of the pack as the leaders went off at a frantic pace over the drying ground. Duncan was relieved to see the grey horse clear the first few fences without trouble as the riders swung left-handed around the course towards the fourth fence. The leader was blazing a trail out in the front, miles ahead. But Duncan had no worries about him; unless he was a world-beater he'd be coming back to the pack before the race was run.

Coming to the water jump, Fee had moved Sammy to the outside and he seemed to be relishing the daylight ahead. He cleared the water with ease. Over the only ditch in the race, the fourth from home, he was lying third. Racing to the top of the hill, Sammy had moved up to the shoulder of the horse in second, Pugilist, the race favourite, ridden by a familiar figure.

'Isn't that Sandy Sanderson just ahead of Fee?' said Lorna.

'Yes.'

'I wonder what he thinks about poor Uncle Willy being warned off?'

Duncan had no idea at that moment. He was concentrating hard on the big grey horse, willing Fee to hold him up for the moment and not to get carried away on the downhill slope to the third from last. Too many animals came a cropper at that point – just like the runaway leader who slipped up on the landing side and threw his rider from the saddle. But Prince Samson negotiated the fence safely and took the next as cleanly, landing just a length behind Pugilist.

As they raced uphill towards the final fence, Sanderson shot a glance over his shoulder. Fee was right there. Duncan could imagine how Sanderson felt about that. He went to work on Pugilist with his stick and his mount responded, opening up a clear three-length lead.

'Oh fooey – I think he's going to win,' Lorna muttered. 'Come on, Fee!' she screamed at the screen, though it was impossible for Fee to hear her.

But, miraculously, it was as if she had. Sammy sailed over the last fence with a magnificent leap that ate up half the distance between him and his rival. Then it was just a race for the line, with both jockeys giving it their all and their horses digging deep into their reserves of strength. It turned out that Prince Samson dug deeper. It seemed to Duncan that Fee toyed with her rival over the last fifty yards, sitting right on his shoulder almost until the post itself, and then darting past him to take a clear victory on the line.

Everyone in the bar was on their feet cheering home the neck-and-neck finish, Lorna among them. Duncan watched her squealing with excitement and on the screen saw a close-up of an ecstatic Fee punching the air as an overjoyed Martin Joyce raced to greet her.

So there was justice in the world of racing after all.

Lorna lay on the sofa that night with Duncan's head resting in her lap. He had his ear pressed to her belly, listening for baby noises, for signs and sounds. It was dusk outside. The evenings were getting lighter. The unmistakable smell of spring was in the air.

'So what do you think?' Lorna was asking him. 'Do you think Uncle Willy was ringing horses?'

'Dunno.'

'You must have some idea.'

Duncan sat up. 'Petie and other trainers have had their suspicions he's done it in the past. But they never felt able to do anything about it. If he didn't have anything to do with it this time, then it would balance up the times that he has, wouldn't it?'

'So you don't think he did it?'

'Not this time. No.'

'Wish I'd known about it. I would have put a thousand pounds on I Am Legend to win.'

'Yes, me too,' said Duncan. 'Only we don't have a thousand.'

'I would have gone round all my friends until I'd got the money. I'd have told them I had a cert. For every one of them who loaned me the stake I would have told them the name of the horse and they could have backed it themselves.'

'Yes, I believe you would have done.'

'Just think, Duncan. It was 33-1 at the beginning of the day.'

'Yep.'

'Somebody made a killing.'

'Yep.'

The unseasonally sun-tanned face of George Pleasance flashed into Duncan's thoughts, spoiling the moment. He erased it.

Then Lorna said, 'It's funny isn't it? That's another of your Dad's enemies gone. Sometimes I wonder who I married.'

Duncan looked out of the window at the dusky sky. The first star of the evening was twinkling. 'You married the father of your child,' said Duncan, 'and the future champion jockey.'

And that's all he would admit to.